Whispering
—to—
Witches

4/0/
17

Whispering to Witches

Anna Dale

BLOOMSBURY

First published in Great Britain in 2004 by Bloomsbury Publishing Plc
38 Soho Square, London, W1D 3HB

A CIP catalogue record of this book is available from the British Library

Hbk ISBN 0 7475 6909 6
Export Pbk ISBN 0 7475 7332 8

All papers used by Bloomsbury Publishing are natural, recyclable products made from
wood grown in well-managed forests. The manufacturing processes conform to the
environmental regulations of the country of origin.

Printed in Great Britain by Clays Ltd, St Ives plc

10 9 8 7 6 5 4 3 2 1

www.bloomsbury.com/whisperingtowitches

To Mary
and in memory of Magnus

Chapter One

An Unexpected Journey

Joe flopped on to the seat and loosened his school tie. His suitcase jutted over the edge of the luggage rack above his head and its label dangled in front of his eyes. It read:

Joseph Binks
c/o Mrs Merle Taverner
2 Cloister Walk
Canterbury
Kent

Joe ripped the label from its piece of string, scrunched it into a ball and threw it into the farthest corner of the railway compartment. The woman sitting opposite him was too engrossed in her newspaper to raise an eyebrow. Joe slumped back into his seat and wished for the hundredth time that day that he was staying in London for Christmas.

It was the twentieth of December. Through the window, Joe could see a few people hurrying along the platform, weighed down with carrier bags. They had the hunched shoulders and haggard faces of typical Christmas shoppers. Yesterday, Joe had been one of them. He and his dad, Nicholas Binks, had struggled home from the supermarket with bags full of sausage rolls, peanuts, crackers and wrapping paper.

Joe sighed and looked at his watch. It was five minutes to four. Exactly twenty-four hours ago, he had been standing at the bottom of a stepladder, his arms filled with tinsel. Joe's father had been at the top of the stepladder, banging drawing pins into the ceiling with the heel of his shoe. Bulging bags of half-unpacked shopping littered the carpet, much to the delight of Hamish who had thrust his nose into all of them.

'Oi! Geddout of it!' Nicholas had shouted when he spied Hamish sneaking under the sofa with a box of peppermint creams. 'Joe, stop that dog! He's about to wolf down Mrs Ingledew's Christmas present!'

Yesterday, Joe had been looking forward to the last day of school and then two glorious weeks of holiday. Just Joe and his father: opening their presents, eating too much chocolate, watching telly, taking Hamish for walks on Tooting Common ...

And then the phone call had come.

It had been well after midnight. A light came on and

seeped underneath Joe's bedroom door. Joe heard his father tramp to the phone. There was a muffled exclamation. Several grunts followed. The phone clicked back on to its cradle and Joe sat up in bed. His father's footsteps padded past Joe's bedroom door and the light went out.

In the morning, Joe almost tripped over his suitcase. The battered brown case was sitting on the landing outside his room. It was draped with gossamer, spun by spiders in the attic. Joe looked at it uneasily. Something was wrong. He hastened down the stairs and passed his father's wine-coloured case which bulged ominously in the hall.

Hamish was playing with his lead in the kitchen. Joe's father was leaning against the sink, munching a piece of toast. He was wearing a suit. 'Listen, son,' he said as Joe appeared in the doorway. 'I'm afraid something ... well, something's come up. My aunt. She's had a fall. You remember Great-aunt Adelaide, don't you?'

Joe stared at his father.

'She was like a mother to me when I was growing up. Anyway, I'm really sorry, Joe, but I'm going to have to go and see her. She's not well at all.' He took a deep breath. 'Here's the plan. A taxicab will be here in an hour, so you'll need to have your suitcase packed by then. The taxi driver will drop you off at school. Then he'll take me to King's Cross station where I'll catch a train to Scotland.' Joe's dad chewed a mouthful of toast. Then he brushed a few crumbs from his lip. 'When school finishes, the same taxi driver will be waiting for you outside the gates. He'll take you straight to Charing Cross. Your train leaves at four on the dot. I've ... er ... I've called your mum. She's expecting you to arrive at Canterbury just before six o'clock tonight. Oh ... you'll be needing some money for the taxi and your train ticket.' Joe's father reached into his wallet and offered his son a sheaf of notes. Joe looked at them blankly.

Nicholas Binks sighed. 'Look, I know you'd like to come with me, but it would be miserable for you, honestly. Scotland's such a long way ... and you'd be hanging around the hospital all the time. It wouldn't be much of a Christmas, would it?'

Hamish sat at Nicholas's feet and gazed longingly at the piece of toast he was holding. Joe's father ruffled the dog's dirty white fur. 'Hamish is going to stay next door with Mrs Ingledew. Don't look at me like that, Joe. He can't come with you. Gordon doesn't like animals, remember.'

Joe slid on to a stool and began to shake some cereal into a bowl. 'Look, Joe ... I'm sorry,' continued his father. 'I know how disappointed you must be, but it might only be for a few days. I could be back before Christmas Day ... Joe! Are you listening to me? Well, say *something*!'

Joe put down his spoon and looked stonily at his father. 'You've got a bit of marmalade on your chin,' he said.

Doors slammed. A whistle blew. The train rattled and began to move jerkily out of Charing Cross station. Joe glanced around the carriage. It was almost full. Passengers sat shoulder to shoulder, their laps filled with intriguing bags and parcels. Joe's gaze rested on the woman sitting opposite him. She smoothed a page in her newspaper and delved into her handbag, producing a green marbled fountain pen. Joe's head began to loll and his eyes closed, flicking open briefly when a man in a pinstriped suit sat down heavily next to the woman and dropped his mobile phone on to the floor.

Joe was woken by another train whizzing past the window. He lifted his icy cheek from the glass, rubbed his neck and looked at his watch. Although he had been asleep for twenty minutes, the woman with the newspaper had not changed her position. She was sitting neatly with her ankles crossed. The newspaper was draped over her knees and her fountain pen hovered over the crossword.

Joe had nothing better to do, so he studied her appearance. She was wearing a salmon-pink woollen suit and black polo-neck jumper. Her hair was short and black, apart from a patch of grey which streaked from above her left temple. Balanced on her nose was a pair of half-moon spectacles, over which she glared nastily when the man's mobile phone began to ring.

The man removed a minuscule mobile from the breast pocket of his pinstriped jacket and slapped the phone to his ear. "'Lo,' he said. 'Yeah, I'm on the train. Not bad. Lef' London miles back. Everyfing's peachy, yeah. Wassat? T'riffic. You're jokin' me! Uh-huh. Uh-huh.'

Joe yawned and glanced out of the window. The man was right. The city had been left far behind. London's big warehouses and rows of squashed terraced dwellings had been replaced by endless lines of great, shadowy trees. In the rapidly descending gloom, Joe thought that they looked like sentinels guarding the railway track.

The sky darkened and, as Joe watched, snowflakes began to whirl against the glass. Joe studied his reflection in the window. He looked pale, ghostly even; and there were dark shadows under his eyes. His sandy hair was tousled and his fringe needed cutting.

Joe tugged off his school tie and allowed himself a brief smile. Usually, he was driven to Canterbury in his dad's clapped-out Morris Minor which had trouble keeping up with the other cars on the motorway. At present, however, the Morris was in the care of Jim the mechanic, having blown a tyre and crashed into a pillar-box three days earlier. For Joe, it was a rare treat to enjoy a comfortable, speedy train journey. He found it exciting to travel on his own, even if his eventual destination was somewhat disappointing. Spending Christmas in Canterbury with his mum, her husband Gordon, and their strange daughter Esme, did not exactly fill him with glee.

By the time the train reached Paddock Wood it was completely dark outside. Joe stared past his reflection in the window and watched the snowflakes falling thickly. He hoped the snow would settle so that he could have a snowball fight the next morning. Then Joe's heart sank when he remembered that his father would not be there for him to pelt snowballs at. Joe doubted whether his seven-year-old sister, Esme, would be a capable opponent, and he knew that Gordon never played any game rougher than tiddly-winks. His mother would be too busy, of course. Joe kicked a bottle top across the floor and sighed.

'Wish I was your age again,' said the man in the pin-striped suit, smoothing back his thinning hair and smiling at Joe. 'I used to be a demon on a toboggan, I did.' He leaned forward and shoved a crumpled paper bag under Joe's nose. 'Like a sweet, lad?'

'Oh, thanks,' said Joe warmly. He took a red one.

The man held out his bag to the woman with the

newspaper but she sniffed disdainfully and shook her head. The man shrugged his shoulders and stuffed five sweets into his mouth at the same time.

Joe looked keenly out of the window every time the train stopped. Each station was as dark and unfamiliar as the last and Joe did not always manage to find the name of the station before the train moved on.

'Was that Chartham?' asked Joe as the train eased away from another platform. The man in the pinstriped suit crunched a sweet and nodded vaguely. Joe squinted as they passed a white sign, but the letters on it were nothing more than a blur. 'If that was Chartham, we'll be stopping at Canterbury in a minute,' said Joe anxiously.

'Don'tcha worry, I've got your luggage.' The man reached up and his navy pinstriped suit strained against his bulk. His sleeves slid back, exposing his wrists, and on one of them, Joe saw a tattoo. It looked like the letter 'S'. The train gave a sudden jolt and the man lurched around the compartment, holding the suitcase above his head, before he flung himself down in the seat next to the woman with the newspaper.

'Phew! What you got in there?' he said, handing the case to Joe. ''Alf a dozen 'ouse bricks?'

Joe grinned and heaved the suitcase on to his knees. 'Just a few books and clothes and stuff.'

'No gold ingots?' teased the man. 'No cannonballs? No –'

'Shh.' The woman looked up from her newspaper and peered past the headrest of Joe's seat down the aisle of the carriage. Joe glanced at the crossword on her lap. Not one of its little white squares had been filled in, even though it had been an hour and three-quarters since they left Charing Cross. Joe thought this was very odd because he was sure that he had heard the nib of her fountain pen scratching away for most of the journey.

The train gave a slight wobble and the woman fell against the man; either that or she nudged him with her elbow. At the same moment, the locks on Joe's suitcase sprang open with a clunk and a wrinkled mass of clothes tumbled on to the floor. Joe felt his cheeks burning with embarrassment as he shoved his clothes back into the case and pressed the lid down. He felt someone patting his arm as he struggled with the locks. It was the woman who had been attempting to do the crossword.

'You've dropped your ticket, boy,' she said urgently. Joe looked down at the floor and scooped up the scrap of paper.

'Thanks,' he muttered. 'Must've slipped ...'

She nodded at him and smiled, then removed her half-moon spectacles, folded her newspaper, and slipped her green marbled fountain pen back into her handbag.

'Excuse me. I do beg your pardon. Is anyone sitting here?' A tall woman carrying a wicker cat basket sat down next to Joe without waiting for an answer. She smoothed the creases from her double-breasted black velvet coat and lifted the cat basket on to her lap, poking her red manicured nails through a tiny barred window in its side.

'What a relief to find a place to perch at last,' she said. 'My darlings have had *such* a long journey. They really are getting quite crotchety.' She shook her long chestnut curls and sighed. 'We've been travelling all day and my coiffure has suffered dreadfully. I'm sure I must look absolutely frightful.' She looked at Joe with unusually pale blue eyes, their lashes coated in black mascara.

'Oh, no,' said Joe quickly. 'You don't. Not at all.' Joe thought she was the most glamorous person he had ever seen.

'Thank you, treasure,' she said, her glistening red lips curling into a smile. Joe was sure that she must be some-one famous. The man in the pinstriped suit certainly seemed to think so. He was gazing at the woman with-out blinking and when she crossed her legs and touched his knee with the pointed tip of her black ankle boot, he looked like he was going to faint.

Joe peered through the tiny window in the cat basket and, just for a moment, he glimpsed a patch of grey fur and the flash of a yellow eye. 'Not too close, my sweet,' cautioned the woman. 'Their claws are like needles and they have been known to bite.' She gave a tinkling laugh and her earrings sparkled as they swung from side to side. 'The little *darlings*.'

The cat basket shifted on her lap as the train began to slow down. Joe gripped the handle of his suitcase and chewed his lower lip. When the platform slid into view, he craned his neck to see if he could spot Gordon's bushy ginger hair or Esme's frantically waving hands. He had not been looking forward to this moment. Once he had jumped down from the train, there was bound to be an awkward silence while they struggled to find something to say to each other. Then Gordon would probably take Joe's luggage, his mother would tell him how much he had grown and Esme would tug at Joe's sleeve with a goofy look on her face.

The man prodded Joe's elbow. 'Your stop, lad,' he said.

As the train juddered to a halt, the lights in the carriage flickered and went out. Joe peered through the window. The platform was swathed in shadow. The only source of light was a feeble beam from a single lamp. Joe squinted and thought he glimpsed a figure standing on the platform. His eyes searched for the name of the station but he could not see it.

'Your stop,' prompted the man again.

Joe stood up, wriggled into his grey school blazer and slammed down the window. Icy air leaked into the compartment. The train engine had stopped and it was so quiet that he could almost hear the snowflakes colliding with each other as they drifted towards the stone platform. He looked at his watch. It was nearly six o'clock. Joe reached through the window and began to fumble with the door handle.

Then a strange sound made him stop.

Joe looked over his shoulder. Shadows had fallen over his travelling companions. The woman with the newspaper had been swallowed up by the darkness. Only her handbag was visible, its clasp winking in a faint glimmer of light. The bag must have been thrown open when the train braked suddenly and it lay on its side, its mouth gaping. Joe listened, holding his breath, and he heard the sound again. A muffled, quivering hiss. Like air escaping from a tyre. There was a slight movement in the handbag and then a thread-like tongue peeped over the clasp, followed by a smooth, shiny head. The tongue flicked in, then out again, and Joe found himself staring into a pair of glittering green eyes.

A light flashed in the compartment and there was a sizzling sound. For a moment, Joe thought that a light bulb was returning to life but, when the searing light flared again, he realised that it was not coming from above his head. What is more, in those brief seconds, he saw a scarlet nail nudge the fastening on the cat basket. Joe heard a frantic scrabbling noise, followed by a creak as the flap of the basket opened. He stiffened and felt an ice-cold shiver slip down his back. All of a sudden, he felt horribly afraid; as if he was in the presence of uncommon wickedness. The darkness seemed to close in around him.

Joe cried out.

The sound of his own voice brought him to his senses. He leaned through the window and joggled the door handle, his eyes wide with panic. The door of the compartment swung open and Joe leaped on to the platform in one bound, his suitcase almost pulling his arm out of its socket.

Filled with relief, Joe slammed the door shut and shrank away from the train. He heard someone blow a whistle and the train's engine began to whirr. The lights in the train came on quite suddenly and Joe shielded his eyes against the glare. Joe saw the glamorous woman standing by the window. She blew him a kiss before sliding the window back up. As the train began to glide out of the station, she continued to stand there, and Joe watched as her smiling crimson lips vanished behind a flurry of snowflakes.

Chapter Two

Spinning Wheels

As the last carriage melted into the darkness, Joe felt his fear dissolving. He walked across the platform and stood underneath the solitary lamp. Its light was comforting and made him feel safe. Reluctant to step into the shadows again, Joe decided to stay put and wait for his mum to locate him.

As the seconds ticked by, Joe tried to make sense of the puzzling series of events on the train. Seeing a snake emerge from somebody's handbag had been a shock. He had been unnerved by its sudden appearance but he was convinced that the snake had not been responsible for making his hair stand on end. Nor had it caused the bolt of fear to shoot through him.

It was the woman, thought Joe. The glamorous woman with the pale blue eyes. He gave an involuntary shudder as he recalled the feverish scratching of claws against wickerwork and the sight of her red fingernail unlatching the cat basket. He shivered again when he remembered the woman watching him from the window as the train pulled away. There had been something disconcerting about her smile. Joe was sure that *she* had been responsible for his distress.

The woman with the newspaper had not seemed the type to carry a reptile in her hand luggage. Joe wondered if the snake had slithered into the handbag without her knowing – or perhaps someone had placed it there as a practical joke. Why had the lights in the compartment suddenly gone out? Was it a coincidence – or had the glamorous woman orchestrated it somehow? And what were the strange flashes of light?

Snowflakes continued to spiral around Joe as he struggled to understand what he had just witnessed. He was so wrapped up in his own thoughts that he barely noticed someone moving towards him along the platform. Then, out of the corner of his eye, he saw a lumpy shape crouching behind his suitcase. As he spun round, the figure jumped to its feet and Joe found himself face to face with a squat little woman in an ankle-length navy coat. Black ringlets escaped from underneath her blue peaked cap. She smiled and two dimples appeared in her cheeks.

'Ticket, please,' she said.

'Wh … what?' said Joe in a startled voice.

'Ticket, young man,' repeated the woman, gesturing towards his suitcase and giving him a wink.

'Oh … yeah. Sorry … it's just …' Joe fumbled in his blazer pocket. 'I had a bit of a scare on the train. Saw a *snake* in someone's handbag and –'

'Tsk!' said the woman. 'What nonsense.' She glanced anxiously down the railway track. Then she prodded Joe with a chubby finger and her dimples disappeared. 'Hurry up, can't you?' she snapped.

'OK, I know I put it somewhere.' Joe searched in his other blazer pocket and produced his train ticket with a grin. The woman snatched it out of his hand without a word of thanks and scuttled away.

'Well, that was pretty rude,' said Joe. He turned up his collar and looked around him. The platform was almost empty. There was no sign of his mum or stepdad. 'Funny,' he said. 'It's not like Gordon to be late for anything. Maybe they're waiting outside in the car. Better go and find them, I suppose.' He picked up his suitcase and followed a trickle of passengers who were making their way to a door marked 'Exit'.

As Joe drew closer, he saw two men arguing in the doorway. One was wrapped up warmly in a thick navy coat and the other was hunching his shoulders in a flimsy white shirt.

'It's sloppy, Derek, there's no other word for it,' said the man in the coat, pulling down the shiny peak of his navy cap. 'Look at the state of you. You're a disgrace to the nation's railways.'

22

Derek shivered and rolled down the sleeves of his thin cotton shirt. 'But Mr Preston, I keep telling you, someone's gone and nicked 'em.'

'Somebody's stolen your hat and coat? Don't be preposterous, Derek. I've heard some excuses in my time –'

'But it's true, Mr Preston, honest. I only took 'em off for a minute, to warm 'em on the radiator while I 'ad a cup of tea –'

'Well, it serves you right, then,' said Mr Preston pompously. 'You should never remove your uniform while you're on duty. You're a careless nitwit. What are you, Derek?'

'A careless nitwit,' repeated Derek miserably.

'That's right. Now, go and dig around in the lost property cupboard and see if you can find an old jumper to wear. Then you can sweep the platform until it's spotless. Spotless, d'you hear?' Mr Preston nodded towards a broom which was standing in the corner.

'Y-yes, sir,' said Derek through chattering teeth.

'Well, what have we here?' said Mr Preston as Joe tried to slip past him. Joe glowered up at Mr Preston and thought about dropping his suitcase on the man's shiny black shoes. Joe did not like the way he had treated poor Derek.

'Excuse me,' said Joe coldly. 'I'd like to get past, please.'

'I'm sure you would, sonny,' said the man, thrusting

his fleshy palm under Joe's nose. 'But I'll have to ask you for your ticket, first.'

'I've given it in already,' protested Joe.

'Sure you have, sonny,' said Mr Preston. 'Come on now. Hand it over.' He wriggled his fingers in front of Joe's face and raised his bushy black eyebrows.

'But I'm telling the truth,' said Joe. 'I gave it to the ticket collector when I got off the train. She had a peaked cap on just like you –'

'Like me, eh? A woman, you say? Well, that's where you're mistaken, sonny. There aren't any female ticket collectors in *this* station.'

'But –' began Joe.

'Mr Preston!' Derek ran over to them, pulling a mustard-coloured jumper over his protruding ears. 'Mr Preston, sir! It must have been an impostor what took the lad's ticket. She must've been wearing my clothes and –'

'You think a thief would whip your coat and hat and then hang about the station collecting tickets? You're thicker than you look, Derek, and that's saying something. She'd have scarpered straightaway. Why ... she'd be halfway to Canterbury, by now.'

'What do you mean?' said Joe, a note of panic in his voice. 'This *is* Canterbury, isn't it?'

'No, sonny, this is Stubble End.'

'Canterbury's five miles down the line,' said Derek helpfully.

'Oh no,' said Joe, covering his face with his hands. 'I've got off at the wrong stop.'

'What am I going to do?' said Joe. He was sitting on his suitcase with his hands plunged into his pockets.

Derek stopped sweeping the platform and leaned on his broom. He chewed the inside of his cheek thoughtfully. 'What's your name, kid?'

'Joe Binks.'

'Well, Joe,' said Derek, 'the phone lines are down, you've missed the last bus, and there aren't no taxicabs – not in a little village like this 'un.'

'How long do I have to wait until the next train?' asked Joe.

'Let's see,' said Derek, glancing at the station clock. He muttered under his breath and began to count on his fingers. 'Er ... that'd be five hours, sixteen minutes, and er ... er ...'

'Great,' said Joe, and sighed. A cloud of warm breath billowed from his mouth and hung in the chilly air like smoke. 'My mum is going to kill me.'

'I'd give you a lift,' said Derek, wiping dust from his baggy navy trousers, 'only I 'aven't got a car.'

'Thanks,' said Joe.

'An' I can't drive.'

'Right.' Joe picked at the red braiding on the sleeve of his blazer. 'Looks like I'm stuck here, then.'

'Least Mr Preston didn't make you pay for another ticket. He's a stickler for rules, he is. You're lucky he's in a Christmassy mood. He's been ever so nice-natured this week.'

'Has he?' said Joe incredulously.

'Oh, yeah,' continued Derek. 'Let me wear this jumper from lost property, didn't he?'

'I suppose.'

'Hang on a minute!' Derek let his broom drop to the ground and whistled through his teeth. 'Joe, I think I've got it! Wait here a sec.' Derek ran up the platform. He reappeared, moments later, with a wide grin on his face and his fingers wrapped around the handlebars of a large orange tricycle.

'What do you think, Joe? Not bad, eh? Once I've pumped its tyres up and lowered its saddle a bit, I reckon it could get you to Canterbury.'

'Well,' said Joe, shrugging his shoulders. 'I could give it a go.' He inspected the tricycle, rubbing his fingers along the scratched paintwork, while Derek tried to straighten a couple of bent spokes in the front wheel. Joe pinged the bell on its handlebars. It made a dull clinking noise. 'Lights work,' said Joe, flicking them on and off, 'and there's somewhere to put my suitcase.' He patted a luggage rack between the two back wheels. 'It's worth a try, but I can't just take it, can I, Derek?'

'Sure you can,' said Derek. 'It's been in lost property for three months and no one's claimed it. Anyone can 'ave it, now. That's the rules. Between you and me, I think Mr Preston 'ad got his eye on it for his son, Malcolm, but you need it more, Joe.' Derek began to pump up the tyres while Joe looked anxiously around the platform. 'Don't you worry about Mr Preston,' said Derek. 'He's in his office with a big mug o' tea and a cream bun. He won't be stirring for –'

There was a deafening roar as a train streamed past the platform, drowning out Derek's words. 'Bet you wish you were on that, eh, Joe?' said Derek when the train had whizzed through Stubble End station.

Joe did not answer. He was thinking about the snake that he had seen slithering from the handbag, half an hour earlier. At the time, he had been certain it was a snake, but now he wondered if it had been a trick of the light. Perhaps it had been nothing more than the woman's green fountain pen. He remembered how scared he had been when he had jumped from the train on to the platform, without being sure of the station's name. Why had he been so convinced that it was Canterbury?

'The man on the train,' muttered Joe. 'I'm sure he said this was my stop. I'm sure he did.'

'Huh?' said Derek, attaching the pump to the tricycle

frame. He patted the saddle. 'Ready to go then, Joe?'

'Yeah.' Joe slid his suitcase on to the luggage rack and Derek fastened it with several pieces of string. Joe wheeled the tricycle through the station entrance and stood looking out into the darkness. He flicked on his front light and snowflakes danced in its narrow beam. He buttoned up his blazer.

'Now, ride careful, won't you?' said Derek. 'Go straight on for about a mile and take the first left. That'll take you on to the Canterbury road. Then you just 'ave to follow the signs.'

'Right. Got it,' said Joe. 'Listen, thanks a lot, Derek.' He shook Derek's outstretched hand. Then he took a deep breath and began to pedal.

Usually, when adults advised Joe to be careful, he rarely heeded their advice, but on this occasion, he decided that Derek's cautionary words should be obeyed. As a result, Joe rode the tricycle extremely sensibly. He pedalled slowly round corners, pressing gently on the brakes so that his tyres did not skid on the slippery road. He tried to avoid potholes so that his suitcase did not bump too heavily and break the string that was keeping it fastened to the tricycle – and as soon as he glimpsed the flash of headlights in the distance, he pulled in to the side of the road and waited for the vehicle to pass before he began to pedal again. As he approached halfway, Joe felt rather pleased with his progress (despite being soaking wet and numb with cold). Then something very peculiar happened.

Joe lost control of the tricycle.

One moment, he was steering it round a corner, and the next, he was plummeting into a ditch, careering up a bank and crashing through a hedge. He tried to turn the handlebars, but they would not budge, and the pedals of the tricycle started to whiz round so fast that his legs were pumping up and down at a frightening speed.

'What's happening?' yelled Joe as the tricycle sped across a field, its mudguards rattling. A tree loomed up out of the darkness and Joe squeezed the brakes but, apart from swerving and nearly throwing him out of the saddle, the tricycle did not slow down. 'This is *crazy*. Just stop, you stupid thing!' shouted Joe as the tricycle smashed through a fence, sending splinters of wood showering through the air. Joe took his feet off the pedals and rested them on the tricycle frame. The pedals continued to revolve by themselves, turning so fast that they started to whine. Joe gripped the handlebars very tightly, closed his eyes and hoped that the nightmare would come to an end.

It did.

The ground became smoother and he heard the growl

of vehicle engines. He opened his eyes and was blinded by a blaze of car headlights. It seemed as if every car was hooting at him. Brakes squealed and Joe felt the tricycle turn sharply and mount a pavement. Astonished people dropped their shopping bags and dived into shop door-ways to avoid Joe and his runaway tricycle.

He recognised a pizza parlour as he flew past it. His mum had taken him there for his twelfth birthday in October. Joe realised that he had reached Canterbury. The tricycle continued to thread its way through shop-pers until it turned down a little cobbled road called Weaver's Lane. It speeded up, appearing to be aiming for a slim, three-storey building with a crooked purple door. Joe squeezed his eyes shut again and grimaced, waiting for the inevitable collision – but it never came. At the last moment, the door swung open and the tricycle skidded on a doormat. Joe lifted his arms to shield his face and was catapulted over the handlebars.

Chapter Three

A Coven Uncovered

Joe slid, face first, underneath a desk, narrowly avoiding a pair of square-toed black shoes with shiny silver buckles. A cat screeched in his ear and sprang on to his back. It sank its claws through his blazer and into his flesh. Joe rolled over to dislodge the cat, which hissed and spat as it leaped on to an armchair.

Joe continued to roll over, his elbows and knees smacking against hard floorboards until his shoulder knocked against a three-legged stool and he came to a stop.

The girl who was sitting on the stool grabbed the seat with both hands as it rocked backwards and forwards. Then both she and the stool toppled over. As the girl fell, the toe of her black boot caught underneath the lid of a desk and flipped it upwards. A little glass bottle dropped to the floor and smashed. Joe heard somebody curse. Then he covered his face with his arms as hundreds of leaves scattered into the air and began to float serenely towards the ground.

'Oof!' said the girl as her body crumpled against the floor. The stool clattered down next to her.

'Er … sorry,' said Joe, spitting out a leaf as it landed in his mouth.

'What's that?' snapped a little woman who was sitting behind a heavy oak desk in one corner of the room. She tucked a few stray wisps of hair back into the coiled plait on top of her head and glared at Joe through her butterfly-shaped spectacles. 'I should think you *are* sorry. Just look at the chaos you've caused!'

Joe brushed several leaves from his blazer and shook a few more out of his hair. 'I really am sorry,' he said, struggling to his feet. 'The tricycle … I don't know what happened. I just couldn't seem to stop.'

'Couldn't stop, eh?' The woman snorted and began to walk towards him. The hem of her long black dress dragged over the bare floorboards.

'Yes, honestly,' said Joe, looking around him.

He had arrived in a room with a low, uneven ceiling, supported by wooden beams. A bare light bulb hung from the ceiling, emitting a soft fizzing noise. The primrose-yellow walls were almost obscured by notice-boards, graphs, pie charts, a calendar picturing a blotchy grey toadstool, and a large map of the British Isles. The floor of the room was easily as crowded as the walls. Every available space seemed to be occupied by an ugly, antiquated item of furniture.

The room's only handsome feature was a rather grand fireplace. A sculpture of an aardvark made from paper-clips rested on its mantelpiece. Below the sculpture, scorched logs stirred and crumbled in a grate while orange flames licked around them. In front of the fireplace were two armchairs: one red and plump, the other blue and rigid. The black cat which had jumped on to Joe's back was perched on the arm of the blue chair. It watched Joe with unblinking green eyes, its tail twitching from side to side.

Unnerved by the cat, Joe stumbled backwards, knocking his shoulder against a sturdy filing cabinet. 'Ouch,' he said, and winced.

'Hurt yourself, have you?' said the grumpy woman. 'Serves you right –'

'Rose!' A young woman with a cropped haircut swivelled round in her chair and stood up. Joe recognised her square-toed shoes with their gleaming silver buckles and realised that it must have been her feet that he had managed to avoid when he was sliding across the floor. The woman was so tall that her short blonde hair almost grazed the low ceiling. She straightened her shoulders, put her hands on her hips and looked sternly at the woman with the butterfly-shaped spectacles. 'There's no need to be so unpleasant, Rose. Why don't you take a look at this boy's tricycle while I check if Twiggy is still in one piece.'

'Why do leaders have to be so bossy?' grumbled Rose quietly.

The young woman crouched down beside the freckly-faced girl who was picking leaves from her tangled brown hair. 'You OK, Twiggy?' she asked, touching the girl's arm.

'Don't fuss, Winifred,' said the girl. She looked over the woman's shoulder and grinned at Joe. 'I'll be fine. I think I might need some more ink, though.'

Fragments of glass crunched under Winifred's square-toed shoes and she nodded gravely. 'Yes, Twigs, it's a pity the bottle was almost full. That stuff is so expensive. I'll have to go to the market and buy some more.'

Joe studied the floorboards with a bemused look on his face. He could see the thin shards of glass glinting like diamonds, but he could not spot the tiniest trace of spilt ink.

'You, boy! Come over here and give me a hand with this contraption!' Rose sucked in her cheeks and looked as if a horrible smell had squirmed up her nose as Joe began to make his way through the cluttered room towards the tricycle.

'My name's Joe, actually,' he said, negotiating a book-case and three cardboard boxes.

'Oh, *is* it,' said Rose.

Apart from the two armchairs, the rest of the furniture in the room was of the type most commonly found in offices. There were five desks of different shapes and sizes but each desk was as battered and old-fashioned as the next. Winifred's desk, at which she had been sitting when Joe burst into the room, was immaculately tidy. Pens sprouted from a pot labelled 'Pens' and paperclips were in a tub labelled 'Paperclips'. Folders were lined up together between wooden raven bookends, and three books called *How to Make Yourself Heard*, *How to Make a Difference* and *How to Make an Aardvark out of Paperclips* were in a pile next to a blank pad of paper. The only object which seemed slightly out of place was a vase of rather droopy-looking weeds.

As Joe passed a spiral staircase and squeezed past Rose's desk, he knocked over a jar full of drawing pins with his elbow.

'Stupid, clumsy boy!' shrieked Rose.

Joe tried to scoop the drawing pins back into the jar but they seemed to slip through his fingers and jump in by themselves. 'This day is turning out to be very weird,' he muttered, rubbing his eyes.

The tricycle was lying on its side on a threadbare rug just inside the door. One of its wheels was still spinning round. Joe touched the tyre with his fingers and it stopped. He gripped the handlebars and heaved the tricycle upright while Rose twittered away to herself and prodded Joe with her bony fingers. Joe stared suspiciously at the tricycle. It seemed so harmless and ordinary but he knew that he would never dare to sit in its saddle again.

'It's almost as if it's been bewitched,' he said, picking up a broken strand of string. He looked around for his suitcase.

'*What* did you say?' said Rose, removing her butter-fly-shaped spectacles and peering at him very closely.

'I ... er ...'

'Speak up!'

Rose's penetrating stare was making Joe feel very uncomfortable. He stepped away from her. 'I ... um ... I only said that ... it seems like this tricycle's been ... *bewitched*.'

'I thought that's what you said.' Rose replaced her spectacles and folded her arms. Joe thought that she looked extremely smug about something. 'Did you hear that, Winifred?' said Rose in a high-pitched, haughty voice. 'This boy thinks his tricycle's been bewitched.'

Joe realised that a deathly hush had fallen on the room. Then Winifred gave a nervous titter. 'Well, what a funny thing to say! Bewitched, indeed! Oh, Joe, you've got quite an imagination, you have. Hasn't he, Twiggy? My goodness!' Winifred picked up a broom and began to sweep up the broken glass. Joe noticed that it was an old-fashioned type of broom. It was nothing more than a bundle of birch twigs tied around the end of a long wooden handle.

Twiggy laughed uncertainly and smiled at Joe but, at the same time, she seemed to be whispering something out of the corner of her mouth.

'Psst … Winifred!' he heard her say. 'Drop *the broom*. Winifred!' Twiggy made a slight flapping gesture with her hands. 'Ditch *the broom* … quick … before he sees …'

'Oh!' Winifred stopped sweeping and let the broom drop to the floor. Then she covered her mouth with her hands and looked worriedly at Joe.

'Poor Winifred,' said Twiggy in a flat voice. 'Have you got a splinter in your hand?'

'What?' said Winifred. 'Oh … yes, that's right.' She held up one finger. 'Ow.'

Joe narrowed his eyes. For some bizarre reason, everyone had begun to act very strangely. He took a few steps backwards and bumped into a hat stand. A limp black hat with a broad rim flopped on to the floor. Joe picked it up by its pointed tip and stared at it. 'Isn't this a witch's hat?' he said.

Rose snatched it out of his hands. 'Of course it's not a witch's hat, you ignoramus. It's the very latest thing in hat couture. Don't you know anything about fashion?'

'Not much,' agreed Joe. He took a deep breath. 'But I know quite a lot about telling huge fibs … and you're not very good at it, Rose.'

'That's it. We've been rumbled,' said Rose sourly. She threw the hat over her shoulder. 'Don't try to hush me, Winifred. The boy's obviously not quite as stupid as I thought. I don't see any point in continuing with this pathetic charade. We might as well admit it.'

'Admit what?' said Joe in a puzzled voice.

'You see?' said Winifred crossly. 'He hasn't rumbled us at all. Oh, why can't you keep your mouth shut, Rose?'

'Yes, I was wrong.' Rose smiled nastily at Joe. 'He *is* as stupid as I thought.'

'Don't be horrible,' said Twiggy. '*I* think he's nice.' She began to clomp towards Joe in her black hobnailed boots.

Joe stared at the girl's faded black tunic. Then he looked very hard at Winifred and Rose. It dawned on him that they were *all* dressed in black. For the first time, he noticed a row of glass jars sitting on a long desk at the back of the room. Brightly-coloured liquid bubbled inside them. The black cat sprang from the armchair and arched its back. Joe's gaze fell on the old-fashioned broom which was lying on the floor.

He felt as if a triangle had been tinged inside his head.

'Crikey!' said Joe, his eyes widening. 'You're not *really* witches, are you?'

He ran to the door, but not before Rose had reached

38

into the folds of her long black dress and produced a thin stick which tapered to a point at one end.

'Is that … is that a *wand*?' Joe gulped as Rose waved the stick in front of his face. 'What are you going to do to me?'

'Rose, please put that down!' shouted Winifred. 'Now, stay calm everybody. The important thing is not to panic –'

'Yippee!' A woman with a large, wobbly body and frizzy grey hair appeared at the foot of the spiral staircase. Wearing a pair of red carpet slippers, she tramped towards the tricycle, knelt on the floor and flung her arms around the front wheel. 'There you are, my little pookums!' she said, smiling blissfully. 'I knew you'd find your way back to your mummy.' The tricycle gave a little jiggle and the woman planted a kiss on its handlebars.

Rose groaned and shook her head. 'Patsy, what on earth are you doing? Have you finally lost your mind?'

The woman ignored her, hugging the tricycle even more tightly. 'Dear, dear, silly old me. I'd quite forgotten what I'd done with you. I must say you make a very splendid tricycle, but I'd better change you back, I suppose.'

'Patsy Bogbean!' said Rose sharply. 'Do you mean to say –'

'Of course I mean what I say,' snapped Patsy, turning her bright green eyes on Rose. 'Otherwise what would be the point of saying anything? Now, do be quiet, you old windbag. You know I can't concentrate with you yapping on.'

Rose made a choking noise and she trembled so much that five hairpins slid from her coiled plait and tinkled against the floorboards. Her plait unravelled like a writhing snake and hung down her back, swinging gently. Joe was tempted to reach for the door handle, but Rose's wand was still an inch away from his nose so he stayed where he was.

Patsy lifted up her tattered black skirt. It was covered with brightly-coloured stains and scorch marks. A wand protruded from the leg of her red bloomers. She pulled it out and swished it through the air a few times.

Rose closed her eyes in a despairing way. 'So unprofessional!' she muttered.

Pointing the wand at the tricycle, Patsy licked her lips. 'Now, let's see,' she said, 'how does the spell go again? I ought to be able to rattle it off. I have to use it enough times!' She took a deep breath and began to recite in a commanding voice:

'By the Stones of Fate
and the Spillikins of Doom,
your former self
you must resume.'

There was a crackling sound as a flurry of green sparks spattered from the end of the wand. The tricycle shivered. Then the handlebars twisted round by themselves and disappeared with a soft pop. The pedals revolved slowly and vanished in the same way. Gradually, the tricycle lost its wheels, its chain and even its bell, until only the bare frame was left. The frame began to ripple before Joe's eyes until, with a loud snap and a rustle of twigs, the tricycle became a broomstick.

'Wow,' breathed Joe. 'I was riding a broomstick and I didn't even know it.'

Patsy stroked the handle of the broom and made soft cooing noises. Twiggy wandered over to her and tugged on the witch's sleeve. 'What are the Spillikins of Doom, Patsy?' she asked.

'I have absolutely no idea, lovey,' replied Patsy. 'But I got the spell out of *Mabel's Book* and it works a treat every time. That woman was a genius.' The witch frowned at Twiggy. 'Why aren't you wearing that nice cardie I knitted you? The one with the itsy-bitsy owl buttons. Go and put it on, petal, or you'll catch your death of cold. It's the middle of winter out there, you know.' Patsy waved her hand at the purple front door and her mouth fell open. 'Hang on a minute,' she said. 'Who's that?'

Joe gave a weak smile and bit his lower lip.

'That's Joe,' said Twiggy brightly. 'He's the one who

brought your broomstick back. He gave us a bit of a shock, but –'

'The boy is a walking disaster,' droned Rose.

'A cycling disaster, to be more accurate,' croaked an elderly male voice from behind a desk in the farthest corner of the room. The desk was piled high with books, newspapers, empty jam-jars and a dusty, old-fashioned typewriter. Joe stood on tiptoe and managed to glimpse a fluffy mass of white hair.

'Oh, go back to sleep, Julius,' said Rose rudely. She prodded Joe with her wand. 'This boy has caused complete havoc. Broke the ink bottle … scattered the leaflets everywhere … knocked Twiggy over. And my poor Ishtar was frightened out of her wits.' The black cat hissed at Joe.

Patsy narrowed her eyes and rubbed her warty chin with a thick, wrinkled finger. 'Who would have thought a little lad like you could do all that!' she said to Joe. 'Well, don't just stand there like a limp lettuce. Come over here so I can get a good look at you.'

Joe ducked underneath Rose's wand and shuffled towards Patsy. He was relieved to have escaped the grouchy witch with the butterfly-shaped spectacles but he was not sure that this one in the red carpet slippers would be any kinder to him. Patsy had cast one spell already and she had been rather too good at it for his liking. He glanced at his watch and saw that it was half past seven. His mum would be very worried by now. Joe did not know how he was going to get out of the room without being turned into a toad, or something even worse.

'Hmm,' said Patsy as Joe stopped in front of her. She placed her hands on his shoulders and gave him a gentle shake. 'Bit puny, aren't you, lad? Still, you've got plenty of time to fatten out.' Joe gulped. He wondered if Patsy was planning to eat him. She tweaked his nose and gave a hearty laugh. Then she wrapped her arms around Joe and gave him a big hug.

'Gnumf,' said Joe as all the air was squeezed out of him.

'Thanks for bringing my broomstick back,' said Patsy when she had finished squashing him. 'I'd completely forgotten that I'd turned it into a tricycle. Where did you find it?'

'Stubble End,' said Joe.

'That's right!' said Patsy. 'I remember now. I nipped down to the station. Couldn't ride my broomstick in broad daylight so I changed it into a tricycle. Bought a ticket from a nice young chap with sticky-out ears and went on a day trip to Margate. I do like riding on those train thingies. Nice, comfy cushioned seats, and you don't have to cope with a crosswind. Don't get me wrong, I love my broomstick, but they're not built with comfort in mind, and ooh ... the draught!'

'We haven't lived at Stubble End for three months,'

said Rose tersely. 'Do you mean to say your broomstick has been missing for that long? That's disgraceful!'

'Oh, hag's knickers!' said Patsy. 'Why don't you mind your own business for once, Rose Threep!'

'She has got a point, Patsy.' Winifred nudged Twiggy's arm and handed her a rusty-red cardigan with owl-shaped buttons. 'This carelessness has got to stop. You're always turning things into something else and then forgetting to change them back. Take Squib, for instance –'

'He's *my* cat,' said Patsy stubbornly. 'I can do what I like with him. Anyway, he loves it. Thrives on the excitement. Not every cat can say they've been a flowerpot, a puff of smoke and a cockroach all in one day.'

'I don't think he does love it,' said Twiggy timidly.

'Who asked you, eh?'

'So where is he, then?' asked Winifred, raising her eyebrows.

'What? Who? What, you mean, er ... you mean Squib? Oh, he's around somewhere ...'

'Where *exactly*?' said Winifred. 'I haven't seen him for a couple of weeks.'

'Neither have I,' said Rose.

'He's fine,' insisted Patsy. 'Happy as a salamander in open-toed sandals. Now, stop interfering, or I won't tell you about the new Re-growing Potion I've invented. It's a classic.' She winked at Joe and slapped him on the shoulder. 'So, Joe, I suppose the Pipistrelles sent you, did they? Miserable bunch of old bat-lovers. They got us booted out of Stubble End, you know. How I miss that quiet old village. So why'd you join Pipistrelle Coven, then, huh? Dora Benton bully you into it, did she? Wouldn't you rather sign up with us?'

'I'm s-sorry,' stuttered Joe. 'I'm afraid I don't know what you're talking about. Nobody *sent* me. I got off at the wrong stop, you see. Derek, the bloke with the sticky-out ears who works at Stubble End station, let me use the tricycle so that I could get home.'

'Oh,' said Patsy and her shoulders drooped. 'So you're not one of us, then?'

'Er ... I don't think so,' said Joe. 'I can't do magic, if that's what you mean.'

'Of course he can't,' sneered Rose. 'I knew as soon as I clapped eyes on him. Nasty common boy. It's obvious he doesn't have the tiniest sprinkle of talent. He's one of *them*.'

'There's no need to hurt the boy's feelings,' said Winifred. 'He can't help it. Now, Joe, why don't you help Twiggy to pick up her leaflets while I make us all a nice cup of dead-nettle tea.'

'I think I ought to go home,' said Joe.

Winifred nodded. 'After you've got a hot drink inside you, I'll take you home myself. How about that?'

Chapter four

The Dead-nettle Witches

Joe scooped up another handful of leaves and placed them carefully on Twiggy's desk, while she sat on her three-legged stool and sorted them into piles.

'Oak for Orpington,' she said, her forehead wrinkling into a frown. 'Sycamore for Sheerness and ... hmm ... that's poplar for Paddock Wood.' She tucked a fountain pen behind her ear and grinned at Joe. 'Thanks for helping,' she said.

'I think this is elm,' said Joe, holding out a leaf with a serrated edge.

'Nope,' said Twiggy. 'Hornbeam. That's for Herne Bay.' She studied it closely and bit her lip. 'Oops,' she said. 'I've made a spelling mistake. Oh, well ... I doubt anyone will notice. We're better at spells than spelling, us witches!'

'What do you mean?' said Joe, leaning over her shoulder and peering at the leaf. 'There's nothing written on it.'

Twiggy gave him a knowing look. 'Oh yes there is. You just can't see it.'

'Why not?' said Joe.

'Because it's written in witchy ink!'

'What kind of ink?'

'Only witches can see it,' explained Twiggy. 'It's invisible to everyone else.' She sighed and scratched her nose. 'I can see you don't believe me.'

'Well ...' began Joe, trying not to laugh.

Twiggy slipped off her stool and ran to the long desk at the back of the room. She groped around the glass jars which were filled with bubbling liquid. Green smoke poured from a rack of little test tubes and Twiggy began to cough.

'What are you after?' asked Patsy, putting her head round the door of a cupboard.

'The, you know ...' Twiggy coughed again and her eyes started to water. She drew two small circles in the air with her finger.

'Oh!' Patsy opened the top drawer of the desk and handed Twiggy a little velvet bag. 'Don't drop them,' she warned. 'I haven't got the patience to make another pair.'

'What are they?' asked Joe, as Twiggy emptied the contents of the bag into her hand.

'Magic spectacles, of course,' she said, holding them up to the light. Their lenses looked as if they were made of liquid. They seemed to swirl and glimmer, changing colour every few seconds. At first they glowed electric blue, but a few moments later they switched to a cloudy pink. Joe reached out and touched the frames. They were extremely thin and fragile-looking.

'What do you think of them?' said Twiggy.

'They're beautiful.'

'Patsy made them,' she said proudly, 'but I helped. There were a lot of ingredients to gather up. I'm good at gathering things.'

'What kind of things?' asked Joe.

'Oh, gossamer, pond slime, hibiscus leaves, a crocodile's tooth …'

'That's quite a shopping list,' said Joe, wondering how it was possible to extract a tooth from a crocodile without losing your entire arm.

Twiggy blushed and shrugged her shoulders. Then she slid the spectacles over Joe's ears.

At first, all that Joe could see was a blurry sparkling mist. After a few seconds, his vision cleared and he stared at Twiggy; at her untidy brown hair, her snubby nose, her rash of freckles and her hazel eyes. There was nothing different about her.

'Don't look at me, you ninny,' said Twiggy, holding up an oak leaf. Joe focused on the leaf and his mouth fell open.

He could see something written on it. The ink was

golden and the messy joined-up writing gleamed from the surface of the dull beige leaf. It read:

Do you wish you were a wiser witch?
Is your coven cramping your style?
Join us at Dead-nettle Coven
if you want to rise above the rest.
Turn south at St Agnes's Mount
and look for the roof with a wonky chimney.

'So that's why Winifred called them leaflets,' said Joe, looking curiously at the floor. A golden stain blossomed on the floorboards where the witchy ink had spilt.

'We're recruiting,' explained Twiggy. 'Well, everyone's recruiting at the moment because there aren't many witches about these days. See that map over there ...' She pointed to the map of the British Isles which was stuck to the wall behind Rose's desk. Little flags had been pinned on to the map. There was a cluster of them in Essex and Kent, and a few scattered in Gwynedd, London and Lancashire, but the rest of the map was practically bare.

'They show where all the covens are in Great Britain. Bit pathetic, isn't it?' Twiggy added sadly.

'What exactly is a coven?' asked Joe.

'Don't you know? A coven is a group of witches. We've all got different names, though. The witches in

Stubble End are called Pipistrelle Coven. Then there's the Bladderwracks – they live on Foulness Island ... and the Vipers hang out in Putney. We're Dead-nettle Coven. Yes, I know. Boring name, isn't it? Well, we're not really a coven ... not properly. You have to have at least six members, you see, and we've only got five. That's why we're having a bit of a recruitment drive at the moment.'

'Here's your dead-nettle tea,' said Winifred, handing Joe a cup of murky green liquid.

Joe sniffed it suspiciously. 'Won't sting my tongue, will it?'

'No,' said Winifred and she laughed. 'Dead-nettles don't have stinging hairs on their leaves. They're quite harmless.'

'Told you,' said Twiggy. 'How dull can you get?'

'Been looking through the magic spectacles, have you, Joe?' said Winifred.

'That is all right, isn't it?' said Twiggy, as Joe hurriedly removed them.

'Yes, of course. No problem.' Winifred smiled at Joe and he felt the tiniest shiver run down his spine.

'Then is it OK if I call Cuthbert? I'm sure he'd like to meet Joe,' said Twiggy.

Winifred nodded and walked back across the room to Julius's desk. She bent close to the old man's mop of white hair and began to whisper something in his ear.

Joe heard Julius say, 'Yes, of course. Right away.' Then there was a creak and the top of Julius's head sank below a pile of books and disappeared.

'Who's Cuthbert?' asked Joe, turning back to Twiggy. She was struggling to open a sash window just behind her desk. It opened suddenly and a puff of wind stirred the piles of leaves. Joe took a swig of the dead-nettle tea and pulled a face. It tasted foul.

'He posts my leaflets for me,' said Twiggy, leaning her head out of the window. She placed two fingers in her mouth and gave a long, shrill whistle. When she withdrew her head it was covered in snowflakes. Joe watched as they melted into her hair.

'What kind of postman delivers leaves?' asked Joe.

'This kind,' said Twiggy, as a gentle gust of wind blew through the window.

'What?' said Joe. 'Where? Do I need to put on those magic specs again? Is Cuthbert invisible?'

'Very nearly ... but you don't need those specs to see him. Just watch.'

Rose was sitting at her desk, coiling her plait on top of her head and replacing the hairpins. A breeze wafted past her, lifting her loose hairs and rippling them in the air. She ducked her head and flapped her hands. 'Get away from me, you revolting little creature. I'm sure it does this on purpose. Eugh! Get away! Twiggy, do something!'

'Rose doesn't like windsprites,' said Twiggy, and she giggled. 'Cuthbert! Come over here. I want you to meet Joe.'

The little flags on the map began to flutter. Then Patsy's frizzy hair blew back from her face as she poured a lumpy green solution into a saucer. Joe felt a breeze on the back of his neck and twisted his head, but he could not see anyone.

'Hello, Cuthbert,' said Twiggy as her hair billowed behind her. 'Can you see him, Joe? You have to look really hard.'

Joe stared at Twiggy's hair and, just for a moment, he thought he glimpsed a sharp pointed chin and the curve of an arm. The air shimmered and Joe saw an agile little body turn a somersault. Then he blinked and the creature vanished.

'Wow!' said Joe. 'He's amazing!'

'You saw him, then! Cuthbert is rather fantastic, isn't he.'

Rose snorted. 'Cuthbert! Pah! How do you know that's its name? Windsprites can't speak. They're nothing but ignorant little show-offs.'

'They are not!' said Twiggy fiercely. 'I know Cuthbert's not his real name but *I* think he *likes* it –'

'Oh, Twiggy,' said Winifred. 'You can't be sure that's the same windsprite. They all look alike.'

'That's not true,' said Twiggy. 'I *know* it's Cuthbert.'

She folded her arms and glowered at Winifred. 'You believe me, don't you, Joe?'

'Sure,' said Joe, and Twiggy beamed at him.

'The kid's right,' said Patsy as she scribbled something in an exercise book. 'That little chap is the only windsprite who bothers to answer her whistle.' Patsy sucked the end of her pen thoughtfully. 'It's a funny thing,' she said, turning to Joe, 'but you don't see many of them about these days. Why, when I was a girl –'

Rose gave a muffled snort.

'When *I* was a girl –' repeated Patsy.

'Before they invented the wheel,' muttered Rose.

'I'll have you know,' said Patsy frostily, 'that I'll be sixty-six next birthday, and the more wrinkles the better, that's what I say. So, kindly shut your trap, Rose Threep. I'm conversing with young Joe, here.'

'You were telling me about windsprites,' prompted Joe.

'Ah, yes.' Patsy smiled. 'When I was your age, I used to see dozens of the little blighters.' She gazed wistfully past Joe's shoulder. 'Saw a whole flock of them flying over a sewage works, once. Lovely sunset there was. Prettiest sight I ever saw.' She blew her nose loudly and shook her head. 'Nowadays, you only see them in ones or twos. It's a downright shame, that's what it is.'

'I'm lucky to have Cuthbert,' said Twiggy, stroking the air beside her head. 'He's ever so helpful. He posts all my leaflets for me. I tell him where they're meant to be dropped and he carries them away. They just look like leaves floating on the breeze. It's clever, isn't it?'

'Yes,' agreed Joe, wishing that he could send a leaf to his mother to tell her not to worry and that he'd be home very soon. He knew that he would be in huge amounts of trouble when he arrived at her house, several hours late. He wondered how he was going to explain what had happened to him.

'Thanks for the tea,' said Joe to Winifred, 'but I think I'd better be going now.'

'I'll come too,' said Twiggy eagerly. A pile of leaves rose off her desk and whisked out of the open window. 'Those are for Orpington,' she called. 'Bye Cuthbert!'

Joe's suitcase was as light as a feather. Winifred had put a spell on it so that it floated weightlessly beside him. Powdery snow had settled on the ground and Joe kept slipping on the stone-flagged path as they took a short cut through Becket Gardens.

'I still don't see why we couldn't have gone by broom-stick,' grumbled Twiggy as she dawdled along, her chin pressed into the red woollen scarf which Patsy had wound around her neck. 'It's dark enough. No one would have –'

'Twiggy, be sensible. It would have been far too dangerous to put Joe on a broomstick.'

'He's ridden one before,' said Twiggy.

'Sort of,' added Joe quietly.

'Don't be impudent,' said Winifred, adjusting the shoulder strap of her bag. Something clinked inside the bag and she put her head down and walked faster. On reaching a wrought-iron gate, Winifred paused and looked behind her. 'Hurry up, you two,' she hissed, before leaving Becket Gardens and turning right.

The High Street was almost deserted, but a few Christmas shoppers continued to press their noses against shop windows, their hands filled with bags and parcels. Most of the shopkeepers were turning out their lights and locking their front doors for the night. Joe could hear faint voices singing carols in the distance.

'Only a few days till Christmas,' said Joe.

'We don't celebrate that,' said Twiggy, 'but it's Yule tomorrow. We're all going to St Agnes's Mount to light a bonfire.'

'If we're invited,' cautioned Winifred. 'Now, Joe, we must be nearing Cloister Walk by now.'

'Yes, I think it's down this little lane and through an archway.'

A few minutes later, they stood at the corner of Cloister Walk and Joe saw the revolving blue lights of a police car outside his mother's house. 'Bye, then,' he said, as Winifred tapped his suitcase with her wand and undid the spell. Joe felt his arm being yanked towards the ground as his case became heavy again.

'Wait a minute,' said Winifred, opening her bag. She produced two jam-jars and a strange-looking funnel. One of the jars contained a swirling turquoise mist; the other was empty.

'No,' pleaded Twiggy. 'Don't do it, Winifred!'

'Get out of my way, Twigs. I don't have any choice.'

Winifred seized Joe's shoulder and dragged him into the shadows. With her other hand, she placed the narrow end of the funnel in his ear. Joe tried to wriggle free but she was holding him very tightly.

'What are you doing?' he said in a scared voice.

'It's painless, don't worry,' said the tall witch. 'Twiggy, get the jars, please. *Now!*'

'I'm really sorry about this, Joe,' said Twiggy, as she unscrewed the lid of the empty jam-jar and held it next to the funnel. Winifred pointed her wand at Joe's head, waved it twice and chanted:

'Tick tock.
Time unlock.
Memory dispel.
Erase
every trace.
Nothing left to dwell.'

Chapter five

An Irksome Girl

Still only half-awake, Joe stretched out his arm and swept the small alarm clock off the bedside table. It landed on the thick pink carpet with a muffled thump.

'Ohhh!' Joe clutched his head and opened one eye. Then he sprang back on to his pillows, yanking the duvet up to his chin. 'What,' said Joe groggily, 'are you *doing* in here, Esme?'

A little girl in a fluffy yellow dressing-gown smiled at him from the foot of his bed. Her hands were clasped around a chunky mug. 'Brought you some milk,' she said. 'I spilt a bit coming up the stairs. If I had a cat, he could have licked it up, couldn't he, Joe? Only Dad won't let me have one. He says that cats leave hairs everywhere and make him sneeze.' She sighed, shuffled forward in her stripy zebra slippers and handed the mug to Joe.

'Er ... thanks,' said Joe, taking a sip.

Esme tilted her head to one side. 'Your hair's sticking

up. It looks funny.'

'Well, I have just woken up, Ez.' He looked at his sister's shiny black hair, neatly cut into a short bob. 'I can see you've brushed yours already.'

'No,' she said. 'I haven't.'

Joe looked at his sister's sleek hair, her glowing skin and her large grey eyes which stared back at him without blinking. 'You're so ... you're so ... *neat*,' he said finally, and Esme beamed at him.

'Have to help with breakfast, now,' she said. 'Don't be long. Mum's taking us shopping later.'

'OK,' said Joe, waving his hand as she padded over to his bedroom door. 'Phew!' he said when he heard Esme going down the stairs. 'I'd forgotten how spooky my little sister is!' He felt that it was unnatural for a seven-year-old to be so tidy and well-behaved. She was a serious little person who was content to play with her dolls in a corner or curl up in a chair with a library book. It had been years since Joe had seen her throw a tantrum, and he found it quite a challenge to make her laugh.

Joe threw back the duvet and slid his legs over the mattress. His toes sank into the soft pink carpet. He bent over, picked up the alarm clock and set it on the bedside table. Joe watched the second hand's stuttering movements as he remembered the events of the day before.

Everything had gone like clockwork at first, thought Joe. The taxi driver had been waiting for him outside the school gates and he had caught the train to Canterbury exactly as planned. It was only when the train stopped at Stubble End that everything had begun to go wrong.

Sitting in the tidy bedroom with daylight filtering through the pink flowery curtains, Joe could not believe that he had been frightened by a woman and the contents of her cat basket – the idea seemed absurd. And I don't believe I saw a snake in that handbag at all, thought Joe, more convinced than ever that his eyes had deceived him. It was dark, he thought, and I couldn't see the fountain pen properly. I must have made a mistake.

Joe frowned as he pulled off his pyjama top. He could not quite recall how he had found himself beside a moonlit river. He remembered sitting on his suitcase on Stubble End station, desperately trying to figure out how he could get home – but his journey to the river was a total blank. Perhaps he had decided to walk to Canterbury and the path beside the river was the quickest route. Yes, thought Joe. That must have been it.

He remembered that he had only been walking for a couple of minutes when he spied a little rowing boat tethered to a landing-stage, and he stepped into the boat without a moment's hesitation. He recalled fitting the oars into the rowlocks and rowing down the river for a long time. He had been surprisingly good at it.

As he held his crumpled pyjama top, Joe examined his hands and was astounded that he could not find a single blister, despite pulling on the oars for over two hours. He shrugged, walked over to his suitcase and rooted around for something to wear. His school uniform was hanging over the back of a chair and he grinned, glad that he would not have to put on the drab grey clothes for two weeks. Joe chose a pair of jeans and his favourite sweatshirt.

He hoped that his mother would be less angry with him this morning. Last night, he had arrived at number two, Cloister Walk to find two stern police constables in the hallway. His mother had dropped her mug of coffee on the carpet when she had spotted Joe. No one had seemed to believe him when he had explained that he had rowed to Canterbury from Stubble End, especially when he had been unable to tell them where he had left the rowing boat. The police constables had lectured Joe about wasting their time and causing needless worry and his mother had spoken to him coldly in a shaking voice. Joe's stepfather, Gordon, had been the only person who had seemed pleased to see him, and Joe had almost warmed to him for a moment. Then Gordon had spoilt things by ruffling Joe's hair in a really annoying way.

Joe opened the pink flowery curtains and wished that his mother had kept her promise to redecorate the guestroom. '*Any* colour would be better than *pink*,' said Joe grumpily.

He yawned. Yesterday had been tiring enough without being woken at a few minutes to midnight by a faint rapping noise on his window. When he had drawn back the curtains and looked out on to the dark snow-covered garden, he had seen someone standing below his window throwing stones up at it.

Joe had been startled at first. He had been tempted to wake his mum and stepdad, but he did not want to be the cause of any more trouble so he had unlatched the window and told the person to go away. It was then that he had realised the person was a girl. As he had slammed the window shut, he had thought he heard her call out his name – but that would have been impossible. All his friends were miles away in London. In Canterbury, the only girl he knew was his sister, Esme. Instead of going downstairs and finding out what the girl wanted, Joe had slid back into bed and fallen asleep.

'Joe! Breakfast!' Gordon was calling him.

Joe gazed down at the garden. It looked smaller and more ordinary in the light of day. The lawn and the roof of the garden shed were hidden under a smooth layer of snow. There were no footprints on the garden path and none below his window either. Perhaps the girl had never been there at all.

'Probably dreamt her,' said Joe.

Gordon was leaning over a frying pan, prodding sausages with a spatula. His blue-and-white striped apron was as spotless as the kitchen itself. Everywhere Joe looked, taps gleamed, utensils shone and dishcloths were neatly folded. Esme sat on a stool beside a pine table with her back to Joe. She was reading a book.

'Careful!' said Gordon, as Esme leaned her book too heavily against a fork. It spun across the table. Gordon left his frying pan for a second, picked up the fork and placed it next to the tablemat. He stroked his ginger moustache with his thumb and forefinger and then reached out to adjust the fork slightly, when he noticed Joe standing in the doorway.

'Ahoy there, sailor!' he said, smiling broadly.

'It was only a rowing boat, Gordon.' Joe perched on a stool and began to pour himself an orange juice.

'Yes, yes, I know. Strange stroke of luck, that … finding it moored in that little river with its oars and all. Still, it was very dangerous, Joe. If the boat had tipped over …'

'I know,' said Joe curtly.

'And how you managed to see your way in the dark, I'll never know –'

'The moon was bright enough.'

'Lot of cloud about, though,' said Joe's stepfather, 'and what with the snow, it can't have been easy.'

'You're as bad as those policemen,' said Joe, slamming

down his glass on the table. 'Why won't anyone believe me? Look, I'm really sorry that I caused you so much worry, but I'm here now, so can't we just drop it?'

'Right you are.' Gordon coughed and prodded the sausages earnestly.

'What's that you're reading, Ez?' asked Joe, eager to change the subject.

Esme peered round the corner of her book. 'It's called *Pigeons in Peril*,' she said, 'and I've just got to a good bit.'

'Oh,' said Joe. 'Sorry.'

'Would you like a fried egg with your vegetarian sausages, Joe?' asked Gordon cheerfully.

'Er ... no thanks. I'd rather have some cornflakes, if that's OK.'

'Of course,' said his stepfather. 'No, no. That's absolutely fine.' Joe could tell that Gordon was disappointed, but he did not feel very hungry. He had gone to bed with a strange taste in his mouth and, this morning, when he had poked his tongue out at himself in the bathroom mirror, it had looked decidedly green.

'Good morning, everybody!' Joe's mother breezed into the room, holding her honey-coloured hair in a pony-tail. She twisted a hair-band around it with nimble fingers. As she bent to kiss the top of Esme's head, her chunky amethyst pendant swung forward and caught her daughter on the back of her neck.

'Ooh, Mum, that hurt,' said Esme.

'Sorry, sweetheart,' said Merle, tapping Esme's nose gently with her finger. 'Your nose is always in a book these days,' she said, 'which is no bad thing, I suppose, but you know how I feel about reading at the table.'

'Mmm.' Esme slipped a piece of paper between two pages and shut the book. 'Can I have one and a half sausages, please Dad?'

'And how are you feeling this morning, Joe?' trilled Merle in an overly jolly voice. She hugged him awkwardly and Joe scowled. 'You gave me such a fright yesterday. Fancy getting off at the wrong station! I think we'll have to give you kids mobile phones for Christmas. I know I just couldn't live without mine.'

'No thank you,' said Esme, cutting a sausage into dainty portions.

'I'd rather have some new trainers,' said Joe.

'You see, Gordon!' said Merle fiercely. She raised her eyebrows and wagged a finger at her husband. 'I told you that something was up. Nick can't even afford to provide trainers for his son.' She placed her hand on Joe's shoulder. 'Is your dad having trouble paying the bills? Is that it? He's not lost his job again –'

'No, Mum!' said Joe. 'Nothing like that. I've taken up cross-country running. My teacher reckons I could be good at it. I get through a lot of trainers, that's all.'

'So, we're going to have an athlete in the family!' said Gordon, opening a cereal packet. He smiled. 'Good for you, Joe! I suppose *I* should do some form of exercise to keep myself in trim – but I've never been what you'd call *sporty*. Pottering about with my metal detector is energetic enough for me!'

'Dad found some *treasure* last week,' said Esme in an awestruck voice.

Gordon blushed. 'Well, only a very tiny piece. I'll show you after breakfast, Joe, shall I?' He put a dish in front of Joe. 'No cornflakes. Sorry. Will muesli do?'

Joe grunted, poking the oats and dried fruit with a spoon. 'Has my dad phoned?' he asked. 'Did he reach Scotland OK? How's Great-aunt Adelaide?'

'She's still poorly,' said Gordon. 'Your dad called last night while you were asleep. He's staying at The Woolly Thistle guesthouse in Tillygrundle, a few miles outside Aberdeen. Snowing something rotten, he said.'

'You can call him tonight,' said Merle briskly. 'Now, eat your breakfast, Joe. If we don't get to the baker's by nine o'clock sharp, they'll have sold out of gingerbread reindeer.'

They had been in a shop called Amulet for fifteen minutes, and Joe was extremely bored. The weird tinkling music which was coming from the tape recorder behind the till was getting on his nerves. Joe sneezed. Incense was burning in a little back room and it made the air thick with the scent of sandalwood. He stopped leaning against a bookshelf which was filled with books about chakras, auras and yogic flying, and began to hunt around for Esme. The shop was small and crammed full of books, posters, candles, jewellery and clothing so it only took Joe five seconds to knock something over.

'Er ... sorry,' he said, picking up some jumpers made from llamas' wool which he had nudged off their hangers. The woman behind the till nodded at him and continued to paint her nails with bright blue varnish. 'Esme,' hissed Joe. 'Where are you?'

'Here!' said Esme, appearing through a rack of tie-dyed shirts. 'Has Mum finished trying things on yet?'

'No,' said Joe and sighed. 'She said the orange one didn't suit her and the red one was too tight. What have you been doing?'

'Finishing *Pigeons in Peril*. The end was rubbish.'

'Oh.'

Esme coughed. 'Joe, what's that funny smell? I feel sick.'

'It's incense, Ez. Tell you what ... why don't we go outside for a minute and get some fresh air.'

Joe was just about to sit next to Esme on the doorstep of Amulet when he saw the girl again. She was standing in the shelter of an archway, with a bag slung over her shoulder, and she was staring straight at him. He had seen her earlier, leaning on the doorpost of the baker's shop, and he had assumed that she was waiting for someone. At the time, it had not occurred to Joe that she might be waiting for *him*. She had been lingering in the shoe shop when he had tried on some trainers, and now, here she was watching him from across the cobbled square. Joe was convinced that he was being followed.

'She must be the girl from last night,' he said under his breath. 'But what does she want with *me*?'

'Right kids, let's go.' Merle nudged Joe's shoulder and waved a large Amulet bag. 'I chose the purple one with the sequins. It fitted me like a dream. OK, where shall we go next? I know this divine little boutique –'

'Not another clothes shop,' pleaded Joe.

Esme held up her library book. 'I've finished it,' she said, smiling hopefully.

'Oh, all right,' said Merle, 'but don't take all day about choosing another one.'

Chapter Six

Jam-jars in the Library

The girl cornered Joe in the sports section. He was flicking through a copy of *Sprinting to the Tape: The Memoirs of Torpedo Travis* when a shadow fell across the photograph of Torpedo winning the Didcot marathon in 1959. Joe looked up and found himself face to face with the mysterious girl who had been trailing him.

Joe slammed the book shut. 'You were in my garden last night and you've been following me all morning. Why?' Joe folded his arms and glared at her.

'You're annoyed,' said the girl calmly. 'I completely understand. You don't even know who I am, do you?'

'Well, of course not!' said Joe, staring at the freckly-faced girl in the tatty black overcoat.

Grimacing, she lifted a heavy bag from her shoulder and rested it on the parquet floor. 'I'm not some kind of loony, you know,' she said. 'You'll just have to trust me.'

'Look, what do you want?' said Joe crossly. 'You're not after the gingerbread reindeer, are you? Because if you are, you're welcome to them. Just *leave me alone*.'

A librarian popped her head round the corner of the sports section and put a finger to her lips. 'Shh there, children. No shouting.' She vanished, then reappeared a moment later, pushing a little wooden trolley with a squeaky wheel. She lifted a book from the trolley and slid it back on to a shelf close to Joe's head.

'Oh great,' said the girl wearily. 'Come on, we'll have to move somewhere else.'

'I don't think so,' said Joe.

'Please, Joe.'

'How do you know my name?'

'Well –'

'Can I help you two at all?' said the librarian. She patted her neck in a flustered manner. 'My name is Lydia. I'm a senior librarian here. Are you looking for a particular book?'

'No ... I mean yes,' said Joe. 'Well, we're just browsing.'

'Then I suggest you pootle over to the children's section. You'll find plenty of books to suit you there.'

'Right. Thanks. We'll do that,' said the girl, yanking the hood of Joe's jacket. She picked up her bag. 'Come on, Joe.'

'OK,' said the girl, when they had reached a dark corner near a rack of picture books. 'Time to get down to the nitty-gritty. We know each other. My name is

Twiggy. We met last night, only you don't remember because Winifred changed your memory. She sucked it out using a Fundibule –'

'A what?' said Joe, edging away from her. 'You must be crazy.'

Twiggy unzipped her bag and drew out a jam-jar. A little apricot cloud floated inside it. 'See. Here it is. This is your memory.'

'You need help,' said Joe, trying to keep his face straight.

'Joe, who drew the snake on your suitcase?'

'Huh?'

'I saw it when we were walking to your house last night. A little coiled viper in the top corner. I don't think Winifred and the others could have seen it or they would have asked you about it. I'm guessing that you're mixed up in something. I need to know how the snake got there.'

'There's no snake on my suitcase,' said Joe slowly.

'It's drawn with witchy ... I mean ... invisible ink. Did you meet someone at the station ... on the train?'

Joe's face turned as pale as a meringue. 'There *was* a woman,' he said shakily. 'I ... I think she was carrying a *snake* in her handbag.'

'Really?' said Twiggy in an excited voice.

'Mmm,' said Joe, finally admitting to himself that the creature had not been a figment of his imagination. He thought back to the moment on the train. When the snake had emerged from the handbag, Joe had been transfixed by its glittering green eyes but, as he had turned away from it, he had noticed something else about the snake. There had been a dark V-shaped mark on its head.

'V for viper,' said Joe quietly.

It was very tricky, but somehow they managed it. Joe wedged the Fundibule into his own ear while Twiggy held up the jam-jar with one hand, grasped a wand in the other and balanced a thick paperback copy of *Mabel's Book* on her knee.

'Right, here we are ... page two hundred and thirty-six. First, I remove your false memory, and then I put back your real one. Wish me luck, I've never done this before.'

'Now you tell me,' said Joe.

'Don't worry, the spells are foolproof. They're from *Mabel's Book*,' said Twiggy, waving her wand.

'Wait!' said Joe. He had heard a squeaking noise moving towards them. But it was too late. Twiggy had already begun to chant the spell.

'Finished!' announced Twiggy, removing the Fundibule from Joe's ear and placing the now empty jam-jar on the floor. The swishing sound in Joe's head grew fainter and fainter until it stopped altogether. He grabbed hold of Twiggy's shoulder to steady himself.

'I feel kind of dizzy,' he said. The rack of picture books swam in front of his eyes.

'I expect that'll wear off,' said Twiggy. 'So ... did it work?'

'Yes, Barbara. I remember everything.'

'*What?*' Twiggy's wand slipped through her limp fingers and clattered on to the floor. '*What* did you call me?'

'Barbara,' said Joe. Then his lips began to twitch.

Twiggy narrowed her eyes and slapped him on the arm. 'You beast!' she said, grinning.

'Well, Twiggy ... that was pretty impressive for a beginner,' said Joe, picking up a jam-jar with a glittering purple mist floating inside it. 'So this is my false memory, is it?'

'No, um ... that sort of escaped,' said Twiggy, casting a guilty look at the ceiling. Joe followed her gaze and saw a little streak of turquoise smoke floating beside a strip light. Twiggy hitched her bag on to her shoulder, rolled up her sleeves and took the jar from Joe. 'This is my spare ... and it's lucky I brought another memory with me because I'm going to have to use it.'

'The squeaky wheel!' said Joe, remembering the sound he had heard as Twiggy began to cast her spell.

'That's right,' she said. 'That nosy old librarian saw everything.'

'There she is,' said Joe, pressing his eye against the keyhole of a door marked 'Private'. He could see Lydia the librarian slumped in an armchair. She was fanning her face with a leaflet advertising the library's Christmas opening times. Joe heard a whistling noise and moved his head slightly. 'Kettle's boiling,' he said.

'Can I see?' Twiggy tried to nudge Joe away from the keyhole.

'Now she's knocking back a cup of tea,' said Joe. 'Wow ... she didn't even bother taking the teabag out. She almost swallowed it.'

Joe saw Lydia wiping her face with a tea towel. Her hair, which had been squeezed into a tight bun, was beginning to come loose, and there were spots of tea down the front of her frilly cream blouse.

'OK, your turn,' said Joe, moving aside so that Twiggy could peer through the keyhole. He straightened up and moved in front of Twiggy, shielding her from any inquisitive people who might be wondering what they were up to. He need not have worried because nobody in the library was paying them any attention. The librarian at the front desk was attaching a piece of mistletoe to a sign above his head, and another librarian was standing on a little wooden ladder in the children's section while Esme pointed at a book on the top shelf. Merle was sitting on a chair by the window. She gave an enormous yawn and looked at her watch.

'Ooh,' whispered Twiggy. 'Lydia's got her purse out. She's tipping some coins into her hand. Now, she's standing up and ... Quick, Joe! Move! She's going to open the door.'

'Can't we just grab her when she comes out?' said Joe as he and Twiggy dived behind a trolley.

'No ... too risky,' said Twiggy. 'She might scream or something. We'll have to wait for the right moment.'

Lydia opened the door timidly and scuttled over to the front desk. The librarian there had finished putting up the mistletoe and was spinning round in a swivel chair.

'Barry,' Joe heard Lydia say to him. 'I'm just popping out for a minute.'

'She can't be going outside,' said Joe. 'She hasn't taken a coat with her.'

'This could be our chance,' breathed Twiggy.

They walked past Barry, who had stopped whirling round in his chair and looked like he was going to be sick. Joe paused in front of a mullioned glass door.

'She's halfway up the corridor,' he said, peering through the glass. 'There's a pay phone on the wall. I think she's going to call someone.'

'Careful,' said Twiggy as he opened the door a crack. 'We'll have to creep up on her. You take the Fundibule and the empty jam-jar and I'll handle the rest.'

Lydia's high-heeled shoes had tapped over the tiled floor, echoing along the empty corridor, but Joe and Twiggy tiptoed behind her without making a sound. Lydia lifted the telephone receiver. She pushed a coin in the slot and Joe noticed that her hand was shaking. She turned her back on Joe and Twiggy and dialled a number.

'Hello?' she said. 'Yes, it's me. Listen ... I've just witnessed something very – Please don't interrupt, dear. I think someone's after me. No – I am *not* being overdramatic –'

'Now!' said Twiggy, and she wrenched the receiver out of Lydia's hand and slammed it back down while Joe put the Fundibule in the librarian's ear. Before Lydia knew what was happening, Joe held up the empty jam-jar, Twiggy pointed her wand and, glancing at *Mabel's Book*, she began to recite the spell:

'Tick tock.
Time unlock.
Memory dispel.
Erase
every trace.
Nothing left to dwell.'

A tiny wisp of pink smoke leaked from Lydia's ear and

settled in the jam-jar. 'Quick! Put the lid on,' said Twiggy.

'But there's only a little bit. Surely we need more than that,' said Joe, peering at the pathetic smudge of pink hovering in the middle of the jar.

'No. It's only about ten minutes' worth,' said Twiggy.

Joe screwed the lid on and Twiggy handed him the jar containing the spare memory – a little cloud of glittering purple mist. It was a heavier jar and the glass had a yellowish tinge to it. The lid was flecked with rust and Joe struggled to unscrew it.

'Ready?' said Twiggy anxiously.

Lydia was swaying slightly with her eyes wide open as if she was in a trance. Joe replaced the Fundibule, held the jar against it and nodded.

'Next page,' said Twiggy, flipping to page two hundred and thirty-seven in *Mabel's Book*. She breathed in deeply, shook her wand and said:

'Tock tick.
Time unpick.
Memory restore.
Leave no
clue to show
what has dwelt before.'

The purple mist uncoiled and wriggled from the jam-jar,

through the Fundibule and into Lydia's car. A tiny puff of glittering mist remained in the jar. 'Good,' said Twiggy. 'There's a little bit of memory left over. With any luck, Julius won't notice that I've borrowed it ...'

'You took that jam-jar without asking?'

'Had to,' said Twiggy. 'He wouldn't have given it to me even if I'd said "please" a thousand times. He thinks I'm too young to do proper magic. All the Dead-nettles do.' She began to stuff everything back into her bag. 'Right, we've finished. Let's go.'

'What memory did you give her?' asked Joe as they hurried down the corridor. Behind them, Lydia had begun to blink her eyes and was banging the heel of her hand against her head.

'No idea,' said Twiggy, and she grinned.

Joe pushed open the door leading into the main part of the library and saw Esme and his mum standing at the desk. Esme was hugging a book to her chest. As Barry the librarian prised the book from Esme's arms, opened its cover and stamped it, Joe heard the pay phone ringing in the corridor.

He glanced over his shoulder. Through the mullioned glass, Joe saw Lydia answering the phone, but he did not think there was anything to worry about.

It had stopped snowing, but a single leaf looped and twirled over the bobbing heads of the Christmas shoppers in the High Street. Joe watched as the leaf streaked downwards and landed on Twiggy's shoulder. He felt a cold draught whoosh past his cheek.

'Bye, Cuthbert,' said Twiggy as she held the leaf in her hand and studied it. 'Oh bother,' she said. 'It's a message from Patsy. I've got to go.'

'What does it say?' asked Joe, staring at the leaf's blank surface. 'Hang on – I thought you'd run out of witchy ink.'

'Winifred managed to salvage a few drops before all the ink soaked into the floorboards,' explained Twiggy. 'The message says: *Get your tush back here. Patsy.* Oh ... there's a P.S. – but the writing's really faint ...' Twiggy screwed up her eyes. '*No ... Yule ... bonfire ... for you.* Drat. What a meany.'

'Aren't they going to let you go to your Yule celebration?'

'Doesn't look like it,' said Twiggy sadly. 'Well, I suppose I asked for it. I promised to help Patsy with this new potion she's invented and then I gave her the slip this morning to come and find you. Bet she's absolutely livid.'

'Sorry,' said Joe.

'It doesn't matter. Actually ...' Twiggy clutched Joe's sleeve and dragged him into a shop doorway, 'it's perfect.

78

They'll be leaving for St Agnes's Mount a couple of hours before midnight. Once they've gone, I'll nip on my broomstick and come and see you. Then I can have another look at that snake on your suitcase.'

'OK,' said Joe, his eyes brightening. He had thought his stay in Canterbury would be dull and dreary, but so far he could not have been more mistaken.

'Don't forget to leave your window open,' called Twiggy, as she ducked under somebody's arm and disappeared into the crowds.

'Joe! Joe!' His mother was calling him. She was standing on some steps beside the statue of a large man wearing a frock coat and a curly wig. Her mobile phone was clamped to one ear. She beckoned to Joe and muttered something into the phone. Joe darted into the crowds and was elbowed and trodden on as he fought his way to the statue. Esme was sitting on its pedestal, reading her new library book.

'I thought you were right behind us,' said Merle, slipping the phone into her handbag. 'You're such a dawdler, Joe. Well, what's happened to your little friend?'

'Twiggy? Oh, she had to go.'

'What a pity,' said his mother, smothering a yawn. 'Anyway, there's been a slight change of schedule. My friend, Brenda, just phoned from the Guild Hall. She's organised a jumble sale for some charity or other and there's a bit of a problem. Two ferrets are fighting over a stuffed old lady – I mean two old ladies are fighting over a stuffed ferret. Brenda says it's turning quite nasty. They've started biffing each other with their handbags. Brenda is at her wit's end. I said I'd go over there and help her sort it out before it turns into a full-scale brawl.' Merle's cheeks were flushed with excitement.

'I'm hungry,' said Esme. Joe's stomach gurgled in agreement.

'Look, I'll tell you what,' said Merle in an irritated voice. She gave a strained smile. 'Why don't you kids have a bite to eat in that little teashop over there and as soon as I've finished restoring calm to the jumble sale, I'll be back to pick you up. OK?' She delved into the pocket of her silver quilted jacket and dropped some coins into Joe's hand. 'Got to fly, now, my cherubs.' She kissed the air twice and scurried down the steps.

'Come on, Esme,' said Joe, wrapping his fingers around his sister's gloved hand. With his other hand, he pocketed the coins and then picked up the bags which Merle had left leaning against the statue.

'Why does Mum always rush off like that?' said Esme. 'Do you think she gets bored with us?' Joe shrugged and forged his way through a stream of shoppers.

The bell above the door gave a welcoming jangle as they entered The Crumbly Sponge teashop. It was warm inside the room. Joe started to unwind his scarf, while

Esme tried to spot an empty table. The teashop was packed with people and there was a constant buzz of conversation interrupted by clinking, slurping and munching.

'Over there,' announced Esme, padding over the floorboards in her yellow wellington boots. She led Joe through a cluster of little round tables, past a glowing coal fire and over to a sprawling cheese plant which looked like it was trying to escape from its pot. Tucked behind it was a table for two, complete with a lacy white tablecloth and two red napkins.

'Well spotted, Ez,' said Joe. He sat down and handed a menu to his sister. Almost immediately, a waitress appeared.

'Can I have a watermelon milkshake with chocolate sprinkles and a toffee muffin, please,' said Esme, undoing the toggles on her duffel coat. Joe ordered a Coke and a ham sandwich. While they were waiting for their food to arrive, Joe heard the scrape of chair legs and the leaves of the massive cheese plant wobbled as someone sat down at the table next to them. Unable to see the new arrivals through the dense foliage, Joe parted a couple of leaves with his fingers.

He breathed in sharply when he saw a hand with scarlet nails place a wicker cat basket on the floor. 'It's the glamorous woman from the train!' he hissed, peering through the leaves of the cheese plant. He caught a glimpse of chestnut curls and a sleeve of black velvet.

'Oh, goody. A cat!' said Esme, putting down her library book.

'No, Ez,' said Joe, remembering the warning that the glamorous woman had given him on the train. 'You mustn't go near the basket. Those cats might claw you.' Joe leaned closer to the cheese plant, curious to hear what the woman was saying. He was so intent on listening that he hardly noticed when the waitress placed his order in front of him.

'That's not good enough!' The glamorous woman seemed to be angry with someone. 'I've kept my side of the bargain, haven't I? You should have found out something useful by now.' Joe did not manage to catch a word of her companion's mumbled response. 'Spillikins of Doom?' snapped the woman. 'Never heard of them.' A black ankle boot with a pointed toe appeared beside the cat basket. 'I'm fed up with your feeble excuses ...'

Pressing his ear against the leaves of the cheese plant, Joe heard the woman's companion mutter something timidly.

'What?' snarled the woman. 'No, you *can't* have another slice of cake.' There was a disappointed sigh and an indistinct murmur. 'The trail's gone cold, I tell you. Of course I questioned them, but the fools wouldn't let anything slip. They'll pay for their silence. They must have got rid of it somehow.'

The woman's threatening tone caused the hair on Joe's neck to stand on end. He was thankful to be hidden from view behind the cheese plant's leaves.

Joe heard the chink of a teacup as it was clumsily placed on its saucer. 'It's time to take some action,' said the woman in a guttural whisper. 'We start tonight. Now drink up. We're leaving.'

There was a movement in the cat basket and Joe saw two pairs of lemon-yellow eyes staring at him. He sat back quickly, slid his knees under the table and picked up his sandwich – but it never reached his mouth. Next to him lay a discarded library book, an empty glass with a chewed straw and a few crumbs on a plate.

The chair was not occupied.

His seven-year-old sister had gone.

Chapter Seven

First Flight Nerves

Joe searched the teashop. He interrupted people's conversations and got down on his hands and knees to look underneath their tables. He cursed himself for ignoring his sister. She had probably become bored and wandered off.

As Joe knelt on a half-eaten doughnut, he had a horrible thought. What if the glamorous woman was behind Esme's disappearance? Joe jumped to his feet. His eyes darted around The Crumbly Sponge but the woman and her cat basket were nowhere to be seen.

'Esme!' shouted Joe, flinging open the door of the teashop, the bell jangling like an alarm. He dashed into the street. 'Esme! Where are you?' Joe's head twisted one way and then another as he tried to catch a glimpse of his sister through the surging mass of people. He started to panic.

'Hey!' called a voice from The Crumbly Sponge. 'Hey, you there!' Joe turned and saw the waitress who had served them at their table. She had taken off her apron and was flapping it in his direction.

Oh, no! thought Joe, his heart sinking. She thinks I've run off without paying the bill!

He hurried towards her, shrugging his shoulders apologetically, but the waitress did not look angry.

'I've lost my sister ...' he began, as she ushered him through the door of the teashop and led him over to the fireplace. There, sitting dreamily behind a coal scuttle, with a fat tabby cat asleep on her lap, was Esme.

'He belongs to the owner,' said the waitress, bending down and stroking the cat's head. 'His name's Dennis ... and it looks like he's found a friend.'

Joe sat on his bed. He shivered and hugged his arms across his chest. Despite wearing woolly socks, a track-suit and a thick jumper, he was freezing cold. The curtains billowed and snowflakes blew in through his window. They wafted gently towards the floor before melting into the pink carpet. Joe looked at his watch. It was three minutes past eleven.

He stood up, unlatched his window and opened it even further. As he leaned out into the dark night, the snowflakes which fell past his face were as grey as ashes. Joe thought about his dad up in Scotland. The weather forecaster on the news had said that blizzards were expected in the Aberdeen area overnight. Joe had telephoned The Woolly Thistle guesthouse in Tillygrundle at teatime. He had spoken to a Mrs Allen but he could barely make out what she was saying. She had sounded as if she were speaking from the bottom of a well. After a few minutes, there had been a buzzing in his ear and the line had gone dead.

'Come on, Twiggy,' said Joe, blowing on his cold fingers. 'Hurry up.'

The alarm clock ticked loudly on his bedside table and its constant rhythm began to send Joe to sleep. His head flopped over to one side and his eyelids flickered.

'Huh? What was that?' He heard a rustling sound and moved over to the window. 'Twiggy?' he said cautiously.

'Out of the way!' called a voice from the darkness and Joe saw a grey shape shooting towards him. He ducked under the windowsill. There was a heavy clunk as something hit the brickwork. Joe heard a muffled scream.

'Watch it, broom,' said Twiggy crossly. 'Hover. Hover. Right … now back up and have another go. Try not to crash into the wall, this time.'

Joe sat on the floor and watched as Twiggy swooped through the open window astride a broomstick. Her boots skimmed the carpet and she landed rather clumsily, knocking over a wastepaper basket.

'Not bad,' she said, patting the broom handle. 'That's

been our best landing so far.' Twiggy dismounted and leaned her broomstick against a wardrobe. 'Hi, Joe,' she said, shaking snowflakes out of her hair. 'Sorry I'm a bit late.'

'You'll have to keep your voice down,' whispered Joe, switching on his bedside lamp. 'Don't want to wake anyone up.'

'Sorry,' said Twiggy. She looked around the room and nodded approvingly. 'Nice room, Joe. Very cosy.'

'You think?' Joe closed the window.

'Oh, yes. Right, where's that suitcase of yours?'

Joe knelt on the floor and slid out the battered brown suitcase from underneath the bed. Twiggy seized it eagerly and turned it over. 'There!' she said, pointing to a corner. 'You see it?'

'Nope,' said Joe.

'Oh, I forgot.' Twiggy reached into the pocket of her hooded cloak and handed him a small velvet bag. 'You'll be needing these.'

Joe loosened the bag's drawstring and the magic spectacles slipped out on to his palm. He put them on and a cloud of muddy colours floated before his eyes. After a few seconds, he was able to see clearly again. Twiggy's finger tapped impatiently against the suitcase and Joe's eyes swivelled to where she was pointing. He gasped and leaned closer.

'I don't believe it,' he said. Right in the corner of the

suitcase there was a coiled snake, about the size of Joe's thumbnail, drawn in golden ink.

'It's definitely a viper,' said Twiggy, peering at it closely. 'Thought as much. So, Joe, tell me about this woman on the train … the one with the snake in her handbag.'

'Er … she seemed pretty ordinary. About fifty, I suppose. Her hair was a bit weird. It was black with a grey stripe. She didn't talk much. Spent most of the journey doing a crossword puzzle … only she was a bit hopeless.'

'What do you mean?' asked Twiggy.

'Well … she couldn't solve the clues. She hadn't filled in any of the squares.'

'Aha!' said Twiggy.

'You don't think –'

'Was she using a fountain pen?'

Joe nodded.

'Witchy ink!' they said together.

'Are you sure this is a good idea?' said Joe, plumping his pillows and stuffing them under his duvet.

'Oh yes,' replied Twiggy. 'You might need to tweak that pillow a bit. That's right … it looks just like you're asleep in bed. I don't think your mum and dad will suspect anything if they poke their noses round the door.'

'It's my mum and *step*dad,' corrected Joe, 'and that

wasn't what I meant.'

'Well, what then?' Twiggy unlatched the window and stretched out her hand to see if it was still snowing.

'Are you positive you'll be able to control that broomstick with both of us riding it?'

'I'll give it my best shot,' she said. 'It might be second-hand, but it's a sturdy little broomstick. Willing, too.' She dropped her voice to a whisper. 'Just not terribly *fast*.'

'I could call round at your place tomorrow. It would only take twenty minutes to walk there –'

'No,' said Twiggy firmly. 'We have to go now while the others aren't at home. They have no idea that I've restored your memory. Winifred would be *furious* if she found out. They won't be back from St Agnes's Mount until dawn so we'll be free to flick through a copy of *Which Witch* and see if this woman is listed.'

'Is that like *Who's Who*?' said Joe.

'Er … yes, I suppose. When you join a coven, you send your personal details to the editor of *Which Witch* and she pops you in. There's a little paragraph about me on page four hundred and seven.' Twiggy smiled shyly and the tips of her ears turned pink.

'I wonder who that woman is,' said Twiggy as she clambered on to her broom. 'I wouldn't be surprised if she turns out to be a member of Viper Coven. That might explain why she was carrying a snake in her handbag – and why she drew a viper on your suitcase.' Twiggy patted the broom handle. 'Hop on, then – and make sure you hang on tight!'

Joe clicked off the light, zipped up his jacket and climbed on to the broomstick, wrapping his arms around Twiggy's waist. He glanced at the jumble of birch twigs behind him. 'Shouldn't proper witches have a cat riding with them?' he said cheekily.

'Oh, don't rub it in,' said Twiggy. 'It was hard enough to persuade them to get me this broomstick. They're meant to be training me to be a witch, but they just treat me like a slave. I spend all day writing leaflets, polishing boots and making endless cups of dead-nettle tea. I've only had three flying lessons, so far. OK, broom – up, up and away!'

Before Joe could change his mind, the broomstick hovered, shifted itself slightly to the left and shot forward. 'Legs up, elbows in,' said Twiggy as the broomstick manoeuvred through the small window. Once they were outside, the broomstick seemed to struggle, sinking with little jerky movements towards the ground. Then Twiggy pulled at the broom handle and shouted a few words in a panicky voice. The broomstick quivered, gave a shake of its birch twigs and started to rise.

Soon they had flown over Joe's back garden, skimmed over somebody's roof (narrowly avoiding a chimney pot) and veered to the right. Joe looked below him. Through the whirling mass of snowflakes he could just make out some glowing spots of light. The broomstick dropped lower on Twiggy's command and Joe realised that she was following a line of streetlamps. The wind buffeted Joe and the snowflakes stung his cheeks but he hardly noticed the discomfort. He felt a strange mixture of fear and excitement bubbling up inside him, and when they finally landed he found that he could not stop grinning.

'You all right?' asked Twiggy, as she opened the crooked purple door with a tap of her wand. 'I think your face has been frozen or something.'

'I'm fine!' said Joe. 'Listen – that was fantastic. I thought you said your broomstick was slow! It whizzed along at about ninety miles an hour!'

'Glad you liked it,' said Twiggy, 'but the newer brooms can go a *lot* faster than that.'

'Vague,' said Twiggy, running her finger down the index at the back of *Which Witch*. '*Very* Vague, Vespertine, Violent ... aah, here we are ... Viper Coven. There are thirteen entries under that. Shouldn't take very long to identify our mystery crossword addict!' Twiggy licked her forefinger and started to leaf through the heavy leather-bound book, while Joe leaned against a red knitted cushion and rested his heels on the pile of books which Twiggy had placed in between the two armchairs.

'Why is one red and the other blue?' said Joe sleepily.

'What?' said Twiggy, her eyes darting across a page.

'The armchairs. They're not very ... matching, are they?' Joe yawned and his eyelids began to droop.

'Patsy and Rose,' said Twiggy without looking up. 'Patsy's mad about red and Rose likes blue. They're very stubborn about it. You should have seen them fighting over the colour of the front door. Both zapped it with their wands at the same moment. That's why it's purple ... Right, did this woman have an eye patch?'

'Huh?'

Twiggy sighed. 'Joe, I hope you're not falling asleep. This is important, you know.'

Joe blinked several times and tried to appear alert. 'No, she didn't have an eye patch. Absolutely not.'

'OK ... she wasn't Olive Creeper. Let's see ... page fifty-nine ...'

Joe's eyes wandered past the fireplace and over to the map of the British Isles. He frowned at the tiny number of flags stuck into it. 'So, how come there's so few witches about?'

'Nobody knows. The numbers have been declining for ... ooh ... twenty years. It's a worry. Aah ... Did she seem allergic to beetroot?'

'How am I supposed to know that?'

'Fair point. All right, did you happen to see if she

had any teeth?'

'Of course she did.'

'That rules out Lottie Grouch, then. Hers fell out in 1950, apparently. She was smacked in the mouth by an enchanted tennis racquet. Nasty. Hmm ...' Twiggy turned over several pages at once.

'So what makes you so special, then?' asked Joe, lifting his feet off the pile of books and selecting the top one. It was Twiggy's paperback copy of *Mabel's Book*. It flopped open at a potion for curing Dreaded Lurgies.

'What do you mean?'

'Well, you look pretty ordinary to me,' said Joe. 'What makes a person become a witch? How do you get your special powers?'

'Oh, that ... I'm not really sure,' said Twiggy. 'It just happens or it doesn't. *So* ...' She plonked her finger in the middle of a page. 'Did she have artichokes growing out of her ears?'

'It doesn't run in the family, then?'

Twiggy shook her head impatiently. 'Patsy says that it's a random thing. Now, concentrate, Joe. Were there artichokes –'

'No.'

'Are you sure?'

'I think I would have noticed.'

Twiggy glared at him. 'Right, what about this one, then – Harriet Perkins. She's forty-six, her favourite colour is pink ... she has a pet snake who can change into a variety of writing implements ... and her hobbies include collecting antique cauldrons and solving difficult crossword puzzles.'

'Yep. That sounds like her,' said Joe, sitting up straight.

'Good.' Twiggy grinned at him. 'Finally, we're getting somewhere. Now, tell me everything that happened on that train ...'

Chapter Eight

Scene of a Crime

'I still can't believe that the man with the mobile phone was a witch, too,' said Joe, stretching his arms above his head and yawning. 'Can men *be* witches?'

'Oh, yes,' said Twiggy. 'But not many covens will let them join. Female witches can be very snooty and set in their ways, you know. It's quite unfair, really. You'll only find male witches in the trendy, modern covens –'

'You've got Julius, haven't you –'

'Or the really desperate ones,' finished Twiggy. 'We're not fussy, here in Dead-nettle. Oh, Joe … if only we could get a sixth member, we'd be treated like a proper coven. That's why we were kicked out of Stubble End, you see. The Pipistrelles took a fancy to the village and that was it. They said they had more of a right to be there. Dora Benton called us "a motley collection of no-hopers".'

'That's a bit rough … making you move out of your own house,' said Joe.

'Oh, no. We still live in the same house,' said Twiggy. 'We just had to move it, that's all. The spell is quite complicated. It nudges two buildings apart and squeezes our house in between them.'

'Don't the neighbours notice?'

'Not generally … as long as you pick the right spot. People just walk along, staring at the pavement, don't they? Gave the milkman a bit of a fright, but Winifred just sprinkled some Befuddle Dust on our front doorstep and that did the trick. The poor milkman was so confused, he couldn't remember whether our house had been there or not.'

'It must be amazing to be a witch,' said Joe enviously.

Twiggy smiled. 'It has its moments, but … well, it can be pretty lonely.'

Struck by the sadness in her voice, Joe looked up at Twiggy. She was lounging in the blue armchair, her legs dangling over its arm. There was a faraway look on her face. Her black tunic was patched and faded, there were holes in her black woollen stockings and the toes of her boots were scuffed and dirty.

Joe thought about the other members of Dead-nettle Coven. None of them was close to Twiggy's age and, although they did not seem to treat her unkindly, the Dead-nettles undoubtedly regarded her as an underling: a servant who had to do what she was told. He remembered the excited expression on her face when he had burst into the room on the bewitched tricycle. Twiggy had not been the least bit annoyed with him when he collided with her stool and knocked her on to the ground. She had acted as if Joe's arrival was the most thrilling thing that had happened all year. Perhaps, for her, it was.

'So, you reckon that the man with the mobile phone is none other than Aubrey White?' said Joe.

'Yes,' said Twiggy, referring to *Which Witch*, 'and Aubrey White just happens to be the leader of Viper Coven. It's really unusual for a male witch to be in charge. He must be *extremely* clever.'

Joe thought back to the train journey. The man had struck Joe as a friendly sort who was rather bumbling and a bit stupid. 'He didn't seem that intelligent to me,' murmured Joe. 'Are you *sure* it was him?'

Twiggy cleared her throat. '"Aubrey White",' she read, sliding her finger across the page, '"was born in Leatherhead. He has the tattoo of a horned viper on his right wrist –"'

'Mmm, that fits,' said Joe. 'I thought it was the letter "S" but I suppose it could have been a snake.'

'"Despite a hectic schedule, as the leader of Viper Coven, he recently passed his Chiromancy exams and is learning to be a professional Charmer at evening classes" ... blah, blah, blah ... aah ... here we are ... "Aubrey is partial to *boiled sweets*, fairy cakes and tripe". There ...

you see,' said Twiggy triumphantly.

'I can't deny it,' said Joe. 'The man on the train did have a bag of sweets. But I'm still not completely convinced.'

Twiggy shrugged her shoulders. Then she leaned sideways and slid out a battered green dictionary from the tall pile of books on the hearthrug. She handed it to Joe. 'Could you look up "Chiromancy" please, Joe. I don't know what it means.' Twiggy told him how to spell it. 'Now, all we've got to do is find out who the glamorous woman is.' She ran her finger down the index of *Which Witch*. 'Maybe she's not in a coven. There's nothing here about cat baskets or red lipstick or ... what kind of boots were they?'

'Black and pointy-toed,' said Joe, scanning the dictionary. 'You know, sort of *sly*-looking.'

'Sly boots, huh?' said Twiggy.

Goosepimples appeared on Joe's arms. 'I ... I saw her in the teashop today.'

'Who? Old Slyboots?'

'Uh-huh. I tried to listen to what she was saying. Slyboots was irritated with someone ... that's for sure. Didn't understand what she was talking about, but she gave me the creeps. I wouldn't be surprised if she *was* a witch.'

'Oh, trust me ... she is,' said Twiggy firmly, 'and it sounds like old Slyboots picked a fight with the two members of Viper Coven on the train. You said the lights went out in the carriage, right?'

'Yes,' said Joe, 'when the train stopped at Stubble End.'

'One of them must have cast the Extinguishing Spell,' said Twiggy, 'so that the other passengers couldn't see what was going on. Bit risky, though. It's not wise to practise magic in front of ... you know ... *your* sort. Tends to cause a bit of a stir.'

'Then I saw these flashes of light as if someone was striking a match –'

'Wands,' said Twiggy knowingly. 'They were probably hexing each other like mad.'

'I didn't hear anything,' said Joe. 'It was deathly quiet, in fact.'

'Hushed combat,' said Twiggy. 'Takes years to perfect. Only the most experienced witches can do it.'

'Do you think the snake and the cats in the basket –'

'They joined in the fight, by the sound of it. Remind me what happened when the lights came on again.'

'Er ... I'd got off the train by then,' said Joe. 'All I saw was Slyboots standing by the window.'

'There was no sign of Harriet or Aubrey?'

'Um ... I didn't see them. No.'

'Oh dear,' said Twiggy softly.

Joe swallowed. He did not like to ask what might have happened to the pair. Plainly, they had lost the fight with

Slyboots. He tried to dismiss the fate of the Vipers from his mind, burying his nose in the dictionary until he found the word he was looking for.

'"Chiromancy is a way of foretelling the future",' read Joe in a solemn voice, '"by studying the lines on somebody's palm."'

'Oh,' said Twiggy, 'that's interesting. Now, look up "Spillikins of Doom". I meant to check its meaning yesterday but I forgot.'

'Spillikins of Doom,' said Joe, wrinkling his forehead. 'I've heard that somewhere before ...'

'Patsy mentioned it in the Disenchantment Spell,' said Twiggy, 'when she turned the tricycle back into a broomstick.'

'Umm ... maybe,' said Joe uncertainly. He scanned a page in the dictionary, finding 'spike-bozzle' and 'spindle', but no word in between. 'It's not in here, you know.'

'It must be!'

'Well, it's not,' said Joe in a tired voice. He handed the dictionary to Twiggy. 'See. There's no mention of the Spillikins of Doom.'

'That's weird.'

Joe sighed. 'Can we stop now? This is too much like homework. Have you got anything to eat? I'm starving.'

'We might have some Yule pudding left over,' said Twiggy, shutting *Which Witch* and wriggling off the armchair. 'And I could make a pot of dead-nettle tea ...'

'No tea for me, thanks,' said Joe quickly. He poked out his tongue to see if it was still green from the mouthful he had swallowed the previous evening. 'I can honestly say I've never tasted anything more disgusting.'

Joe heard rattling noises coming from the kitchen, the entrance of which was hidden behind a large filing cabinet. Then Twiggy emerged from the room, carrying a plate which was covered with brown smudges.

'I'm sure there was a big slice of Yule pudding on this plate, but it's gone,' she grumbled as she tramped towards Joe. 'Nothing left but crumbs! Something funny's going on,' she said grimly.

'No kidding,' said Joe, standing beside Patsy's desk. He was holding the velvet bag containing the magic spectacles, which Twiggy had asked him to replace in the top drawer. 'I think you should take a look at *this*.'

Twiggy's jaw dropped open. 'How on earth did *that* happen?'

The top of Patsy's desk was as cluttered as usual. Assorted jars and bottles stood next to saucers filled with powder and racks of cloudy test tubes. In front of these containers was an exercise book which lay open at a particular page. Patsy had scrawled 'Re-growing Potion' at the top of it. The desk was covered in stains and scratches, but especially noticeable was a tiny lime-green blob about the size of a peanut; and protruding just below this blob was the small branch of a tree, with glossy oval leaves sprouting from it.

'Beech,' said Twiggy gloomily. She plucked a leaf and let it float to the floor. 'Same as the desk, of course.' Twiggy gave a heavy sigh and raised her hand to her forehead. 'This means trouble.'

Joe glanced at the exercise book. 'Re-growing Potion,' he murmured. 'Are you trying to tell me that the desk has started to grow back into a tree?'

'Yes,' said Twiggy. 'Exactly. It's Patsy's new potion: the one I was supposed to be helping her with when I followed you around Canterbury today. She's really proud of it, and no wonder! If more than that tiny drop had been spilled, we'd have a tree poking out of our roof.'

'Would it work on this?' asked Joe, drawing a small flake of metal from his pocket. 'My stepdad was showing me what he'd found with his metal detector. I had to pretend to be interested. He gave this to me. Said it could be part of an old coin or something. I was going to throw it away.'

Before Twiggy could stop him, Joe had dabbed the scrap of dull yellow metal into the spot of Re-growing Potion. He held it in the palm of his hand and watched as it began to swell into a small triangular pendant with a dark red stone in its centre.

'Wow! Gordon will go wild when I show him this! It must be really, really old. I think it's real gold – and the stone must be a garnet. Have a look, Twiggy. That potion is brilliant.'

'Oh,' said Twiggy. 'Mmm.' Joe was disappointed that she did not seem the least bit interested in his pendant. It was the branch that appeared to fascinate her. She stared at it with a baffled expression on her face. Then she looked at the empty plate in her hand. Her eyes grew large and her mouth dropped open. '*Joe*,' said Twiggy, seizing his arm. She looked distractedly around her.

'What is it?' said Joe.

'Shh!' Twiggy put a finger to her lips. 'They might still be here,' she whispered.

'Who?' said Joe, grappling with Twiggy as she tried to put her hand over his mouth. 'What are you talking about?'

'The thieves,' whispered Twiggy. 'We've been burgled.'

'You sure?' said Joe. He glanced around the cluttered room and tried to assess whether anyone could have rifled through the witches' belongings. The room looked remarkably normal: a mishmash of books, papers, weird ornaments and far too much furniture for such a modest space. He found it impossible to tell if anything had been disturbed.

'I'm positive,' said Twiggy in a fretful whisper. 'They stole the last piece of Yule pudding and they took Patsy's Re-growing Potion. It was sitting on her desk in a conical flask when she left for St Agnes's Mount. Patsy made me promise not to touch it. The thieves must have sneaked in when I came to get you this evening. They must have spilled a bit of the potion.' Twiggy peered nervously around the room. 'I wonder what else they pinched. Maybe they're watching us right now.'

'That's it,' said Joe as he clomped noisily down the spiral staircase. 'We've searched the whole house and nobody's here. Don't you have a witches' police force or something you could call?'

'No,' said Twiggy, clasping her wand very tightly and holding it out in front of her, 'but I think I should send a leaf to Winifred and the others straightaway.' Suddenly she clutched Joe's arm and squealed hysterically. 'Oh, no! We've run out of witchy ink.'

'Can't you use normal ink?' said Joe calmly. 'After all, it is an emergency.'

'You're right. Yes, I will. Normal ink. Good thinking.' Twiggy walked over to her desk and lifted the lid. 'Now, where did I put those spare leaves …'

'It's a shame about Julius's trunk,' said Joe. He

crouched behind the old man's desk and ran his fingers over the trunk's splintered wooden lid. The locks had been broken, and the contents of the trunk thrown on to the floor. Jam-jars containing colourful mists had rolled into shadowy corners or wedged themselves under Julius's desk. Joe began to pick them up and replace them carefully inside the trunk. Then he gathered up a few books which had been slung to one side.

He came across a thick journal whose brittle, yellowing pages had separated from the spine. There was a smudged footprint on one of the pages and Joe rubbed away the dirt with his finger. Underneath was a diary entry, dated nineteen years ago on the 31st of August. The words were written in faded indigo ink.

'"Porridge for breakfast",' read Joe. '"Attended auction at Ilfracombe. Purchased splendid curio – belonged to F.F.! Buttered crumpets for tea. Bath. Bed."' Joe smiled. It seemed that Julius had always been a man of few words. He slipped the page between the rest and enclosed them in the battered cover.

'Finished,' said Twiggy, putting down her fountain pen and reading through her message on the leaf. 'Thanks for clearing up, Joe. The thieves made a bit of a mess, didn't they? It's a shame they broke those locks on Julius's trunk. A simple Unfastening Spell would have done the trick.'

'Mmm,' said Joe and he smiled at Twiggy. 'You'd

know about that, wouldn't you? You must have broken into this trunk to steal the jam-jar with my memory in it.'

'Maybe,' said Twiggy, twiddling her hair round her finger, 'but it wasn't *stealing*. Not *really*.'

'Uh-huh,' said Joe. 'So, how does it work, then? How do you manage to suck out the exact bit of memory?'

'It's technical.' Twiggy stuck her head out of the window and whistled.

'Well?' said Joe when she had withdrawn her head.

Twiggy folded her arms and tutted. 'Why are you so interested? All *right*,' she said when Joe looked pleadingly at her. 'If you must know, it's a matter of concentration. You have to fix the date and time-span in your mind.'

'Is that all?'

'Yes,' said Twiggy irritably. 'Sorry to disappoint you, Joe. It's very difficult, actually. Once you've started the spell, you can't afford to get distracted or you might wipe the person's entire memory.'

'That's why you couldn't stop in the library,' said Joe, 'even when you realised that Lydia was watching you.'

'That's right,' said Twiggy. She gazed out of the open window, the breeze gently ruffling her hair. 'Oh, where *are* you, Cuthbert?'

Joe placed the damaged journal on top of a small pile of books in Julius's wooden trunk. Then he closed the lid, straightened a few items on Julius's desk and walked over to the window to join Twiggy.

'Any sign of him?' asked Joe.

'Nothing,' said Twiggy, clutching the leaf in her hand. 'Cuthbert's never taken this long before. I don't understand what's keeping him.' Her shoulders drooped and she gave a little sob. 'Oh, Joe ... if only I'd stayed here! I could have hidden when the thieves got in. At least I'd know who they were. How am I going to explain this to Winifred? She'll want to know where I was when the break-in happened. I'll have to confess everything. She might even throw me out of Dead-nettle Coven ...'

'I'm sure Winifred wouldn't do that,' said Joe. 'It's a shame you don't have a watchdog. My dog, Hamish, would have barked his little head off at the first sign of an intruder.'

'If only Rose had left Ishtar behind,' said Twiggy.

'Yes,' said Joe, fingering the sore places on his back where Rose's cat had sunk her claws into him the day before.

'Oh,' said Twiggy. 'Oh, that's it. Squib. I'd forgotten.'

'Huh?' said Joe.

'Squib is Patsy's cat,' explained Twiggy, her cheeks flushing with colour. 'She's always transforming him into something else ... poor old thing. He's been missing for weeks and I'll bet he's somewhere in this room. He will have seen *everything*.'

'What use is that?' said Joe. 'Unless you're fluent in *cat* language.'

A smug grin appeared on Twiggy's face.

'You're *not*, are you?' said Joe. 'Can you really talk to cats?'

'Oh, yes,' said Twiggy. 'It's easy. Striking up a conversation with Squib won't be a problem.' She surveyed the crowded room and her smile faded. 'Of course – we'll have to *find* him, first.'

Chapter Nine

The Midnight Market

There were two heaps of paperclips on Winifred's desk. Joe picked up a single paperclip from the much smaller pile and held it aloft.

'A bit higher, please,' said Twiggy, as she licked her lips and prepared to point her wand at the paperclip. Joe felt his head beginning to nod forward and the paperclip wavered in the air. 'Stay focused, Joe,' said Twiggy. 'You have to keep it still.'

'Ready?' said Joe. Without waiting for her to reply he looked at the copy of *Mabel's Book* which lay open on the desk in front of him. '"By the Stones of Fate ..."' he read wearily.

'It's all right,' interrupted Twiggy. 'I've memorised it now, thanks.'

'I should think you have,' said Joe moodily. 'This is the one hundred and fifty-ninth paperclip after all. Can't you just wave your wand over all of them at once? It would be a lot quicker.'

'You know the spell doesn't work like that, Joe. You can only use it on one object at a time. Now, hold the paperclip steady …'

She cleared her throat before chanting:

'By the Stones of Fate
and the Spillikins of Doom,
your former self
you must resume.'

The tip of her wand made a sizzling sound and a few green sparks dribbled rather pathetically on to the paperclip. Nothing happened.

Joe glared at Twiggy and dropped the paperclip on to the larger heap. 'Surprise, surprise,' he said. 'Like I said before, I really don't think that Patsy would have changed her cat into a paperclip. What's Winifred going to say when she finds out that you've dismantled her sculpture of an aardvark for no good reason?'

Twiggy ignored him. 'Next,' she said curtly.

'All right. There are only a handful left, anyway.'

A couple of minutes later, Twiggy had finished casting the Disenchantment Spell on every single paperclip in the headquarters of Dead-nettle Coven and none of them had proved to be a black cat called Squib.

'What now?' asked Joe, covering an enormous yawn with the back of his hand. 'You've tried the doormat, three rolls of tape, all the bottles on Patsy's desk, and one hundred and sixty-six paperclips – unless I've miscounted. Please don't say you're going to start on the drawing pins.'

'*You* make a suggestion, then,' said Twiggy, searching desperately around the room. 'Squib vanished two weeks ago – so we're looking for an object that's appeared recently, something easy to overlook ...'

'Who is this Mabel person, anyway?' said Joe grumpily as he leafed through her book.

'Mabel Crump is only The Greatest Witch Who Ever Lived,' replied Twiggy, before pointing her wand at a toadstone paperweight and muttering the spell under her breath. The paperweight remained unchanged and Twiggy sighed. 'Mabel lived in Elizabethan times. She was mind-bogglingly brilliant, you know. Most of the spells and potions we use now were invented by her all those hundreds of years ago. Patsy's a bit of an inventor herself and Mabel is her absolute hero. Careful, don't crease it,' said Twiggy as Joe flipped the book over and studied the blurb on the back cover.

'"In 1596, at the tender age of twenty-two,"' read Joe, '"Mabel Crump wrote the greatest work in the history of witches' literature: *A Book of Spells, Potions and Other Snippets of Witchery*, which later reverted to the simpler title of *Mabel's Book*. Since its translation in 1848, *Mabel's Book* has become a worldwide bestseller."'

Twiggy nodded proudly. 'And you'll *never* guess where she was born.'

'Where?' said Joe.

'Stubble End!'

'Oh, so *that's* why everyone wants to live there,' said Joe. 'It's the birthplace of the famous Mabel Crump!'

'Yes,' agreed Twiggy, 'it's a great honour, you see.'

'Hang on a minute,' said Joe, rereading the information on the back cover of the book. 'Mabel was English, wasn't she?'

'Mmm,' said Twiggy vaguely, leaning over Joe's shoulder.

'So why did the book need to be translated?' Joe's eyes widened. 'And why wasn't it translated for over two hundred and fifty years? Was it written in code or something?'

'No,' said Twiggy, picking up the vase of wilting weeds on Winifred's desk.

'Well, what then?'

'You really want to know?'

'Yes.'

'All right ... Mabel had dreadful handwriting. Nobody could read a word of it. Then, about two hundred years ago, this language expert got hold of the book and managed to make some sense out of it. It was a lifetime's work, mind you.'

'Oh,' said Joe disappointedly.

'Here,' said Twiggy. 'Hold this.' She shoved a limp plant with heart-shaped leaves into his hand.

'Not very pretty, is it?' said Joe, holding it up. 'I don't know why Winifred bothered putting *this* in a vase. I would have chucked it straight on to the compost heap.'

'It's a dead-nettle,' said Twiggy huffily. 'Winifred always keeps one on her desk. It *is* our emblem, after all. I know it's not very inspiring ...' She spoke the Disenchantment Spell and flourished her wand.

As the green sparks touched the drooping leaves, there was a hissing sound and tiny black hairs began to sprout on the leaves, thickening and spreading until Joe was holding a black furry dead-nettle in his hand. The plant continued to swell and writhe. Then two little triangular bulges appeared. The furry creature was becoming heavier and heavier so that Joe was forced to lower his hands and hold it in his lap. Sharp needles sank into his palms and he cried out. Then two green eyes flicked open and stared at him.

'Squib!' shouted Twiggy excitedly. The cat flattened his ears and spat at her as she stroked his tangled fur. 'Look at you! Your paws are all wet. How long have you been standing in that vase, hey? Oh dear,' said Twiggy, as Squib swiped at her hand with his claws. 'He's in a bit of a mood, isn't he?'

'Can you blame him?' said Joe, scratching the cat gently under his chin. Squib's tail twitched but he crouched lower on Joe's lap, closed his eyes and started to purr.

'Well, he seems to like you.'

'Probably because I'm not a witch,' said Joe, but he was secretly pleased. 'Why don't we give Squib a saucer of milk or something. Then you can start to ask him some questions.'

'Oh, yes … er … right.' Twiggy vanished behind the filing cabinet and appeared again a few moments later, carrying a chipped red saucer. Milk slopped over its sides as she placed it on the floor under Winifred's desk. Squib stood up on Joe's lap and stretched himself. Then he sniffed the air before springing lightly on to the floor and lapping the milk with his small pink tongue.

'There's a s-l-i-g-h-t problem,' said Twiggy, fidgeting nervously.

'What do you mean?' asked Joe.

'Um … I can't question Squib at the moment because we're out of Lingo Liquorice. I won't be able to understand him without it, you see.'

'You didn't say anything about needing whatsit liquorice –'

'We could pop out and get some,' said Twiggy quickly. 'The Midnight Market is just round the corner. Won't take very long.'

'But it's well past midnight,' said Joe, looking at his watch.

'Doesn't matter. The Market will be there until dawn.' Twiggy pulled on her tatty black overcoat. 'Come on, Joe.'

'Don't you think someone should stay here with Squib?' he said. 'The poor cat's still in shock … and what if the thieves come back?'

'Squib will hide if he hears any strange noises. Or … I could try and turn him into a –' The cat's tail lashed from side to side as Twiggy picked up her wand.

'I don't think that would be a good idea,' said Joe, snatching the wand out of her hand. 'OK, you win. I'll come with you. Better close the window before we leave, though.'

'I wonder what's happened to Cuthbert,' said Twiggy sadly, as she scrunched up the leaf on which she had written her note to Winifred, and threw it into the wastepaper basket.

The snow had almost stopped falling. Occasionally, a stray snowflake drifted past Joe's nose and became invisible as soon as it merged with the snow which had already landed on the pavement. There had not been time for an icy crust to form on the powdery sheet of white, and Joe's trainers made muffled croaking sounds as he padded over it.

The moon had blanched everything that was not smothered by snow and, when Joe glanced at Twiggy's face, he saw that her skin had a pale silver tint. Unlit doorways were draped with dusky shadows. The only colour came from the streetlamps, which threw puddles of buttery light on to the snow-covered street.

Joe plunged his hands deep into his pockets as he and Twiggy walked side by side. An empty crisp packet fluttered briefly and became still again. A cat darted across the road and disappeared down a dark alley. Nothing else moved.

'I thought you said it wasn't far,' said Joe in a low voice. There was no need to whisper, but he did not like to break the silence of the early morning.

'You see that little stone archway up ahead?' said Twiggy. 'The Midnight Market is just through there.'

When they reached the archway, Joe leaned against its smooth, cold stones and peered into a small courtyard enclosed by a high wall on two sides and a hawthorn hedge at the far end. As far as Joe could see, the courtyard was completely empty.

'I think we're too late,' he said. 'Everybody's gone home.'

Twiggy shook her head and smiled at him. '*Listen*,' she said.

Joe was feeling weak with tiredness but he decided to humour her, for a couple of minutes at least. He tugged the hood of his jacket over his head, closed his eyes and waited.

At first, all he heard was a very faint clinking sound like faraway wind chimes shifting in a breeze. Then came an indistinct murmuring which grew stronger and stronger until Joe could make out individual voices. He opened his eyes.

The courtyard was no longer deserted. Misty shapes fused and separated and, as Joe watched, the images became more defined, until he found himself staring at a bustling marketplace. Striped canopies with scalloped edges sagged under the weight of freshly-fallen snow. Beneath them were trestle tables loaded down with jars and bottles, cages and baskets, pots and cauldrons. Lanterns swung and candles flickered. People milled about in front of Joe's eyes.

Twiggy grinned and nudged his elbow. 'Gone home, have they?' she said.

Joe wanted to pause at every market stall, but Twiggy kept tugging at his sleeve before moving off into the meandering stream of people. Unlike ordinary shoppers, Joe noticed that these people were almost entirely dressed in black, apart from the odd brightly-coloured scarf, pair of earmuffs or neckerchief.

Joe stopped beside a stall hung with holly and juniper garlands. Strings of dried rosebuds had been wound round the table legs and quartz crystals were suspended from the canopy to look like icicles. Joe picked up a bag which contained delicious-smelling spices.

'What will you give me for it?' asked the man who was standing behind the table.

'Oh … I don't want … I mean, I haven't got any money,' said Joe, hurriedly replacing the bag on the table. The man, who was wearing a three-cornered hat, winked at Joe and grabbed a handful of oranges from his display. He began to juggle with them.

'Hey,' said a voice in Joe's ear. 'I thought you were right behind me. We've got to find the Lingo Liquorice, remember? Now, come on.' Twiggy yanked Joe's sleeve so hard that he nearly tripped over his own feet.

They passed an elderly witch who grinned at Joe with her one tooth. She was ladling steaming liquid into small tankards. 'Hibiscus Syrup?' she said, beckoning to Joe. She dipped her ladle into another cauldron. 'Or maybe you'd prefer a Cinnamon Posset? What do you say, boy?'

'Sorry,' said Joe, shrugging his shoulders. The air was filled with mouth-watering smells and he was beginning to feel rather hungry. He hoped that the Lingo Liquorice, when they eventually found it, would be extremely tasty.

'Would you like a sip of Pumpkin Mead?' said the old witch hopefully.

'No time,' said Twiggy briskly, dragging Joe away.

'Just look at these!' gasped Joe, as they passed a table crowded with wooden cages. In each cage, on a plump cushion, sat a sleek black cat. Even Twiggy could not resist poking her fingers through the bars and stroking their fur.

'Don't handle the merchandise,' snapped a tall, sour-looking witch from behind the table.

Twiggy rapidly withdrew her fingers. 'Old bat,' she muttered rudely. 'Oh, Joe! Come and see this one!'

In a varnished rosewood cage, asleep on a purple velvet cushion, was the most magnificent cat that Joe had ever seen. His handsome fur was black and glossy, all apart from a sprinkling of silver hairs on the point of each ear and the tip of his tail. Disturbed by Joe and Twiggy's excited whispering, the cat opened his eyes.

'Wow!' breathed Joe. He had expected the cat to have green eyes like Squib and Ishtar, but this cat was staring disdainfully at Joe with two pools of mottled gold.

'It's an Amber-eyed Silver-tip,' said Twiggy in an awestruck voice. 'The crème de la crème of witches' cats. They're *incredibly* expensive. Oh, Joe ... isn't he *beautiful*!'

The cat yawned as if he were bored by the praise that was being heaped upon him. Then his golden eyes narrowed to slits and he went back to sleep.

'I don't understand why it's so busy,' said Twiggy, squeezing through a small crowd of people who were

119

grouped around a table in the corner. 'Everyone should still be at the Yule celebrations.' She edged past a woman holding a spiky-leafed plant and stood on tiptoe. 'Joe? Where are you?'

'Right behind you ... ouch!' said Joe as a spiky leaf jabbed him in the head. He smoothed down his hair and joined Twiggy in front of a table packed with tall glass jars.

'Steady, there. There's no need to shove, madam,' said a stout, bright-eyed man wearing a stripy apron. He waved his scoop in the air and then rapped it on the table. 'Settle *down*, please, ladies and gents. You'll all get served. Now, who was next?'

About nineteen people shouted at once.

'I think it was you, missie, wasn't it?' said the man, raising his eyebrows at Twiggy. 'What can I get you?'

'I'd like some Lingo Liquorice, please.'

'Ah,' said the man. 'Now, would that be for bats, rats and black cats, or for dogs, frogs and hedgehogs? I've only got the two sorts at the moment, you see.'

'Bats, rats and black cats ... if you don't mind,' said Twiggy politely.

The man put his hand on a few jars and twisted them round so he could read the labels. 'This is the one,' he said, tapping the lid of one jar and smiling.

'Yuk, that looks revolting,' whispered Joe, as he watched the man shovel a few limp black strips into his scoop and drop them into a paper bag.

'That all right for you, missie?' said the man, expertly twisting the corners of the bag. Twiggy nodded and he held out his hand. 'So, what have you got for me, then?'

Twiggy delved into the pocket of her overcoat and brought out a squashed cardboard box. 'Dead-nettle teabags,' she said anxiously. 'I made them myself.'

'That's … er … super, little miss.' The man took the teabags and placed the bag of Lingo Liquorice in her hand. 'Pleasure doing business with you. Right, who's my next customer?'

'That's a funny way to pay for something,' said Joe, when they had pushed their way free of the crowd. 'Haven't you witches heard of money?'

'Oh, we don't bother with that,' said Twiggy. 'Swapping things is a much fairer way of paying, don't you think?'

Joe considered this for a moment. 'Well … I suppose mouldy-looking liquorice and stinky dead-nettle tea *are* about as stomach-turning as each other.'

'I *made* those teabags,' said Twiggy indignantly.

'I was joking,' said Joe and he began to laugh. 'But you must admit –'

'Don't make fun of me, Joe.'

'I'm not!' He gave her arm a little squeeze. 'Why don't we have a look around a few more stalls and then –'

'We have to get back right away,' said Twiggy, frowning. 'I just need to get some witchy ink and then we're leaving.'

'Oh, don't be such a grump.'

'What?' Twiggy pursed her lips together. 'You're the one who didn't want to come in the first place.' She prodded Joe's stomach with her finger. 'You were worried about Squib half an hour ago, and now ... well, you couldn't care less about him.'

'That's not true!'

'I don't know why I bothered to give you your stupid memory back,' shouted Twiggy. She was almost in tears. 'I thought you could be my friend and all you do is ... *insult my teabags*!'

'Twiggy!' yelled Joe as she turned and ran away from him. He watched her tousled head bobbing in a sea of black cloaks and pointed hats. But after a few seconds, he had lost sight of her.

Chapter Ten

Squib Speaks

Joe bent down and rooted around in a soggy cardboard box full of mildewy books. Muttering to himself, he picked up a copy of *Low-fat Slug Recipes for the Single Witch* and thumped it back down again.

The woman behind the table cleared her throat and folded her arms. Joe continued to mumble as he ferreted through the box. He was annoyed with Twiggy for getting upset over nothing but, at the same time, he could not help feeling guilty. She had risked the wrath of Dead-nettle Coven to restore his memory to him. What is more, Twiggy had missed out on the Yule bonfire on St Agnes's Mount, which was probably the highlight of her year, and she had not moaned about it once.

Joe began to regret having criticised her teabags. Perhaps witches' taste buds were different to those of normal people. Dead-nettle tea might taste like cabbage water to him but, perhaps, to the magical fraternity, it was like drinking liquid chocolate.

'I'm sorry,' said the witch behind the table. She narrowed her eyes suspiciously at Joe. 'I doubt you'll find any teabags in there.'

'Pardon?'

'That is what you are looking for, isn't it?'

Joe realised that he must have been thinking out loud. 'Oh ... oh. It's my ... my *aunt*, you see. She collects them ... teabags, that is. I wondered if you had a book on the ... the different flavours?'

Evidently the witch did not believe him, because she did not bother to answer. She raised an eyebrow and drummed her fingers against her elbow. 'Uh-*huh*,' she said.

Joe smiled weakly and pretended to be extremely interested in a copy of *Mabel's Book* which he had found at the bottom of the box. It was a very old copy with thick yellowing pages. On the front cover, underneath the author's name, it read: 'Translated from the illegible by Fleur Fortescue.' He began to flick through the pages, aware that the witch was watching him closely. When he got to page five hundred and twelve, he stopped.

'Excuse me,' said Joe, holding up the book. 'It looks like somebody has ripped out a page.' He ran his finger down the centre of the book and felt the jagged remains of the page which had been torn out. 'Page five hundred and thirteen is –'

'Missing,' finished the witch. 'I know.'

'Oh, I ... I just thought –'

'In fact,' she said frostily, 'everybody knows ... all except *you* that is.'

'What do you mean ... everybody knows?' said Joe, wondering if the witch were slightly mad. 'How ... how can they?'

'It's traditional,' said the witch, closing her eyes despairingly. 'In the original book, which Mabel Crump wrote in 1596, the five hundred and thirteenth page was removed.' The witch raised her hand as Joe opened his mouth to ask why. 'The reason is unknown,' she continued, 'but it is assumed, in learned circles, that the page contained a powerful, destructive magic. At the last moment, Mabel realised the potential harm it could cause, and thus, extracted it.'

'So every copy of *Mabel's Book* has the same page missing, does it?'

'That is so,' said the witch, looking down her nose at Joe. 'Why has no one told you of this before? To which coven do you belong?'

'Oh ... er ... er.' Joe picked up a battered board game called 'The Stones of Fate', held it to his ear and rattled it.

'Well?'

'Oh ... um ... um ...' faltered Joe. 'Dead-nettle,' he said and bit his lip.

'That,' said the witch coldly, 'explains it.'

'Oi, smiler.' A man raised his black trilby hat at Joe and beckoned to him. Joe stared blankly at the man before shuffling over to his stall.

'Cold, are you?' asked the man. 'Aah … shame.' Joe shrugged his hunched shoulders and shoved his hands deeper into his pockets. 'Could I interest you in this quality garment?' said the man, holding a furry mustard scarf against his checked jacket. He stroked the scarf and nodded at Joe. 'Lovely and warm. Genuine Peruvian camel hair. Want to try it on?'

'No thanks,' said Joe miserably.

'Oh,' said the man, winking at Joe. 'Got the *hump*, have you?'

'Huh?'

'It's a joke, lad.'

'Oh, yeah,' said Joe. 'Yeah. Very funny.'

The man gave Joe an odd look. 'What's the matter? Crashed your broomstick or something? You need cheering up, you do. How about this?' He picked up a book and started to flick through it. '*Magical Mishaps and Bewitching Bloopers*. It'll make you split your sides. Listen to this … "A witch who was sunbathing on a beach in Morecambe had to change the memories of one hundred and eighteen people when she covered herself in levitating cream by mistake." Ha! Now is that hilarious or what?'

'Mmm,' said Joe vaguely.

The man took off his trilby hat, slicked his hair back with one hand and replaced his hat. 'Blimey,' he said. 'You're a bundle of laughs, you are! Face as long as a drainpipe. What's your name, lad?'

'Joe.'

'Well, Joe. What's up? Nothing can be that bad, can it?'

'Had an argument with someone,' mumbled Joe, 'and now I can't find her.'

'Oh.' The man whistled through his teeth. 'Upset your girlfriend, have you?'

'She's *not* my girlfriend,' snapped Joe, 'but I think it was my fault. I said something rude about her teabags.'

'Sounds serious,' said the man, his lips beginning to twitch. 'Tell you what lad, why don't you –'

'What's that?' said Joe. He had heard a feeble, high-pitched wail. Joe leaned over the stall and tilted his head. 'I think it's coming from behind you.'

'Huh?' The man moved to one side, revealing a wooden cage which was perched on a stool. Inside the cage, curled up on a patchwork blanket, was a sleepy black kitten with silver tufts on the tips of her ears and a smattering of similar hairs at the end of her tail. She blinked her eyes slowly. They were the colour of clear honey.

'Hang *on*, that's an Amber-eyed Silver-tip, isn't it?' said Joe. 'Oh, if *only* ...'

'She'd make a lovely present, wouldn't she?' said the man, unlatching the cage. 'Want to hold her for a minute?' The kitten gave a little mew as the man scooped her roughly into his hand.

'I can't afford –' began Joe. Then he felt something lying in the bottom of his pocket and he smiled as his fingers closed over the garnet pendant.

'Bought yourself a new scarf?' said Twiggy and she sniffed.

'What?' Joe dipped his chin and saw a corner of the patchwork blanket hanging over the zip of his jacket. 'Er ... yeah,' he said, his hands clutched over his stomach. Twiggy stuck her nose in the air and continued to march at a brisk pace along the snow-covered pavement. Joe struggled to keep up with her.

'Well, actually, no,' he said, stopping in a pool of light cast by a streetlamp. The snow glittered around his feet. 'As a matter of fact ... it's a gift for you ... to say that I'm –'

'Joe!' Twiggy put her hands to her mouth and her cheeks reddened. 'You didn't have to ... I shouldn't have made such a fuss about a few silly teabags.'

'Well ...' Joe shrugged. 'I upset you, and I'm sorry.'

He began to unzip his jacket. Several woollen squares tumbled forward and a furry black head popped into view.

'Ohhh,' breathed Twiggy. 'A kitten!'

'Not just any kitten,' announced Joe proudly. 'This is an Amber-eyed Silver-tip!' The kitten wriggled as Joe carefully disentangled her from the blanket. 'Of course, it *could* just be a very furry tadpole,' said Joe, grinning. Then his mouth fell open. 'I don't *believe* it. That double-crossing cheat! He hoodwinked me.'

Twiggy took the kitten from Joe as he examined the sleeves of his jacket. 'Look at that!' he said, rubbing his finger against a silver streak. 'It's *powder paint*.' Joe stared at the kitten, which was purring in Twiggy's arms. There was a trace of silver at the tip of one ear but the other was completely black and the kitten's eyes had faded from amber to a pallid lime-green.

'Right,' said Joe firmly. 'I'm going to go back to that market and …' His voice tailed off as he watched Twiggy press the kitten against her cheek. Her eyes were filled with tears.

'Thank you, Joe,' said Twiggy. 'She's *gorgeous*.'

'What shall I call her?' Twiggy waggled a feather on the floor and the kitten pounced on it.

'How about … Fake,' said Joe sourly as he knelt beside the fireplace. He dropped a fresh log into the grate and it landed on the glowing ash with a whump. 'Or Gut Bucket … I think that would be a very suitable name for her, judging by the way she tucked into those kippers …'

The log shifted and orange sparks shot up the chimney. Joe sank into the red armchair and stretched out his hand to stroke Squib, who had fallen asleep on the knitted cushion.

'Are we going to try out this Lingo Liquorice then, or what? My eyes are struggling to stay open and I need to get home.' Joe glanced at his watch. 'Crikey, it's nearly quarter past four!'

'All right,' said Twiggy with a sigh. She tickled the top of the kitten's head. 'I think I've decided what to name her. It was something you mentioned –'

'Not Gut Bucket!'

Twiggy glared at him. 'Of course not. I'm going to call her Tadpole.'

'You can't call a *cat* Tadpole!'

'Why not?'

'Well, for one thing, it doesn't sound very sophisticated and, more importantly, she's not going to grow into a *frog*, is she?'

'I don't care,' said Twiggy stubbornly. 'I think it suits her.' Her face softened. 'You don't mind, do you, Joe? It *was* really nice of you to give up your garnet pendant like that.'

Joe shook his head and smiled. He opened his palm and thrust it at Twiggy. 'Liquorice, please,' he said.

Twiggy patted the pocket of her overcoat which she had slung over a stool. She pulled out the wrinkled paper bag and handed Joe a strip of lank black liquorice. Joe nibbled the end of it, cautiously.

'Not bad,' he said, stuffing the whole strip in his mouth.

'You're not meant to eat the whole thing,' said Twiggy, tearing off a tiny piece of liquorice before chewing it delicately. 'You've just gobbled up several hours' worth.'

The log in the fireplace hissed and popped as flames licked over it. Squib woke up and stretched out his front legs, digging his claws into Joe's trousers.

'Ow!' said Joe.

'My apologies,' said Squib in a deep, growling voice.

Joe gasped, stuck his finger in his ear and wiggled it around. 'He spoke then, Twiggy! Did you hear that? Squib ... go on. Say something else!'

'You're starting to annoy me,' said the cat.

'Listen, Squib ... dear, *darling* Squib,' said Twiggy as she crouched beside the red armchair, stirring a cup of dead-nettle tea with a spoon. 'We need your help.'

The cat yawned rudely.

'Somebody broke into this house earlier tonight. They stole a slice of Yule pudding and Patsy's Re-growing Potion –'

'Ha ha,' said Squib bitterly.

'Did you see anything?' asked Joe. He scratched Squib very gently behind his ear and the cat's whiskers began to quiver.

'Mmm … mmm,' purred Squib. 'Only one perrrson. Lady. Clumsy. No thin stick …'

'I think he means "wand",' whispered Twiggy, clinking the spoon against her teacup.

'Searrrching for something.' The cat closed his eyes and purred even louder. 'Spillikins. Spillikins. Spillikins of Doom.'

'*That's* where I heard it!' shouted Joe, knocking the cup of dead-nettle tea out of Twiggy's hand in his excitement. 'The teashop. That woman –'

'What, old Slyboots?' said Twiggy.

'Yes! I'm positive I heard her say *Spillikins of Doom.*'

Squib, who had stopped purring when the teacup clunked against the hearthrug, jumped on to Joe's lap, shooting little pinpricks of pain into his legs. His tail swelled up like a bottlebrush and his olive-green eyes bulged out of his head.

'What's the matter, Squib?' said Twiggy.

'Hide! Have to hide!' yowled the cat, springing off Joe's lap and slinking underneath Rose's heavy oak desk.

'Pick me up!' squeaked the kitten, who was cowering by Twiggy's ankles.

Seconds later, the front door of Dead-nettle Coven flew open with such force that it slammed into the wall and rattled on its hinges. Accompanied by a gust of wind and a shower of snowflakes, four witches appeared in the doorway.

Chapter Eleven

Dunkel and fleck

'Oh, h-hello,' said Twiggy in a tremulous voice. She gulped and tried to conceal Tadpole in the pocket of her cardigan. 'Y-you're back early.' Joe flattened himself against the armchair and stayed as still as possible. He hoped that the witches' unusual eyesight did not enable them to see through furniture.

'Tell me about it,' snarled Patsy. Joe heard the witch stomp her feet on the doormat. Then she gave an ear-splitting sneeze.

'Why can't you ever put your hand over your mouth?' complained Rose in a familiar scolding manner. 'You've just sprayed gelatinous spit all over my –'

'WILL YOU TWO PUT A CORK IN IT!' The normally calm Winifred sounded very close to breaking point.

'Did you have a nice time at the Yule bonfire?' asked Twiggy timidly.

'What Yule bonfire?' said Patsy, and Joe heard a

clattering noise as if the witch had hurled her broom-stick on the floor.

'How many hours did we wander about, like half-witted ninnies, on that *stupid* hill?' said Rose.

'Nearly as long as we had to listen to you whining about it,' growled Patsy, and Joe heard a brief commotion followed by two slaps which rang out as clearly as cracks from a whip. Rose began to snivel and Winifred commented that her hand felt numb.

'I believe,' said Julius's wavering voice, 'that the *precise* duration was four hours and twenty-three minutes.'

'I think the bonfire must have been cancelled, Twigs,' said Winifred wearily, 'only no one bothered to tell us. Be a sweetheart and make a pot of dead-nettle tea, hey? It's been a *very* long night.'

Twiggy did not move.

'And a freezing one, too,' said Patsy. 'I'm so cold, I've got goosepimples on my goosepimples. What I need is forty winks in my nice, comfy armchair in front of the fire ...'

Every trace of colour drained from Twiggy's face and Joe's rapid heartbeat thundered in his ears. He heard Patsy tramp towards the chair. It's jam-jar time again, thought Joe sadly. His muscles tensed. Twiggy's mouth dropped open. A floorboard creaked.

And Patsy stopped.

'Oh my word!' Joe heard her say. 'Is that a *tree*

growing out of my desk?'

'Which *chump* left this saucer of milk –' began Julius.

'Isn't that *Squib* lurking in the corner?' said Rose.

'Hey!' said Winifred in a voice shaking with outrage. 'What's happened to my aardvark?'

Joe did not have to see the witches to know that they were all staring expectantly at Twiggy. He saw her shuffle her feet and tuck a few straggly hairs behind her ear. Then she placed one hand on the kitten-sized bulge in her cardigan pocket and gripped the arm of the chair with the other.

'Ah,' said Twiggy, swaying slightly. 'I can explain …'

'In the olden days, they would've turned him into a toad without a moment's hesitation –'

'Yes. Thank you, Rose,' snapped Winifred as she paced around the room with her arms folded. 'We are *not* going to transform the boy into a warty amphibian. This is *not* the Middle Ages.'

'It's what he deserves,' said Rose, circling Joe in a menacing way. 'Pesky nuisance … always poking his nose into our business.' Joe staggered back against the map of the British Isles and felt a pin jab him in the neck.

'It wasn't his fault –' began Twiggy.

'I'd keep quiet, if I were you.' Rose's eyes glinted behind her butterfly-shaped spectacles as she rounded on Twiggy. 'You're in quite enough trouble already.'

'Patsy,' said Winifred in a worried voice. 'What do you think we should do about Joe?'

'Don't care,' said Patsy sulkily. She slouched on a stool beside her desk and stared at the lime-green blob which was all that remained of her Re-growing Potion. Every now and then, she sniffed loudly and muttered rude things about burglars under her breath.

'Shall I fetch a couple of jam-jars, Winifred?' Julius tottered across the room, wearing a maroon smoking jacket and bow tie. He clutched a long-handled pair of eyeglasses in one hand. His fluffy white hair made him look as if he had a small cloud hovering over his head.

'Thank you, Julius,' said Winifred. 'I think it's really our only option.'

Joe began to edge along the wall, past the calendar with the picture of the toadstool on it. Without taking his eyes off the front door, he stepped over Squib and sidled up to the hat stand, which held several broad-brimmed black hats. Melted snowflakes dripped from their soggy pointed tips and splashed on to Joe. He stood very still and waited, gradually becoming wetter and wetter.

'Please, don't,' wailed Twiggy, grabbing Winifred's arm. 'Not after everything I've told you. There's something sinister going on and we have to find out what it is. Joe is a witness.'

'Don't be ridiculous!' said Rose. 'He just saw a few witches having a spat on a train. It was careless of them. Yes. But I wouldn't call it *sinister*.'

'What about the snake that Harriet Perkins drew on Joe's suitcase?' said Twiggy desperately. 'It was a message –'

'It was graffiti,' said Rose. 'The woman was bored and fancied having a bit of a doodle. We've all done it.'

Winifred raised an eyebrow disapprovingly.

'The break-in!' said Twiggy, her face turning purple with frustration.

'We were unlucky,' said Rose and shrugged.

'But Joe's my friend!' shouted Twiggy. 'He bought me a kitten!'

'Yes,' agreed Winifred, trying to loosen Twiggy's vice-like grip on her arm. 'I'll admit that was very generous but –'

'No!' shrieked Julius, peering through his lorgnette. 'Calamity! Look what those thieving scoundrels have done to my trunk!'

It was the moment Joe had been waiting for. The witches were distracted for a few seconds. Rose, Winifred and Julius had turned their backs on him and Patsy was too grief-stricken about her stolen Re-growing Potion to notice Joe's hand moving towards the doorknob. He twisted it firmly and sneaked out of the house. By the time the witches' enraged cries reached Joe's ears he had sprinted past six lampposts and had almost arrived at the corner of Weaver's Lane.

Joe did not go straight home. He knew that a broomstick was capable of overtaking him in a matter of minutes, so he turned right instead of left at the end of the street and kept to the shadows. Every now and then, he slowed to a jog and tilted his face towards the sky, but he did not see a single broomstick diving after him. He ran for several miles, loping along at the steady pace he used when he was cross-country running at school. He had never run over snow in the darkness before but the familiar feeling of striding out on his own was strangely comforting. It was bitterly cold, but the air seemed to blast his tiredness away and, when Joe came to a standstill, he did so reluctantly. He had heard voices.

Joe peered uneasily around him. There were no streetlamps. The only source of light was the moon, fleetingly glimpsed through a mass of shredded cloud. There was no pavement beneath his feet, either. In his anxiety to escape the witches, Joe realised that he must have run through the outskirts of Canterbury and into the countryside. He was in a narrow lane, overhung by trees which creaked eerily in the still night.

Joe heard the echoing voices again. They were drawing closer but he could see no sign of movement in the dark lane. The bodiless voices began to reverberate in Joe's ears and he felt his heart fluttering with panic. Then he heard a scratching sound which seemed to be coming from a nearby ditch and it occurred to him that the owners of the voices might be underground. Joe crouched next to the ditch and listened.

'A wasted evening, don't you think so, Dunkel?' said a harsh male voice.

'Indeed,' replied a female voice. 'Our mistress will not be pleased. She becomes more impatient every day.'

'We must find it for her at all costs,' said the first voice gruffly.

'Yes, Fleck.' Joe heard a sigh. 'It's puzzling, is it not?'

'That a mere piece of paper could be so valuable?'

'Yes,' said Dunkel. The scratching sound stopped. 'We were in the right village, weren't we, Fleck – and in the right house?'

'Of course, my dear! Stop fretting.'

'A piece of paper is so easy to miss,' continued Dunkel worriedly. 'You don't think we failed to notice it –'

'Impossible!' said Fleck. 'We ransacked the entire building. Plenty of bat droppings but no sign of her precious document.' The scratching noise resumed.

'What made her imagine that it was there?' asked Dunkel meekly.

'A hunch, nothing more,' said Fleck. 'Our mistress suspects every coven in the district. It's her belief that the prisoners managed to slip the piece of paper to someone – most likely a local witch – before she started that skirmish on the train.'

Dunkel sniggered. 'I do enjoy a lively fight. We knocked the stuffing out of them, didn't we Fleck?'

Joe heard a wheezing chuckle and then the voices became muffled. 'Do you think we'll be punished for not succeeding in our task?' said Dunkel.

'Undoubtedly, my dear. Prepare yourself for another spell in … *The Basket*.'

'Oh,' said Dunkel in a distressed voice. 'That cramped, hateful little box. How I loathe it! My whiskers get horribly squashed.'

'Have courage, my dear …'

A movement caught Joe's eye and he saw two dark shapes slinking out of the ditch. It's the cats from the wicker basket! thought Joe as he spied two long tails dragging over the snow. Lucky I ate that whole strip of Lingo Liquorice. Wait till Twiggy hears about this!

The shrouded moon burst through a break in the cloud and the lane was illuminated for a second. It was just long enough for Joe to glimpse the naked tails and hunched grey backs of two rats as they reared on to their hind legs and sniffed the air. Then they scuttled over the snow towards a pinprick of light that winked through the trees.

Chapter Twelve

Two Hoots

Joe opened his eyes. He did not need to switch on his bedside lamp because daylight had already seeped into every corner of the room through the thin flowery curtains. He sat up in bed and was surprised to find that his duvet was flat and unruffled, as if he had not stirred in his sleep.

No wonder I slept so soundly, thought Joe, feeling a dull ache in his leg muscles. He remembered the events of the night before. He had been tempted to follow the rats into the trees but he had known that he would need to save all his energy for the long run home. By the time he had reached the corner of Cloister Walk, Joe had been ready to collapse. He had half-expected Winifred to be waiting for him, armed with a Fundibule and jam-jars, but he had crept through the front gate and sneaked round the side of the house into the back garden without anyone confronting him. The spare back door key had been in its usual place: under a flowerpot beside the garden shed. By the time his head had sunk on to his pillow, dawn had been breaking and Joe had fallen asleep to the fluting call of a blackbird.

There was a mug of hot chocolate on Joe's bedside table. He peered at the wrinkled layer of skin which had formed over its surface and decided that it must have been sitting there for some time. Joe glanced at the alarm clock.

'What?' he shouted, throwing back his duvet. It was almost midday.

Joe thumped down the stairs with his T-shirt on inside out. His socks slid over the tiled hall and he popped his head round the kitchen door. There was a delicious smell coming from the saucepan on the cooker. Joe was amazed to see that his mother was stirring the saucepan. Her forehead was creased with frown lines and she looked as if she was in a trance.

'Mum,' said Joe.

'Hello, Joe!' she said brightly, her frown disappearing. Her eyes widened and she let the wooden spoon drop into the pan. 'What's the matter?'

'Nothing,' said Joe, staring at his mum. 'I've just never seen you … wearing an apron before.'

'Oh!' Merle seemed relieved. 'Haven't you?' She rubbed her hands down Gordon's blue-and-white striped apron. The shoulder straps were too long for her, exposing the first four buttons of her denim shirt. She picked up the spoon again. 'It's carrot and coriander soup. That *is* your favourite isn't it?'

'Yes,' said Joe in a bewildered voice. 'Why didn't you wake me? Where's Gordon?'

'At the supermarket with Esme. You know how she loves to tick things off the shopping list. She's a funny one.' Merle smiled at Joe with glistening eyes. 'You looked so peaceful lying in your bed, I didn't have the heart to wake you. I expect you're ravenous. Lunch won't be long …'

A car door slammed outside. About a minute later, a key rattled in the front door and Joe heard Esme's high-pitched chatter.

'Need any help?' asked Joe as Gordon appeared holding a cardboard box and three bulging carrier bags. Esme was carrying a handsome plant with red leaves.

'It's a poinsettia,' she said proudly.

'Thank you, Joe,' said Gordon. 'There are a few more bags in the car. But put a jumper on. It's perishing out there.'

'Has anyone seen my sweatshirt?' said Joe. 'I can't find it.'

Esme fixed Joe with her big grey eyes, bit her lip and shook her head.

'Don't worry about the washing-up,' said Gordon, after they had finished their lunch. He patted Joe on the shoulder. 'Why don't you go and watch some telly.'

'The television's broken ... remember?' Joe's mum slapped Gordon on the arm with a rubber glove. 'Fancy forgetting that.'

Gordon laughed. 'Yes ... yes. Silly me. We must see about getting it fixed. Well, you could play a game of cards with Esme, then. If you *want* to, that is.'

As Joe left the kitchen, Gordon and his mother began to whisper. Pausing in the doorway, Joe said, 'Is something up?'

'No,' said Gordon, scratching his nose.

'Nothing,' said his mum, plunging her hands into the washing-up bowl.

'Weren't you meant to be helping with a Christmas raffle this afternoon, Mum?'

'What?' said Merle casually. 'Oh ... that. No, no ... I don't think I'll go. Brenda can cope on her own.'

'Oh,' said Joe. 'Right.'

He sauntered into the living room. Esme's latest library book *Toffee-nosed Tara* was lying abandoned on the carpet beside the Christmas tree. His sister was nowhere to be seen. That's strange, thought Joe as he picked up the book and smoothed its crumpled pages. It's not like Esme to be so careless with a library book. Joe placed it on the coffee table. I wonder where she's got to, he thought.

'Esme!' he called, cupping his hands around his mouth. There was no answer.

Joe walked over to the bookcase and slid out *A Street Atlas of Canterbury*. He found the page which showed the city centre and tried to figure out which route he had taken the night before. He was moving his finger along a road called Swingletree Lane when the doorbell rang.

'Someone for you, Joe,' shouted Gordon.

'Your mum's a bit of a fusspot, isn't she?' said Twiggy, patting a lump of snow between her red mittens.

'Not usually.' Joe removed a garish bobble hat and a pair of earmuffs which his mother had insisted he put on. He stuffed them in his pockets. 'She's behaving a bit oddly today.'

'If your dad –'

'*Step*dad,' insisted Joe as he skidded on a slush-covered paving slab.

'Yes, well if *he* hadn't persuaded her, she'd never have allowed you to come outdoors.'

'I'm not sure it's a very good idea, anyway,' said Joe, looking suspiciously up and down Cloister Walk. 'You're not leading me into an ambush, are you?'

Twiggy hurled her snowball and it landed with a splat

on somebody's gatepost, leaving a white smudge. 'I told you already. Winifred's had second thoughts. She's decided to leave your memory alone.'

Joe snorted. 'I don't believe that for a moment,' he said.

'She has,' said Twiggy, 'honestly, Joe. Winifred can be a bit bossy, but she's quite a reasonable person.'

'I'm not going to be turned into a toad instead, then?'

'Don't be silly. Winifred sent me to apologise to you, on behalf of all the witches in Dead-nettle Coven.'

'Wow.' Joe was very impressed. He stared at Twiggy. 'How did you manage to change their minds?'

'Well,' said Twiggy, 'I did my best, but I think it was the certificate that persuaded them in the end.'

'What certificate?'

'It arrived, by windsprite, just after you left,' said Twiggy. 'It was from our Head Office.'

'Is that in London?' asked Joe, thinking about the small terraced house he shared with his father and Hamish in Tooting. It seemed unlikely that he would be returning there before Christmas. Joe heaved a sigh.

'London?' said Twiggy in a puzzled voice. 'No. Why should you think that? Our Head Office is in Fingringhoe.' Joe looked blank and Twiggy rolled her eyes. 'It's in Essex,' she said. 'Anyway, they sent a leaf, addressed to Winifred, along with the certificate.' Twiggy reached into the pocket of her overcoat and produced a crimson maple leaf. She began to read from it:

'*Dear Miss Whirlbat*

We have been informed by Mrs Veronica Snipe, deputy editor of Which Witch, *that you have recruited a sixth member of Dead-nettle Coven. Therefore, we are sending you the Golden Cauldron Certificate recognising your official status as a coven. Congratulations.*
Yours bewitchingly
Freda Snaggletooth
Governor of Covens

P.S. It was noted that your newest member showed a considerable lack of knowledge about Mabel's Book. Please rectify this immediately.'

'Crikey,' said Joe, remembering the stern witch behind the bookstall at the Midnight Market. 'Veronica Snipe must have been the woman who told me about the missing page in *Mabel's Book*. She really believed me when I said ...'

'Mmm?' said Twiggy.

'I ... er ... told her that I belonged to Dead-nettle Coven.'

Twiggy smirked. 'Never mind. Winifred and the

148

others are *really* thrilled about the certificate ... even if it wasn't exactly deserved. By the way, Veronica Snipe sent a form for you to fill in. They need your biographical details for *Which Witch.*'

'But what happens when they find out that I'm not the least bit magical? Won't you get into trouble?'

'Oh, yeah ... heaps,' said Twiggy, 'but if we *admit* you're not a witch, we'll get it in the neck as well. Let's just hope nobody finds out, eh? Now, which way are we going?'

They stopped in a narrow alleyway beside the white-washed wall of a Tudor house. Joe unzipped his jacket and produced *A Street Atlas of Canterbury.* He began to flick through the pages. 'You'll *never* believe what happened to me last night –' he began.

'*I* had to polish eleven pairs of boots, sweep the floors, cook breakfast and fetch some ingredients for a new batch of Re-growing Potion,' said Twiggy without pausing for breath, '*and* I wasn't allowed to use any magic. They may be pleased about their certificate but they're still furious with *me.*

'Julius is ever so upset about his trunk being smashed open. He reckons the thieves have stolen one of his books. But – *even worse* – he's noticed that the purple mist, in that jam-jar I borrowed, has all but disappeared. He's absolutely gutted! Said it used to belong to a famous academic. I didn't dare tell him that I used it on that feeble librarian.

'Winifred says that if I disobey her one more time, she'll take away my kitten, Patsy is seething about her stolen potion ... and you'll *never* guess *what* ... Squib seems to have vanished again.' Twiggy screwed up her freckled face and put her hands on her hips. 'Oh, sorry,' she said, noticing that Joe's mouth was hanging open. 'Were you going to say something?'

'Yes,' said Joe, 'I was.' He took a deep breath and could barely keep the excitement out of his voice. 'When I escaped from your place last night, I decided to ... take the long route home, and I overheard a fascinating conversation on the way. It was about Slyboots –'

'No!' said Twiggy, stepping to one side as a man came down the alleyway with a border collie at his heels. Joe waited for them to pass before continuing.

'Remember I told you that Slyboots had a wicker cat basket with her when she was on the train? I assumed that there were cats inside it, but ...' Joe's voice dropped to a whisper, 'in actual fact, they were *rats* –'

'Ooh,' interrupted Twiggy.

'– called Dunkel and Fleck. Thanks to the Lingo Liquorice, I could understand everything that they were saying. They'd been up to some mischief. Said they'd ransacked a house on Slyboots's orders –'

'Not *ours*,' said Twiggy eagerly. 'Not Dead-nettle Coven?'

'No,' said Joe. 'No, I don't think so. Squib didn't mention anything about a couple of rats, did he? Our burglar was acting alone. Anyway, these rats said they were looking for a piece of paper –'

'A piece of *paper*?' said Twiggy. 'Is that all?'

'Yes,' snapped Joe. He wished Twiggy would allow him to finish. 'A very *valuable* piece of paper that Slyboots is desperate to get hold of, apparently. Dunkel and Fleck reckon that two prisoners must have given the piece of paper to some witch on a train …'

'*Aubrey White and Harriet Perkins*,' breathed Twiggy, leaning closer to Joe. 'The Vipers! Old Slyboots must have *captured* them. That means they're still alive! I didn't tell you, before, because I didn't want to scare you, but I thought old Slyboots might have bumped them off. What do you think the piece of paper was? A letter?' Twiggy grabbed Joe's arm and her eyes bulged in their sockets. 'Crumbs, Joe, what if the Vipers didn't pass it to a witch? What if they gave it … to *you*!'

'But it makes perfect sense,' said Twiggy sulkily as she dawdled behind Joe. 'They might have slipped a sheet of paper into your suitcase without you noticing. Didn't you say it burst open on the journey?'

'Yes,' said Joe, striding ahead, his nose buried in *A*

Street Atlas of Canterbury. 'It did, but ... hang on. I think we should have turned left at that crossroads back there.'

'Are you *sure* you know where you're going?' said Twiggy, as Joe turned round and began to march towards her.

'Of course,' snapped Joe, 'but it all looked very different in the dark.'

'I can't feel my toes,' moaned Twiggy as she waded through the snow. 'If we'd waited until tonight, we could have flown here on my broomstick.'

'Oh, stop grumbling.'

'*You* stop being so bossy, then.' Twiggy brushed a neat band of snow from a road sign. 'Did you say you were looking for Swingletree Lane?'

'Yes,' said Joe.

'Well, it's down here,' said Twiggy, glancing over her shoulder and promptly sinking into a ditch.

It took several minutes for Joe to pull Twiggy out of the snow-filled ditch because they were both laughing so much. When they scrambled on to the roadside again, Joe's jeans were soaked, his fingers burned and there were bobbles of snow clinging to his hair. As they walked side by side along Swingletree Lane, Twiggy persisted with her theory about his suitcase.

'What about when you –'

'I didn't see any piece of paper when I unpacked,' declared Joe.

'Are you positive? They could have folded it up really small.'

'I'm certain,' said Joe, staring at the interweaving branches above his head. 'OK, stop a minute. I think this is where I heard the rats. I remember that tree.' He pointed to the trunk of a dead oak tree which was smothered in twisting strands of ivy. A rotting branch had dropped to the ground. It leaned against the trunk like a crutch supporting a stooping man.

'Here!' said Joe, kneeling beside a patch of disturbed snow. 'This is where I crouched last night ... and I saw them emerging from the ditch a little further along.' Joe and Twiggy stepped on to the snowy verge as a black Mini zoomed past them, spraying them with grimy slush.

Twiggy burrowed in the snow while Joe prodded in the ditch with a stick. 'I've found something,' he said, feeling the stick pressing against a solid object. Scooping out handfuls of snow, Twiggy cleared the area around the stick. Gradually, she uncovered the end of a terracotta drainpipe.

'It must run underneath the fields,' said Joe, peering through a hedge. 'I wonder where the rats were coming from.'

'The nearest village in that direction is Stubble End,' said Twiggy.

Joe closed his eyes, trying to re-create the darkness of the night before.

'What are you doing?' asked Twiggy.

'I'm trying to remember where that light was coming from.' Joe swivelled round blindly. 'The rats came out of the ditch and ran off through the trees towards a light. I think we should find out what it was.'

'Could have been somebody's torch,' suggested Twiggy.

Joe shook his head. 'The light wasn't moving.' He opened his eyes and pointed to a dense thicket of naked trees and twisting brambles. 'Over there in that wood,' he said.

The snow reached up to Joe's knees in some places and, after every few steps, he had to stop to disentangle himself from a particularly prickly bramble bush. Twiggy squealed every time her hair snagged on a low branch. Their progress was slow. It was impossible for Joe to tell if he were heading in the right direction and he began to doubt whether it had been wise to enter the wood at all.

'Those rats were having a snoop around Pipistrelle Coven last night,' said Twiggy. She turned sideways and inched past a holly bush. 'Don't you reckon?'

'Yeah,' said Joe, following behind her. 'Quite a coincidence, isn't it? Two covens, within a few miles of each other, getting burgled on the very same night.'

'Do you think the woman who broke into our coven was looking for the same bit of paper?' asked Twiggy.

'I don't know,' said Joe, slipping on a tree root. 'It's

possible, I suppose – if this letter, or whatever it was that the rats were after, has anything to do with the Spillikins of Doom.'

'Slyboots burgled Dead-nettle,' said Twiggy firmly. 'I'm sure of it.'

'That's my hunch, too,' admitted Joe. 'But why wouldn't she bring her wand with her? Remember? Squib mentioned that the burglar didn't have one. And why would she steal … what was it?'

'A slice of Yule pudding,' said Twiggy, 'Patsy's Re-growing Potion and one of Julius's old maths books about graphs or something.'

'Weird,' said Joe. 'Well, she must have taken them for a reason.'

Glimpsing a dull orange patch of colour through the trees, Joe gasped and hastened towards it. He stumbled over the uneven ground, snapping twigs beneath his feet and bumping against tree trunks. Joe drew nearer and nearer until he reached a crumbling brick wall over which he could see the roof and upper storey of a cottage.

The wall was pitted with holes where the cement had started to wear away and Joe found it easy to wedge his trainers in the holes and scramble over the wall. He jumped down into a small garden with raised flowerbeds and clusters of large clay pots. There was a murky pond in one corner and shards of ice floated on its surface.

'"Two Hoots",' whispered Joe as Twiggy landed next to him. He pointed to the name of the cottage, each letter of which had been nailed to an owl-shaped block of wood in the porch. 'Spooky sort of name ...'

'And look!' said Twiggy, nudging Joe with her elbow. 'Look what's hanging above it ... a lantern!'

'The light!' said Joe eagerly. 'The one I saw last night! This is *definitely* where the rats were headed.'

Ivy crept up the walls of Two Hoots, surrounding each of the ground-floor windows with a ragged fringe of dark leaves. Joe walked across the garden to the nearest window, rubbed his sleeve on the misty glass and looked in. At first, he could barely see anything but, as his eyes adjusted to the gloom, he made out a pile of notebooks on a desk, a rocking chair and something which looked like an empty fish tank.

'Nothing out of the ordinary,' muttered Joe.

'I think we should leave, now,' said Twiggy anxiously. 'We're trespassing, and anyway, this house gives me the shivers.'

Joe's fingers gripped the windowsill as his eyes caught sight of something half-hidden behind the rocking chair. 'It's the cat basket!' he said. 'Slyboots must live here!'

'Let's go, Joe.'

'All right,' he said with a sigh. 'But why don't we come back tonight and –'

There was a muffled squeak from Twiggy and Joe

turned round. Standing behind him, with one hand clamped over Twiggy's mouth, was a witch. In her other hand, she held a wand.

'I think you might find that your plans have changed,' said the witch icily. She prodded Joe with the tip of her wand and her lips stretched into a cruel smile.

Chapter Thirteen

A Batty Gathering

The black Mini hurtled through the countryside like a runaway roller skate. It skidded round corners, roared up hills and seemed to lurch into every available pothole. Joe and Twiggy spent most of the journey bouncing up and down on the back seat with their hands over their eyes.

'Who is this maniac?' said Joe, his teeth rattling. The witch had not answered any of their questions as she herded them between the trees and back on to Swingletree Lane. Her Mini had been parked in a rather haphazard fashion, with its bonnet hanging over a ditch.

'Not ... not ... not ... not sure,' said Twiggy, as the Mini went over several bumps. 'I *think* I know her from somewhere ...'

Joe peered through his fingers and studied the witch's face in the Mini's rear-view mirror. She was about the same age as Winifred, Joe supposed. Faint creases were beginning to form at the outer corners of her eyes and

her cheeks were sallow and sunken. Two dark eyes darted from side to side under a heavy auburn fringe. The
witch checked her mirror and saw Joe looking at her.
She scowled at him and yanked at the steering wheel.
There was a squeal of brakes and Joe was thrown against
his seatbelt as the Mini clung to a sharp bend. Joe had a
horrible feeling that the carrot and coriander soup,
which was slopping about in his stomach, would be making a reappearance very shortly.

Twiggy parted her fingers and looked at Joe. 'Your
face has gone green,' she said. Joe chose not to reply, as
it would have involved opening his mouth.

The Mini rocketed down a steep slope, almost
becoming airborne before swerving around a duck pond
and shooting over a narrow bridge. Then the witch
crunched her gear stick; the Mini's engine growled and it
careered to a halt outside an old, ramshackle barn.

Joe and Twiggy breathed simultaneous sighs of relief.

The witch leaned around her seat and glared at them.
She unfastened their seatbelts with two jabs of her wand
and a few inaudible words. '*You* and *you*,' she said, thrusting a bony forefinger in their faces. 'Follow *me* ... and
no funny business.'

'What do we do?' whispered Joe as the witch opened
her door and shouted somebody's name.

'I left my wand back at the coven,' said Twiggy and
she shrugged when Joe gave her a despairing look.

'Well,' she said crossly, 'Tadpole wanted to play with it. I guess we'll have to go with the flow … it's what Winifred would do. There's no point panicking.'

Joe wriggled out of his seat and closed the slush-spattered door of the Mini. He was still feeling queasy from the car journey and did not resist when the witch gripped his shoulder and steered him towards a door at the side of the barn. As the witch released their shoulders to open it, Twiggy nudged Joe's elbow.

'We're in Stubble End,' she hissed, 'and this is Pipistrelle Coven.'

'What do you think they want?' asked Joe.

'Apart from driving lessons, you mean?' Twiggy shook her head. 'Don't know … but you belong to Dead-nettle Coven, remember?' She smiled nervously and winked at him as they followed the witch through the door.

The inside of the barn was surprisingly cosy. In the middle of the floor, a small fire burned brightly, sur-rounded by a circle of stones. Smoke spiralled upwards past a number of bats hanging upside-down from the rafters, and vanished through a hole in the roof.

A plump witch with black ringlets was snoozing on a sofa with her feet resting on an upturned cauldron, and several other witches were lying in hammocks with their limbs dangling over the sides. Joe counted nine black cats curled up on a couple of hay bales in the corner and another four were stretched out beside the fire. The only sound was a faint rumble of contented snoring.

A mixture of smoky, musty smells tickled Joe's nose and he sneezed. One of the cats beside the fire opened its green eyes and stared at him. Then the auburn-haired witch clapped her hands and disrupted the peaceful scene.

'Up! Everybody up!' she shouted. 'I have something important to tell you.'

The witch on the sofa scratched her head and yawned. She blinked very slowly and smiled, causing a dimple to appear in each cheek. 'Who've you got there, Sarah? A couple of guests?' She squinted at Twiggy. 'Why, you're Marjorie, aren't you? From Bladderwrack Coven?'

'Nope,' said Twiggy.

'Oh,' said the witch in a disappointed voice. 'I could have sworn ...'

Sarah, the auburn-haired witch, walked briskly over to the sofa and rescued a pair of spectacles that the plump witch was squashing beneath her elbow. 'Try these, Dora,' she said wearily.

'Oh, very well,' grumbled the woman, brushing aside her black ringlets and hooking the spectacles behind her ears. The hammocks swayed as some of the other witches, who had been asleep, began to stir. They sat upright, with ruffled hair and crumpled polka-dot pyjamas, training their bleary eyes on Joe and Twiggy.

'Drat and double drat!' said the witch called Dora, straightening her spectacles. 'It's one of those beastly Dead-nettles!'

'Yes,' said Sarah, sucking in her sallow cheeks. 'Prunella Brushwood – if I'm not mistaken.'

'Prunella?' Joe stared at Twiggy in astonishment. Her cheeks reddened and she scratched her nose self-consciously. 'Your real name's *Prunella*?' said Joe, touching Twiggy's arm. The name did not seem to suit her at all.

'Nobody calls me that,' said Twiggy in a tight voice. She frowned at Sarah. 'I prefer to be called by my nick-name, which is Twiggy.'

'Twiggy,' repeated Sarah sneeringly. She cocked an eyebrow. 'Is that because your hair resembles a bird's nest?' There was a ripple of laughter from the other members of Pipistrelle Coven. Twiggy stared miserably at the floor.

'Well, what's the annoying little brat doing here? The Dead-nettles moved out of this village months ago. Now, go on … scram!' Dora made a swatting motion with her hand as if she thought Twiggy were an irritating insect. 'Sarah, why are you wasting my time? What's your important news? Don't tell me it's something to do with that useless bunch of droopy Dead-nettles?'

Twiggy stuck out her trembling chin. 'We're not use-less! Patsy's the best spellbinder there is, and …

Winifred's a fantastic leader –'

'That namby-pamby stick insect!' said Dora. 'Pah! Winifred Whirlbat wouldn't know the first thing about being the leader of a coven. Oh.' She smiled slyly. 'I was forgetting. The Dead-nettles aren't a *proper* coven, are they?'

'Yes, they are!' said Joe, stepping forward. 'And I'm their newest member.' There had been something familiar about the witch on the sofa and, when she started being rude to Twiggy, Joe remembered where he had seen her before. Dora Benton had been wearing a long, navy coat and a peaked cap on the station platform, and she was wearing a pair of black silk pyjamas now; but the dimples were the same and so was her brusque manner.

'I know you,' he said boldly. 'You're the woman who stole Derek's uniform and took my train ticket under false pretences.'

'And I know *you*!' declared Dora, beaming from ear to ear. 'Oh, well *done*, Sarah. Wherever did you find him?'

'On Swingletree Lane.' Sarah reached into the inside pocket of her black velvet jacket and produced a small square of paper. She unfolded it and Joe craned his neck to see what was written on it. There were no words – just a pencil drawing of a boy with shaggy hair, a sturdy chin and a rather bemused expression on his face. Sarah held the piece of paper next to Joe's head. 'An excellent likeness, don't you think?'

Dora grunted. 'I don't know why you felt the need to interrogate that bumbling oaf at the station. My description of the boy was –'

'Worse than useless,' finished Sarah. 'Derek was most informative. It doesn't take much talent to impersonate a ticket collector, Dora – but a policewoman is quite a challenge. I was very convincing, even if I say so myself. Once I'd fooled Derek into thinking the boy was a runaway, he was only too willing to help. Described the boy in meticulous detail. Even sketched this picture for me.' Sarah's tone hardened. 'Don't glare at me, Dora. You know as well as I do that your eyesight is terrible. You need to wear those spectacles *all the time*.'

'That's quite enough from you,' snapped Dora. She glowered and folded her arms. 'I think you're forgetting that *I'm* the boss around here.'

'After all,' continued Sarah fearlessly, 'if you'd been wearing them that night, you would have noticed straightaway that the boy had given you a worthless, ordinary train ticket instead of –'

'SHUT UP!' roared Dora and a witch who had been asleep promptly fell out of her hammock. 'Anyway, where is it?' Dora stomped towards Joe and held out her podgy hand. 'Give it here, you little worm.'

'W … what?' said Joe. 'I don't understand …'

'THE PAGE!' screamed Dora, her black ringlets quivering. 'I know you've got it. The Vipers gave it to you, didn't they? I was expecting Harriet and Aubrey, of course, but when I bent down to tie my shoelace, I saw their little picture on your suitcase. I may not have the eyesight of an eagle,' she said sourly, 'but I'm not as blind as a bat, you know.' Dora glanced in the direction of the rafters. 'No offence intended,' she added meekly.

'You're wrong,' said Joe. 'I haven't a clue what you're on about. Nobody handed me any *page*.'

'He's in Dead-nettle,' hissed Sarah. 'They know nothing about the recent emergency. Head Office didn't want to involve them in the matter. A wise decision, if you ask me …'

'Have we been left out of something?' said Twiggy indignantly. 'That's not fair. We're a proper coven, now. Why won't anyone take us seriously? I don't understand why you dislike us so much.' Twiggy looked beseechingly at Dora and Sarah. Neither witch uttered a word. 'Is it because of Julius?' asked Twiggy. 'And Joe, too? Don't you agree that men should be allowed to join covens? Well, I think they should, so there! Winifred says that mixed covens are the way forward. She says that we should embrace change –'

'We don't have a problem with male witches,' interrupted Sarah.

'As long as they don't join *my* coven,' added Dora with a scowl.

'It's Rose Threep we disapprove of,' said Sarah stiffly.

'Rose?' said Twiggy in a mystified voice.

'Winifred should be ashamed of herself,' said Dora, 'letting a witch like *that* into her coven.'

'A witch like what?' said Twiggy. 'What have you got against Rose? She can be a bit spiteful, but –'

'The page, Dora,' said Sarah impatiently. She ushered Joe and Twiggy over to the sofa. 'They'll have to be told. There's no avoiding it, now.'

'Very well,' said Dora, pushing the bridge of her spectacles up her nose. She began to pace around the room in an agitated manner. Joe sat next to Twiggy on the edge of the sofa. A black cat began to rub its head against Joe's legs.

'You've heard of *Mabel's Book*, I imagine,' said Dora.

'Of course!' they said together.

'Then you'll know about the missing page.'

'Yes,' said Joe, remembering what Veronica Snipe had told him at the Midnight Market. 'There was a dangerous spell on page five hundred and something. Mabel ripped it out so that nobody could use it.'

Joe felt Twiggy nudging his elbow. 'How do you know about that?' she whispered.

'You are partly correct,' said Dora. 'Some witches still insist that Mabel Crump removed the page … but they are wrong! The page was ripped out by the *translator* of the book: a witch by the name of Fleur Fortescue.'

'Fleur …' Joe wrinkled his forehead. 'Of course! Her

166

name was on the front cover of the old copy of *Mabel's Book* that I found in the cardboard box.'

'Do you *mind*?' said Dora angrily. 'Pay attention when I am speaking. Now, where was I?'

'You were about to tell them about Fleur,' said Sarah. 'When she translated the five hundred and thirteenth page, Fleur realised the calamitous power of its spell and tore it out. She destroyed her translation immediately but she decided to hide the original page where no one would ever find it –'

'Except they did,' said Dora, glaring at Sarah. 'Now shut up, you. *I'm* telling this story.'

'Where'd they find it?' asked Joe.

'In Germany,' said Dora quickly, before Sarah could open her mouth.

'I know all this,' grumbled Twiggy. She received an instant dig in the ribs from Joe.

'Shh,' he whispered. 'I don't.'

'About twenty years ago,' continued Dora, 'a dog named Strudel dug it up in a forest. The page had been rolled up inside a fountain pen and wedged underneath a tree root. The dog owner's daughter was a witch and she stopped him from throwing the piece of paper away. The owner thought it was blank, you see …'

'Because *Mabel's Book* was written in witchy ink,' said Twiggy.

'Yes,' said Dora, her hand pressed over her heart. 'For

twenty years that page has been passed from witch to witch and from coven to coven.'

'Why?' asked Joe.

'For a very obvious reason, you little numbskull,' said Dora. She looked cautiously over her shoulder and lowered her voice. 'There are people,' she said fearfully, 'who want it. People who will stop at nothing to get it.'

'But I thought no one could read Mabel's handwriting,' said Joe.

'Fleur managed it, didn't she?' said Sarah. 'One day, someone will translate those words again and then ...' She clapped her hands. 'Kerboom!'

'Who *knows* what would happen,' said Dora.

'Why don't you just rip up the page,' said Joe, 'or throw it on the fire? Then you wouldn't have to worry about it any more.'

'How dare you!' thundered Dora. 'Have some respect, boy. Mabel Crump is a legend! This barn stands on the very spot where she scribbled her famous work of genius. Destroy it?' Her eyelids flickered as if she was going to faint. 'The very idea.'

'Don't you think we've tried to get rid of it?' said Sarah, giving Dora a disgusted look. '*Mabel's Book* is indestructible. She must have soaked each page in Durable Potion so that its words could be read in hundreds of years to come.'

'Or *not*,' said Joe, remembering Mabel's appalling

handwriting.

Sarah ignored him. 'Two days ago, we received a leaf from Head Office informing us that the page had to be smuggled out of London post-haste – and that they had chosen *our* coven to be involved in the operation.'

'Such an honour for Pipistrelle,' murmured Dora.

'Aubrey White and Harriet Perkins, from Viper Coven, had volunteered to travel incognito on the four o'clock train from Charing Cross,' explained Sarah. 'They were supposed to alight at Stubble End and deliver the page to Dora who would be disguised as a ticket collector. Only ... something went horribly wrong – they never got off the train, and they haven't been seen since.'

'Slyboots,' said Joe gravely. He shivered as he remembered the frantic scratching noises which had been coming from the wicker cat basket on the train. '*Rat* basket,' he said, correcting himself. He felt a prickling sensation at the nape of his neck.

'OK ... that's enough,' snapped Dora. 'We haven't brought you here for a cosy chit-chat. Now, where's the page?'

'I haven't got it,' said Joe. 'Honestly. I haven't got the slightest idea where it is.'

Dora clutched her head and howled. 'I can't stand it!' she moaned. 'First the Yule bonfire is cancelled so we decide to go broomstick racing instead and I fall off into the duck pond. Then we arrive back at the coven for a nightcap and a bit of shut-eye and we find the place in a complete mess! And now … AND NOW! This … insolent little pipsqueak says he hasn't got the page! I told Head Office that everything was under control. What am I going to tell them now? HUH? They'll pickle my eyeballs for this!'

'Er … Dora,' said a young witch timidly. She shuffled up to the leader of Pipistrelle Coven, clutching a red maple leaf in her hand. 'This must have arrived this morning. It's from Head Office.'

Dora made a choking noise and snatched the leaf out of the young witch's hand. Then she closed her eyes and thrust it at Sarah. 'Read it, would you? I can't face it.'

'Very well,' said Sarah, staring at the leaf. 'Oh, my. What disastrous news.'

Dora wailed and sank down on to the sofa, almost crushing Joe in the process. 'My career is over,' she said, putting her head in her hands.

'There's been a robbery,' said Sarah solemnly, 'at the National Museum of Witchcraft in Piddock's Cove. Somebody's stolen the original copy of *Mabel's Book*.'

Chapter fourteen

The Monsters of Much Marcle

It had been easy to escape. The witches had been so traumatised by the news from Head Office that no one had noticed when Joe and Twiggy had tiptoed towards the barn door. Half the witches had been huddled together, hugging each other and weeping, and the other half had collapsed into their hammocks with stupefied looks on their faces.

Beside the door, there had been a barrel filled with broomsticks and Twiggy had taken one to ensure a successful getaway. In minutes, Joe and Twiggy had flown over the hump-backed bridge and soared past the duck pond. She urged the broomstick to fly higher and they became immersed in a freezing mist that seemed to wrap itself around Joe's body, chilling him to the bone. Snowflakes began to float past his face.

'Twiggy! Do we have to fly so high?' The wind whipped Joe's words away almost as soon as they had left his mouth. He had to shout to make himself heard.

'Yes!' replied Twiggy. 'We have to stay in the clouds. Witches aren't supposed to use their broomsticks in daylight. It would be too risky to drop any lower. Somebody might see us!'

Joe looked beneath him but all he could see was a thick grey fog. 'How will you know when we reach Canterbury?' he yelled.

'We're not going to Canterbury,' said Twiggy. 'At least, not yet.'

'We're not?'

She shook her head firmly and ordered the broomstick to veer to the left. 'I thought we'd take a little detour to Piddock's Cove!'

The blanket of cloud began to drift apart as the broomstick dived downwards. Clear patches appeared through the weak swirls of mist and Joe was able to glimpse choppy grey water laced with white froth. They swooped lower and Joe realised that Twiggy was following a coastline. Below them, the sea ebbed and flowed on beaches the colour of oatmeal. Joe glanced to his right and saw steep cliffs topped with fields of snow. Snaking stone walls severed each field and broke up the endless spread of white.

Joe clasped Twiggy's waist even more tightly as the broomstick plummeted towards a huge rock which was being buffeted by waves. At its centre was a hole shaped like a doorway and Twiggy urged the broomstick through it. Joe ducked as they shot through the gap and ascended rapidly. The broomstick performed a loop the-loop before streaming into the next cove, gliding over the cliff-top and landing beside a cottage. It had lilac walls and a slate roof.

Joe climbed off the broomstick and straightened up with difficulty. He had been crouched over the broom for nearly an hour and his joints were stiff and painful. Twiggy raised her arms in the air and made a whooping noise.

'Was that fun or what?' she said. 'Winifred would have fainted on the spot if she'd seen us zoom through that rock! I don't think my little broom would have been able to pull off a stunt like that, but this one is a top-of-the-range model.'

'You *are* going to give it back?' said Joe.

'Oh, yes. I've only *borrowed* it.' She patted its birch twigs and grinned at him. 'I bet Dora Benton is hopping mad by now!'

'So, this is Piddock's Cove?' said Joe, looking down on to a crescent-shaped bay. The waves had littered the empty beach with seaweed and driftwood and a lone boat was anchored near the shore.

'Yes,' said Twiggy. 'We're on the coast of Dorset.' She walked up the front path of the cottage, popped the broomstick in an umbrella stand in the porch and rang the doorbell. 'I came here last summer with Winifred,' she said, 'but the museum was closed. I had a lovely paddle in the sea, though.'

'You think Slyboots was behind the robbery, don't you?' said Joe.

'Mmm,' said Twiggy, 'but we need to find out for sure.'

'I don't understand why she'd want the book,' said Joe. 'Page five hundred and thirteen has been torn out and the whole book has been translated –'

'Into seventy-four languages,' said Twiggy.

'So what can she possibly learn from it?' Joe stepped back a couple of paces as he heard muffled footsteps on the other side of the door. The flap of the letterbox was lifted up and a chin covered with white hairs appeared in the rectangular gap.

'My name is Arthur Poppleweed. I am the curator of the National Museum of Witchcraft,' said a gruff voice from the letterbox. 'Kindly state your business.'

'Er … we are Joe and Twiggy from Dead-nettle Coven,' said Joe. 'We've come to look around the museum ... because we're very interested in … er … old artefacts and things.'

There was a long pause before the white bristles

moved again. 'Very well,' said the voice, 'you may enter, but be warned! I am armed with a hefty cudgel and a water pistol filled with Petrifying Potion … and I'm not afraid to use them.'

'What's Petrifying Potion?' said Joe to Twiggy as the curator unlocked the front door.

'It turns you into a statue,' replied Twiggy. 'Patsy uses it for making garden ornaments.'

If Joe had been a passer-by, he would never have guessed that the picturesque little cottage was the National Museum of Witchcraft. There were no signs on the gatepost or the front door to advertise this fact. However, as soon as Joe had stepped over the threshold, he smelt the familiar stale, musty odour of decaying objects which had been present in every museum he had ever visited.

'Welcome,' said Arthur, and he asked Joe to hold his cudgel while he scratched his beard. The old man wore a pair of patched corduroy trousers and a blue sailor's smock. The top of his head was bald and speckled like a bird's egg and there was a big sticking plaster on it.

'Got knocked out by the robber,' said Arthur, pointing at his injured head with the tip of his water pistol. 'That's why I've had to step up security, you see.'

Joe and Twiggy followed him down the dark hallway and into a small room with the curtains drawn at the windows. The room was lit entirely by candlelight.

'You have a wander and if you've got any questions, I'll be right here,' said Arthur, sitting in a wooden chair by the door. He rested the cudgel and the water pistol in his lap.

'Here it is!' said Joe, standing in front of a shattered pane of glass. Inside a display case was a tray lined with faded green velvet and in the centre of the tray was a small patch of velvet which had kept its original vibrant colour. It was about the size of a pack of playing cards. Underneath the bright green rectangle was a dog-eared piece of card which said:

```
Exhibit 122: 'A Book of Spells, Potions
and Other Snippets of Witchery' by the
supremely-talented (and rumoured to be
quite good-looking) genius, Mabel
Crump. It was written in the month of
March 1596 (or it could have been
April) in totally unreadable handwrit-
ing and was translated into English in
1848 by Fleur Fortescue who was a right
know-it-all. Today, it is known simply
as 'Mabel's Book', and is to be found
on every witch's bookshelf (though I
did know a witch who kept it in her
cutlery drawer).
```

'I never realised the book was so tiny,' said Joe, staring at the green patch where the book had resided.

'Oh, yes,' said Arthur. 'Pocket-sized, you might say.' He gave a heavy sigh. 'Very easy to steal, at any rate.'

'Can you remember what the thief looked like?' said Joe eagerly.

'Well, I didn't see much of them,' said Arthur. 'One minute I was frying eggs and bacon for my breakfast and the next ... I was face down on the floor with a bump on my head the size of a pomegranate. The thief was a woman – I remember seeing her hand just before she zapped me with her wand. She had these long red nails ...'

Joe nodded. 'It sounds like Slyboots all right.'

'Slyboots?' said Arthur in a puzzled voice.

'Over here, Joe,' called Twiggy gleefully. 'I've found a photograph of Rose.'

'Crikey,' said Joe as he leaned over a dusty display case in the corner. He looked at a photograph of two girls dressed in black tunics which reached down to their ankles. One girl, who had her hair in bunches, was glaring at the camera. The other had a long plait wrapped around her neck like a scarf and she was sticking out her tongue. Joe read the typed card below the photograph:

Exhibit 062: A rare photograph of The Monsters of Much Marcle (who were a

right pair of little horrors). Expelled
from Brimstone Coven at the age of ten,
Rosemary Threep and Logan Dritch ter-
rorised the village of Much Marcle for
eleven months before being captured and
sent to The Penitentiary for Wayward
Witches in Papua New Guinea.

Joe's eyes wandered over the rest of the objects in the display case. Exhibit 063 was a paintbrush which the girls had dipped in witchy ink and used to daub rude messages all over Much Marcle. Exhibit 064 was a stick of purple chalk which was all that was left of Much Marcle Primary School after Rose and Logan had whipped up a tornado one August afternoon. The card quoted Rose as saying that they had sent it crashing into the empty building 'for a laugh'.

'Now we know why the Pipistrelles bad-mouthed Rose,' said Joe.

'And that's why everyone has got such a low opinion of Dead-nettle,' said Twiggy. 'Because one of our members was a famous hooligan in her youth. I can't imagine *Rose* doing all those terrible things. She's such a prim old crosspatch.' Twiggy laughed and pressed her finger against the glass. 'Look at her ... sticking her tongue out!'

Joe studied the photograph earnestly, but he was not

interested in Rose. Instead, he looked at the other girl, Logan Dritch. She had a penetrating stare and her hair was a deep reddish-brown. He noticed her strong, determined jaw and the curl of her lips. The face of the glamorous woman on the train flashed into his mind.

'It's Slyboots!' said Joe suddenly, grabbing Twiggy's arm. 'The other girl! The other Monster of Much Marcle.'

'You sure?' said Twiggy.

Joe nodded. 'I'm positive. Slyboots and Logan Dritch are one and the same.'

Chapter fifteen

Out of the Woods

The pier was deserted apart from the huddled figure of a fisherman in shiny yellow waterproofs, seated on a collapsible stool. One of his hands clasped a fishing rod which jutted over the edge of the pier, a fine silken thread dropping from its tip and vanishing into the swirling waters below. The fisherman's other hand gripped the brim of his sou'wester. He pulled the waterproof hat firmly over his eyes.

Twiggy battled to land her broomstick. The same strong gust of wind that was trying to dislodge the fisherman's hat was doing its best to blow her off course and deposit the broomstick and its passengers into the foaming, steel-grey sea.

Twiggy's hair tickled Joe's face. 'Nearly there,' she said, leaning into the wind and holding the broomstick steady. The broom hovered like a dragonfly about to touch down on a lily pad. Joe felt his trainers knock against a metal railing and, a few seconds later, they landed safely at the end of the pier.

'Nicely done,' said Joe, approvingly. He was relieved to feel the solid wooden planks beneath his feet. 'Time for some refreshments,' he said, patting a swollen pocket in his jacket. He glanced over to the other side of the pier where the fisherman sat with his back to them, one hand still tugging at his sou'wester. The fisherman seemed completely unaware of Joe and Twiggy's arrival.

Joe sat down and reached into his pocket. He produced two parcels of food, wrapped in greaseproof paper, and handed one to Twiggy.

'It was nice of Mr Poppleweed to make us a snack,' said Twiggy, unwrapping two enormous sandwiches and a thick slice of fruit cake. She lifted up a slice of bread with her finger. 'Yum ... roast chicken and piccalilli.'

'It's lemon curd, actually,' said Joe, speaking with his mouth full, 'but it's rather delicious all the same.' A screeching cry caused Joe to raise his head, and he saw a pair of seagulls wheeling and swooping above the fisherman as he tried to unhook a squirming fish from his line.

'Is that a boat?' asked Twiggy, pointing to a dark smudge on the horizon.

Joe squinted. 'Yeah, quite a big one. Probably a tanker.'

'I've never been on a boat,' said Twiggy. She licked

her fingers before taking a second bite of her sandwich.

'I went on a cross-channel ferry, once,' said Joe, 'with the rest of my class. It was a school trip to Calais. The weather was foul. Never seen such gigantic waves. My friend, Drew, spent the whole journey with his head over a toilet bowl.'

'I wish *I* could go to school,' said Twiggy yearningly. 'It must be a *wonderful* place.'

'I'd hardly call it that,' said Joe. 'We get mountains of homework and some of the teachers are a nightmare. Take Mr Tripp, for instance. I told him that Hamish had eaten my essay on "The Nomadic Tribes of Northern Africa" and my stupid teacher refused to believe me … even when I showed him the soggy remnants, complete with a dog's teeth-marks. Mr Tripp gave me detention for a whole week. How unfair is that?'

'Pity you didn't have any Re-growing Potion,' said Twiggy, brushing crumbs from her lap.

'What do you mean?'

'Well,' said Twiggy, 'a few drops of the stuff and your essay would have reproduced itself.'

'Yeah,' said Joe, finishing off his fruit cake and wiping his hands on his jacket. 'Yeah …' he said thoughtfully. Then he scrunched up the greaseproof paper and jumped to his feet.

'Quick,' said Joe. 'We've got to leave.' He picked up the broomstick and thrust it at Twiggy.

'Huh? But, Joe, I haven't finished –'

'We've got to get back. It's really important. I've figured it out!'

'You're not making any sense,' said Twiggy, shaking her head. She prepared to take a bite of fruit cake.

'I know why Logan stole the original copy of *Mabel's Book*,' said Joe, seizing Twiggy's shoulder. 'She's already got the Re-growing Potion, remember –'

'Page five hundred and thirteen!' said Twiggy, the slice of cake falling from her fingers. 'Logan's going to re-grow it! Oh, Joe, we have to stop her.'

It was a wobbly take-off. Twiggy's panicky instructions seemed to confuse the broom and it shot forward, clipping the fisherman's sou'wester as it left the pier. In his astonishment, the fisherman dropped his fish and there was a soft plop as it landed back in the water. With his face entirely hidden by his yellow hat, the fisherman stood up and shook his fist.

'Ruddy seagulls!' he shouted.

'Landing on a pier in blustery weather was a cinch compared to this,' said Twiggy as she tried to manoeuvre the broom through layer upon layer of intertwined branches. 'It would have been quicker to dismount on Swingletree Lane and walk the rest of the way.'

'No it wouldn't,' said Joe firmly. 'I'd rather arrive with scratches and bruises and twigs caught up in my hair than reach Logan's cottage a few minutes too late.'

'Be practical, Joe,' said Twiggy, knocking her elbow against a branch. A sprinkling of snow fell to the ground. 'Logan must have returned from Piddock's Cove hours ago.'

'Assuming she rode on a broomstick,' said Joe.

Twiggy snorted. 'Water-skied to Dorset, did she?'

'There's public transport,' persisted Joe, 'and how do we know she doesn't own a car? That witch from Pipistrelle Coven had a Mini. Logan Dritch doesn't strike me as the type to suffer a long, uncomfortable, freezing cold journey.'

Twiggy's back stiffened and Joe realised that he might have offended her. 'Of course, *I* wouldn't have missed today's trip for the *world*,' he said quickly.

'Glad to hear it,' said Twiggy. There was a ripping noise as her hooded cloak became snagged on a branch. 'Oh, I'm fed up with this,' she said. 'We're making such slow progress. I'm going to crash through and hope for the best. Hold on, Joe,' she said, tilting the broomstick at a sharp angle. 'This might hurt a bit.'

Twiggy crouched low over the broom and Joe buried his face in her cloak as they plunged towards the ground. Joe's ears filled with a cacophony of snapping twigs. With his eyes closed, they sounded like hundreds of crackers being pulled. Joe winced and gritted his teeth when his leg thudded into a branch. He heard Twiggy squeal. Then the broom hopped sideways and Joe slipped off. He landed on all fours in a deep drift of snow.

'Joe! Are you OK?' Twiggy knelt beside him, holding the broomstick. Its birch twigs were looking quite dishevelled and it kept making little twitching movements. Twiggy stroked its handle soothingly.

'Miraculously, I'm fine,' said Joe, spluttering slightly. He wiped snow from his face and struggled to his feet. 'What about you?'

'I think I'll have a few impressive bruises, but there's nothing broken,' said Twiggy. 'I'm more worried about the broomstick. It seems to be a bit traumatised. If it doesn't recover fairly quickly, we might have to walk home.'

'Poor thing,' said Joe, giving the broomstick a sympathetic pat. He glanced around him. The trees had become silhouettes and the air was grainy. Dusk was settling. Joe rubbed his eyes. 'Where's the lantern? Do you see it?'

'Over there,' said Twiggy, pointing to a golden disc of light. They tramped through the snow towards it.

They reached Two Hoots within five minutes. Joe slithered over the wall. 'The coast's clear,' he hissed, and a moment later he caught the broomstick as Twiggy tossed it into the garden. Her hands appeared at the top of the wall. Then, with a grunt, she hauled herself over the crumbling brickwork and landed beside him.

Nothing stirred in the garden. Joe put his finger to his lips and trod cautiously through the snow until he reached a window with a chink of light gleaming from between its drawn curtains. Twiggy and Joe crouched underneath the windowsill and listened. Joe's heartbeat thumped in his ears.

'This is stupid,' whispered Twiggy, hugging the trembling broomstick. 'I haven't got my wand with me ... and, with the broom in this state, our chances of a quick getaway are *nil*.'

'We'll have to be extremely careful, then, won't we?' Joe stood up slowly and pressed his cheek against the window. His warm breath steamed up the cold glass and he had to keep rubbing its clouded surface with his sleeve so that he could see clearly. Joe gasped. Through a tiny gap in the curtains, he could see a small kitchen and stomping angrily around it was Logan Dritch.

'It's her,' said Joe softly, 'and she's in a furious rage.' He watched as Logan kicked the door of an old-fashioned cooking stove and threw three saucepans across the room.

'Let's have a look,' said Twiggy, standing on tiptoe and peering through the same gap in the curtains. 'Wow, so that's old Slyboots ... I mean Logan Dritch, is it? She's a bit of a glamour puss. I like her outfit. That shade of green really suits her. The feather boa's a bit over the top, though, and I bet she dyes her hair.'

'Where's the book?' said Joe, his eyes searching the kitchen. Logan walked over to the kitchen table and swept a crystal glass and a bottle of champagne on to the floor. Frothing liquid gushed from the broken bottle, flooding over the kitchen tiles. Two objects remained on the table. One was a conical flask. Logan seized the flask and raised her hand as if she were going to smash it, but something made her change her mind and she replaced it carefully on the table.

'The Re-growing Potion,' whispered Twiggy in Joe's ear.

The second item was a tiny book bound in tawny leather. Logan picked it up and opened it at a page stained with lime-green droplets. Her face contorted into an expression of disgust and she parted her crimson lips and screamed.

'*Mabel's Book!*' said Joe.

'I don't believe it,' said Twiggy, rubbing the glass with a corner of her cloak and jamming one eye to the window. 'Logan tried to re-grow the missing page *but it didn't work!*'

'I don't understand,' said Joe. 'It looks like the page has grown back, hasn't it?'

'Yes,' said Twiggy, an amused smile on her face. 'But

there's nothing written on it! The paper has grown back *but Mabel's words haven't!*'

Twiggy and Joe hugged each other and tried to stifle their laughter. 'No wonder she's in such a bad mood,' said Joe. 'Imagine going to all that effort for nothing!' He peered through the window again. 'Hang on a minute, where's she gone –'

Twiggy shrieked and Joe staggered backwards as the curtains were swept aside to reveal Logan Dritch filling the window frame. She roared with fury and Joe's hair stood on end. 'R-run for it,' he stuttered.

Joe sprinted across the garden. He grazed his fingers on the rough bricks as he scrambled desperately up the wall. Pausing at the top, he looked over his shoulder and saw a sight that horrified him.

The garden was in darkness. Light blazed from the kitchen window and threw a bright rectangle into the garden where Twiggy was lying spread-eagled in the snow. The broomstick was pinned underneath her body. Joe guessed that she had tripped over it in her haste to get away. A shadow fell across Twiggy as Logan slid her legs over the windowsill. Joe saw that the witch was holding a wand in her hand.

Joe shouted a warning to Twiggy but, to his dismay, she did not make any attempt to run. She remained face down in the snow and Joe heard her murmuring something as if she were talking to herself.

The pointed toes of Logan's black ankle boots made contact with the snowy ground. Joe shook his fringe from his eyes and did the only thing that he could think of.

He threw a snowball.

It landed, with expert precision, smack in the middle of Logan's face. Before the witch had time to react, Joe lobbed another. It caught her on the side of the head. Joe began to mould a third snowball between his hands when he noticed that Twiggy seemed to be rising from the ground. She had not been talking to herself, after all; she had been speaking to the broom-stick which had been lying beneath her. Twiggy sat up and grasped the handle with both hands. She instructed the broom to fly towards Joe and to wait on top of the wall so that he could climb on. Releasing his final snow-ball (which hit Logan between the eyes) Joe settled himself on the back of the broom and they sped away into the darkness.

The broomstick made a valiant effort and managed to reach the edge of the wood before sinking to the ground. Then Joe carried the broom over his shoulder and ran as fast as he could along Swingletree Lane. After ten min-utes, he stopped and waited for Twiggy to catch up.

'Come on,' said Joe as she dropped to her knees beside him. He grabbed her hand and pulled Twiggy to her feet. Joe cast anxious glances over his shoulder. 'Do you think we're being followed?'

Twiggy shook her head. 'Don't worry,' she said breathlessly. 'There's nobody behind us.'

Chapter Sixteen

Brainwaves and Bombshells

'You're coming to the pantomime and that's final,' said Joe's mum, opening her compact and applying her lipstick. 'Now, hurry up and get ready. Don't pout at me like that, Joe. It was very kind of Gordon to arrange such a lovely treat.'

Joe made no attempt to move from the sofa in the living room. He pretended to yawn. 'But I'm really tired. I'll only fall asleep in the theatre.'

'You will *not!*' snapped Merle, shaking his elbow. 'It's your own fault if you've worn yourself out. When I said you could go for a walk I didn't expect you to be gone for the whole afternoon.'

Gordon walked into the living room, dressed in a twill jacket and a woolly hat. 'Is there a problem?' he said, resting his hand on his wife's shoulder.

'No,' said Merle, patting his hand. She turned to Joe. 'Please, darling. You'll enjoy yourself. It'll take your mind off –'

Gordon cleared his throat.

'Why don't you wear that sweatshirt you're so fond of,' said Merle sweetly.

'Oh, all *right*,' said Joe. 'I'll come.' He dragged his feet across the living room carpet and stamped upstairs. He emptied his chest of drawers but could not find his favourite sweatshirt. Instead, Joe tugged a green jumper over his head and combed his hair with a total lack of enthusiasm.

'I'm too old for pantomimes,' grumbled Joe as he scuffed his feet in the snow on the way to the Marlowe Theatre. Esme clung to his hand, her eyes shining with excitement. She yanked Joe's arm as she skipped along.

'Last year it was *The Wizard of Oz*,' said Esme in a thrilled voice. 'The wicked witch was *really* scary.'

'Mmm,' agreed Joe. 'Witches can be frightening, can't they?' He thought about his encounter with Logan a few hours previously. Clearly she had suffered a minor setback when her plan to re-grow the page had failed, but Joe suspected that Logan's resolve would not be weakened.

'She won't stop until she's found that page,' murmured Joe and, for the rest of the short walk to the theatre, he remained deep in thought, trying to deduce the whereabouts of the missing page.

'I'm sure this is the seventh glass of milk you've had today,' said Merle, reaching in the fridge for a pint of milk while Esme held up a glass with a pleading look on her face.

'I'm just thirsty, Mum,' said Esme as a stream of milk flowed into her glass. She began to sip it slowly.

'It's late, Esme. As soon as you've finished, go and change into your pyjamas.'

Joe sat on a kitchen stool and flicked through the theatre programme. He had surprised himself by thoroughly enjoying the pantomime. He had even shouted 'Look behind you' and 'Oh no he hasn't' with the rest of the audience, albeit not as heartily as his stepfather.

'Cup of tea, Joe?' said Gordon, filling the kettle. Joe nodded. 'Have a good time, did you, then?'

'Yeah,' said Joe, 'actually I did.'

'Splendid,' said his stepfather. '*Robinson Crusoe* is a bit of a classic, isn't it? Very realistic palm trees, too.'

'Dad,' said Esme. 'Please could I have my theatre ticket?'

'Want to keep it as a souvenir, do you?' said Gordon, plucking a ticket from his wallet. He offered it to Esme but, before she could take it, the ticket slipped from his fingers and on to the floor. 'Oops,' said Gordon. 'Dropped it. Clumsy me.' As Gordon bent down to pick it up, Joe felt a shiver run down his spine.

'Of *course!*' he said out loud, and he stood up so quickly that his stool fell over. 'The ticket! *The ticket!*'

'What about your cup of tea?' called Gordon as Joe left the kitchen and raced up the stairs to his bedroom.

Joe threw open his wardrobe doors and checked the pockets of his school blazer. Apart from a chewed pen lid and a piece of string, there was nothing in there. He searched the pockets of his grey trousers, which had been washed and neatly ironed by Gordon, but they were empty.

Where is it? thought Joe desperately.

He tipped up a wastepaper basket and sorted through its contents but he did not find what he was looking for.

Joe sank on to his bed and held his head in his hands. He cursed himself for being so stupid. Harriet Perkins had given him the missing page from *Mabel's Book*, only he had not realised it. She must have seen Logan Dritch coming towards her down the aisle of the train and had pretended that Joe had dropped his train ticket. The piece of paper he had scooped up from the dusty floor of the railway compartment had not been a train ticket at all. It had been the five hundred and thirteenth page of the greatest work in the history of witches' literature. Joe had been urged to get off at Stubble End so that he could hand the page to Dora Benton, but he had given her his train ticket instead. Joe knew that he must have brought the page home with him – but where was it?

Once he had turned his own room upside-down, he dashed across the landing into the bedroom belonging to his mum and stepdad. He was about to slide open a drawer in his mum's dressing table when he saw a pile of photographs lying in front of her mirror. Every single one of them was a picture of his father.

'Joe! What are you doing in here?' said his mum, standing in the doorway.

'I was looking ...' Joe held up a photograph of his dad's smiling face. 'Why were you –'

Merle gasped and raised her hands to her mouth. Gordon appeared beside her and put an arm around her shoulders. 'I think it's time we told him,' he said quietly.

'What?' said Joe, staring at their solemn faces.

'We needed to find some photographs of your dad ... to give to the police,' said Gordon. 'There have been terrible blizzards in Scotland, Joe. Your dad took a taxi-cab from the hospital last night, but it never arrived at Tillygrundle. The taxi and its driver were found early this morning, but your dad had gone to fetch help. I'm afraid he's still missing.'

Chapter Seventeen

Joe's Proposal

Out of the corner of his eye, Joe saw a hunched black figure scuffing through the snowy precincts of Canterbury Cathedral. The person drew closer until a pair of boots with creased toes and frayed laces stopped beside his own trainers.

'Morning,' said Twiggy.

Joe did not bother to reply. He leaned his chin on his hands and stared sullenly at the ground.

'Your mum told me you'd be here.' Twiggy's red mitten reached out to pat Joe's shoulder but he shrank away from her. 'She explained ... about your dad, Joe. I'm really, really sorry.'

'Yeah,' whispered Joe, smiling weakly at Twiggy. She sat down next to him on the wooden bench. Joe did not mean to be so gruff with her but he was finding it very difficult to speak to anyone at the moment. He was too concerned with the mixture of feelings which were churning inside him.

Joe felt distressed and anxious about his dad but he was also angry with his mum and Gordon for being so secretive about his dad's disappearance. They had received a visit from the local police the previous morning while Joe had been asleep. Deciding to keep quiet and spare Joe any worry, his mum and Gordon had treated him with exaggerated tenderness, hoping against hope that his dad would be found.

I thought something was wrong, thought Joe, remembering how his mum had chosen to stay at home and cook his favourite soup rather than help at a Christmas raffle.

Joe's hand gripped the arm of the wooden bench as a great wave of guilt engulfed him. He had been so wrapped up in the affairs of Dead-nettle Coven and the search for the missing page of *Mabel's Book* that he had barely given his father a second thought.

It had been three days since Joe had spoken to his dad. Joe remembered how sulky he had been on the way to school. He had mumbled goodbye to his father and slammed the door of the black taxicab. His dad had wound down the window and waved, his tie rippling as the taxi pulled away. By the time Joe's class had filed into assembly, his dad must have travelled across London to King's Cross station and boarded the train that would take him to Scotland.

Scotland.

It was so unbearably far away. Joe had measured the distance in an atlas. It was five hundred miles to Tillygrundle and, although Joe had begged his mum and stepdad to take him there, they had refused. They had said the journey would be too long and, even if they reached the Grampian Mountains, which was unlikely because of the hazardous weather, there was nothing that they could do to help with the search. Joe felt as if he could explode with frustration. He could not bear to be in Canterbury surrounded by people who were excitedly preparing for Christmas, while his dad was lost on a Scottish hillside, battling for his life in a blizzard.

'Want to hold Tadpole?' said Twiggy gently. When Joe did not respond, she placed the kitten in his lap and he felt the tension inside him slowly ebb away as he stroked Tadpole's soft fur. 'I can't afford to let her out of my sight, now,' said Twiggy.

'Why?' Joe scratched the kitten under her chin and she began to purr.

'Winifred's on the warpath. She got a really nasty leaf from the Pipistrelles, saying how insufferably awful I was. That broomstick I took belonged to Dora Benton and she's not too happy about it, I can tell you. Winifred's over at Stubble End right now, trying to smooth things over, and I'm in total disgrace. I'm afraid Winifred will carry out her threat and take Tadpole away from me.'

'Oh, no,' said Joe, his thoughts drifting from his missing father for a moment. 'That would be too cruel. Haven't you explained to Winifred about Logan Dritch?'

'Well, I tried,' said Twiggy gloomily, 'but as soon as I mentioned the Monsters of Much Marcle, she put her hand over my mouth and told me to shut up. Apparently, it's taken *years* for Rose to forget about her misspent youth and put the past behind her. Winifred was so cross; she wouldn't listen to another word I said. She kept going on about giving people a second chance and keeping my nose out of other people's business. Things are looking pretty bleak, aren't they?' said Twiggy, heaving a sigh.

'They certainly are,' said Joe, heaving an even louder one.

'We've *got* to find the missing page of *Mabel's Book* before Logan Dritch does,' said Twiggy, 'but I have to admit I'm completely stumped.'

'Mmm,' said Joe. Then he sat up straight and his eyes widened. 'Twiggy,' he said eagerly, 'wasn't there a potion in *Mabel's Book* for curing Dreaded Lurgies? Do you think it would work on frostbite or ... or hypothermia?'

'Shouldn't think so,' said Twiggy. 'They're caused by exposure to really low temperatures, aren't they?' She screwed up her face. 'A Thawing Potion might do the job. Patsy said she was given that potion when she visited her pen-pal in the Arctic Circle. Poor old Patsy froze on her broomstick. Couldn't move a muscle.'

'Would you make it for me?' said Joe. 'And would you fly me to Scotland?'

'To Scotland? No way!' said Twiggy in a horrified voice.

'OK, then … do you think I could borrow your broomstick?'

'What?' said Twiggy. 'Are you out of your mind? You wouldn't be able to ride it by yourself, unless you smeared it with Flying Ointment. As for making the Thawing Potion … I'd have to find all the ingredients. Anyway, Winifred's bound to spot me and ask me what on earth I'm up to. No, I couldn't possibly. I'd be *expelled* if I was caught.'

Joe frowned and stared at her. 'Would you do it if I showed you where the missing page was?'

'*Mabel's* page? You know where it is? Well, tell me, Joe! Quick!'

Joe shook his head firmly. 'Not unless you make the Thawing Potion and bring me your broomstick. Then I can fly to Scotland and save my dad.'

'But that's *crazy*!' Twiggy was silent for a few minutes. 'All right,' she said at last. 'I think I've got some Flying Ointment in my Broomstick Rider's Starter Pack that Winifred gave me – but it will take me … I don't know … about six hours to make that potion.'

'Fine,' said Joe coolly, glancing at his watch. 'I'll meet you, tonight, at half past five behind my garden shed.'

Twiggy scooped up her kitten and shot a worried look at Joe. Then she scuttled through the Cathedral precincts. Joe watched her until she was out of sight.

'Right,' he said. 'I've got six hours to find that page.'

By half past four, Joe was beginning to panic. He had rooted through his wastepaper basket seven times, crawled on his hands and knees into every corner of his room, shone a torch into the tiniest crevices of his wardrobe, and even checked on top of his lampshade. The page was definitely not in his room. Neither was it in any other room in the house.

On the pretence that he needed to keep busy and be distracted from thinking about his father, Joe had insisted on doing some housework. With a duster in his hand and a vacuum cleaner by his side, he slid his hands underneath the seat cushions of the sofa, inspected all the kitchen cupboards, upturned every rubbish bin and scrutinised every square inch of carpet. When he had finished he even sifted through the vacuum-cleaner bag, coating his hands with a film of dust but, apart from finding thirty-two pence, his search proved to be fruitless.

Joe squashed some clothes, a sandwich box and some pages torn from the atlas into a lightweight rucksack and fastened it securely. He slipped a torch and compass into the pocket of his jacket. Then he sat on his bed and chewed his nails, desperately trying to urge himself to remember what he had done with the page. He looked at his watch. It was twenty minutes to five.

Squeezing his eyes shut, Joe tried to replay the crucial moment in his mind, when Harriet Perkins had patted his arm and told him that he had dropped his ticket. The events played in slow motion inside his head. He saw himself bend down, his fingers closing around the piece of paper. Then he straightened up, his hand sliding into the pocket of his trousers.

'Of course,' said Joe, his eyes flicking open. 'When I handed my train ticket to Dora Benton I found it in my *blazer* pocket. *The page must have been in my trousers.*'

Joe was tempted to rifle through the pockets of his grey trousers for the umpteenth time when a horrible thought struck him. 'Oh, no!' breathed Joe. 'They've been in the washing machine – but the page is indestructible ... so ...'

Without warning, a clear picture of the page flared inside Joe's head. For a few seconds, he saw it in sharp detail. The tiny page was pale yellow with a ragged edge along one side where it had been torn from *Mabel's Book*.

'I've seen it,' said Joe, when the image had vanished

from his mind as quickly as it had appeared. 'Not on the train ... but somewhere *here* in this house.' He tried to conjure up the picture of the page again, but he could not manage it. All that remained with him was a firm belief that the page was in someone else's possession.

Joe remembered how tired he had been when he arrived at number two, Cloister Walk three nights before. After he had tried to convince the policemen that he had rowed home from Stubble End, he had eaten a small supper and dragged himself upstairs to the guest bedroom.

Joe had not bothered to unpack his suitcase. Neither had he hung up his school uniform in the wardrobe. He had thrown his clothes over the back of a chair before pulling on his pyjamas and collapsing into bed. It was possible that the page had fallen out of his trouser pocket and on to the carpet – but it had not been there the next morning. Or had it?

'Esme!' said Joe, slapping both hands against his mattress. 'She was in my room when I woke up. She brought me a mug of milk!' He took less than ten seconds to spring off his bed, yank open his door, sprint across the landing and fling open the door of Esme's bedroom.

'Ez, I need to ask you something,' said Joe urgently.

'Mmm?' said Esme. She was sitting on her bed, leaning against a pillow. Her face was completely hidden behind her library book. Esme lifted her head and peered over the top of *Toffee-nosed Tara*. 'Oh, hello, Joe,' she said, picking up a plate and raising it towards him. 'Would you like some of my gingerbread reindeer? I've eaten the hooves and the antlers but you can have the rest if you like.'

'No thanks, Ez,' said Joe, perching on the end of her bed. 'I've got a question for you. It's very important.'

'Oh, good. I like questions,' said Esme, sitting cross-legged and resting the library book on her zebra slippers. She looked at Joe expectantly.

'I've lost a piece of paper,' said Joe in an unsteady voice. 'It's very small and has a yellowish tinge ...'

'Like parchment?' said Esme brightly.

'Yes, Ez. Exactly,' said Joe, a little astounded by her intelligence. 'There's nothing written on it. It looks like a worthless scrap of paper but it's *not*. I really need to find it, Esme. Have you seen it?'

'Um.' Esme tilted her head and pressed a finger to her lips. 'I think so,' she said slowly, her cheeks flushing. 'I might have picked it up ... but I didn't know it was precious, Joe. Honestly.'

'Doesn't matter,' said Joe, clenching his hands together. 'Where is it?'

Esme bit her lip and looked at the library book which was balanced on her slippers. A theatre ticket poked out from between the pages.

'That's it!' said Joe, instantly remembering where he

had seen the page from *Mabel's Book*. His sister had been using it as a bookmark. When he came down to breakfast on that first morning, he had seen Esme slip a piece of yellow paper into her book to mark her place.

Joe smiled warmly at his sister. 'Where's the bit of paper now, Ez?'

'I might have left it in *Pigeons in Peril*,' said Esme, clutching her slippers.

'Uh-huh,' said Joe, looking eagerly around his sister's bedroom. 'Is that in your bookcase?'

'No,' she said in a timid whisper. 'I took it back to the library.'

Chapter Eighteen

Searching by Torchlight

Joe crept across the lawn. The snow was topped with a thin icy crust and, despite treading carefully, he made a crunching noise with every step. Joe glanced back at the house but all the windows were closed, trapping the warm air inside. No one would be able to hear him. Avoiding the patch of light which streamed over the snow when Gordon turned on a lamp in the living room, Joe kept to the edge of the lawn, stumbling every now and then into the flowerbed. Although the air was bitterly cold, he could feel droplets of sweat prickling against his hairline. Joe checked the time. It was nearly half past five.

Gordon had been in the process of sprinkling parmesan cheese on a broccoli soufflé when Joe made his announcement. Explaining that he felt like spending the evening on his own, Joe had insisted on preparing a hasty meal of beans on toast, putting it on a tray and taking it to his room. Joe had faked several yawns before leaving the kitchen. He pretended that the housework had exhausted him and that he would probably read for a while before going to bed early. On hearing Joe's plan, his mum had seemed slightly relieved and Gordon had reacted sympathetically, assuring Joe that baked beans were bound to be much tastier than his broccoli soufflé.

In the privacy of his room, Joe had dressed in two pairs of tracksuit bottoms and two thick jumpers. Then he had crammed a hat with furry earflaps into the pocket of his rucksack. He had been in the middle of stuffing pillows underneath the duvet when he heard footsteps on the stairs. Joe had managed to jump into bed a few seconds before Gordon knocked softly on the door and brought in a mug of hot chocolate. When Gordon had said goodnight to him, Joe had felt uncomfortable – and not just because he was wearing so many clothes. He hated lying to his mum and stepdad, but it could not be helped. If they were not prepared to take him to Scotland, then he would have to sneak off by himself.

Joe reached the corner of the garden, slipped into the narrow gap between the shed and the privet hedge and waited. The seconds ticked by. Twiggy was late.

Joe crouched down and the jagged edge of a broken flowerpot dug into his ankle. He was about to kick it aside when he heard a noise – a muffled thump, and then another. Joe put his ear against the shed and caught the brief murmur of a voice. There was somebody inside! It could not be Gordon because he was in the living room doing a jigsaw and his mum was upstairs having a bath. Joe had heard her singing to herself when he had tiptoed down the stairs.

It must be Twiggy, thought Joe. Perhaps she thought I said we'd meet *inside* the shed ... but how did she get the key ... and who is she talking to? Joe moved stealthily round the corner of the shed and put one eye to a knot-hole in the door.

She had her back to him but Joe knew at once that it was Esme. Her yellow wellington boots were an instant give-away. She was kneeling down beside a cardboard box, an empty glass in her hand. Esme muttered something and stood up to rest the glass on a workbench, beside a large red torch. Joe could not prevent himself from gasping as the contents of the cardboard box were revealed to him. He saw a black cat sitting on a blanket, washing itself with its paw. A china saucer rested on the floorboards next to the box and there were little white speckles surrounding it. Joe took another look at the cat, barely able to believe his own eyes. But there was no doubting the cat's identity.

It was Squib.

Joe lost his footing for a moment and leaned against the door, dislodging the latch. 'Who's there?' said Esme's worried voice. Joe had half a mind not to answer but he did not want to frighten his sister.

'Don't worry. It's only me,' said Joe, opening the door

and stepping inside the shed. 'Looks like you've been keeping a secret.'

'His name's Charlie,' said Esme. She reached down and picked up the cat, holding him around his chest so that his back legs dangled in an ungainly manner. Squib did not seem to mind. He gazed lovingly at Esme and began to purr.

'I found him yesterday morning,' said Esme, 'while I was making a snowman. He was hiding in the flowerbed, watching me. Poor Charlie hasn't got a collar and I'm sure he doesn't belong to anyone. I really love him, Joe, but I don't think Dad would feel the same way. He says cats are hairy and smelly. That's why I've been keeping Charlie in here.'

'And that's why you've been guzzling so much milk ... or rather Charlie has.' Joe smiled and then his face fell. 'Hey!' he said, taking a closer look at Squib's blanket. 'That's my favourite sweatshirt, isn't it?' He picked it up and tried to shake the black hairs from it.

'Charlie was cold,' said Esme.

'Well, couldn't you have found something else?'

'What's going on?' said a voice from the doorway. Twiggy entered the shed and put a hand to her mouth. 'Isn't that Squib?'

'No, it's Charlie,' said Esme, squeezing the cat in her arms.

'I *knew* he liked you,' Twiggy said to Joe. 'Winifred

must have mentioned where you lived. She was going to come after you on the night you escaped and then the Golden Cauldron Certificate came from Head Office and she changed her mind. I guess Squib decided to move to your address. Can't blame him, really. He's probably had enough of being a witch's cat.'

'Huh?' said Esme.

'She's only joking,' said Joe hurriedly. 'Have you got the stuff, Twiggy? Right, then … it's time we left.'

'Where are we going?'

'To the library,' said Joe, cupping his hand around his mouth, but he did not say it quietly enough.

'It won't be open,' said Esme confidently. 'The library closes at half past five and it will be closed tomorrow because it's Christmas Eve. It's not open on Christmas Day or Boxing Day either.'

'The page is in the library?' said Twiggy in a bewildered voice.

'Yes,' said Joe, 'in a copy of *Pigeons in Peril*, believe it or not. Next week will be too late,' he said, thinking of his father. Joe shook his head. 'I *can't* wait that long. We'll have to go tonight … find an unlocked window or something.'

Esme was appalled. 'Joe, that's against the law. And anyway, I thought you told Mum and Dad that you were going to bed early.'

Joe put his hand on his sister's shoulder. 'Look, Esme.

I promise not to tell anyone about Charlie, if you keep my trip to the library a secret. OK?'

Esme nodded. 'OK,' she said, 'but only if Charlie can have his blanket.'

'It's a deal,' said Joe, dropping his sweatshirt into the cardboard box.

Closing the door gently behind him, Joe leaned into the gap behind the shed and retrieved his rucksack. 'Where's the potion, then?' he said to Twiggy.

'In my bag. It was ever so tricky to make,' she said. 'Took me a whole hour to find the right kind of candle-wax, and the camel's eyelash wasn't easy to come by, either.'

Twiggy slid on to her broomstick. 'I've brought my own, today,' she said, patting the handle of her second-hand broom. 'Had to give the other one back to Dora Renton. Apparently, she nearly blew a gasket when she saw the condition it was in.'

'Will it recover?' said Joe, remembering how the gutsy little broom had saved their necks.

'Oh, yes,' said Twiggy as Joe climbed on behind her. 'It'll be back to its normal self after a few visits to the broom therapist.'

'Good,' said Joe, not quite certain if Twiggy was joking.

As they hovered above the privet hedge, Joe thought he heard a pattering sound coming from the woodpile in the farthest corner of the garden. He glanced at it just in time to see two naked tails slithering over the heap of logs before vanishing into the shadows.

Beneath them, the sky was illuminated with an amber glow. Streetlamps shone and shafts of light stretched over pavements from shop doorways. In a cobbled square the coloured lights on a giant Christmas tree winked and sparkled.

Twiggy kept stroking the broomstick encouragingly, urging it to fly higher. They needed to keep in the dark portion of the sky where they could fly without the fear of being seen. The broomstick was struggling. The extra weight of Joe's rucksack and Twiggy's shoulder bag was causing it to pitch and jerk.

'Look for a place to land!' shouted Twiggy in an alarmed voice. 'Preferably somewhere dark and deserted!'

'How about down there?' replied Joe, pointing to an unlit area beside a steepled building.

'Perfect,' said Twiggy. 'Dive, broom!'

The broomstick did not need to be told twice. It descended at an incredibly steep angle so that Joe had to cling on with all his might to remain seated. Cold air blasted in his face, preventing him from being able to take a breath. Joe saw the ground rush towards him at a terrifying speed. Twiggy yanked the broom handle and screamed. At the last moment, the broomstick pulled up and Joe tumbled on to the ground, banging his knee on an upright stone slab.

'Phew,' said Twiggy, emerging rather gingerly from a holly bush. 'I really must finish reading my *Flying Manual*. I'm sure there's a chapter on "Crashing with Panache".'

Too dazed to make any comment, Joe leaned on the slab and rubbed his injured knee. He glanced around the shadowy place. It was eerily quiet and shrouded in darkness. Blurred grey shapes seemed to float in the gloom. Joe snatched his hand away from the stone slab when he realised where they had landed.

'It's a graveyard,' he whispered. 'Let's get out of here.'

It was Joe's idea to snap off a few sprigs of holly and push them in amongst the broomstick's birch twigs before they left the graveyard. Joe told Twiggy that she would look like a girl carrying a slightly peculiar Christmas decoration rather than a witch holding a broomstick. As a result, they were able to walk through the streets of bustling shoppers with nobody giving them a second glance.

In less than ten minutes, they had found their way to the High Street and Joe caught sight of the limestone façade of the library. He hurried towards it, eager to retrieve the page and embark on his journey to Scotland. Twiggy trotted by his side, clutching her broomstick in one hand and holding Tadpole against her chest with the other. The kitten had been travelling inside Twiggy's shoulder bag, wrapped in her red cardigan, but had been joggled awake when Twiggy started to run. Tadpole had mewed until Twiggy lifted her out of the bag and cuddled her.

Joe bounded up the worn stone steps leading to the main entrance of the library. There was a notice on the door confirming the Christmas opening times. 'Esme was right,' he said, but he could not resist turning the door handle to check if it was definitely locked. 'We'll have to find another way in,' said Joe, shrugging his shoulders. He looked up at the blank windows set into the smooth limestone wall, but they all appeared to be fastened shut.

'Let's go and see if there's a back entrance,' said Twiggy, nodding her head towards a dark alleyway which ran along the side of the building.

In a shadowy courtyard behind a couple of dustbins, they found the back door of the library. Joe rattled the doorknob but the door failed to open. 'Now what do we do?' he said gloomily.

Twiggy grinned and asked him to hold Tadpole for a moment. Then she lifted a copy of *Mabel's Book* out of her bag. 'Time for a bit of magic,' she said, delving in her bag for her wand. Joe held his torch over the book as Twiggy searched for a suitable spell. 'Right. Here we are ... this should do it ... The Unlatching Spell. It impinges on hinges and jolts bolts, apparently. Hold the torch steady, Joe.' Twiggy stretched out her arm and pointed her wand at the doorknob.

'Yield to me, sealed door.
Tremble at your very core.
Bolts and latches, locks and catches,
hinder me no more.'

As soon as she had uttered the words, Joe heard a scraping sound like bolts being drawn back and the doorknob began to turn of its own accord. There was a sharp click and the door swung open.

Joe went first, the torch beam sweeping in front of him. They were in a small room, crowded with boxes of books. On a rickety table was a tray containing dust jackets and a mug of congealed brown sludge which might have been coffee several days earlier. Somebody had written 'I'm bored' thirteen times on a piece of paper and there was also a scribbled caricature of a peevish-looking woman with her hair scraped back into a tight bun. Joe suspected that it was supposed to be Lydia the librarian, whose memory they had tampered with.

He found a door leading into a corridor which was

decorated with peeling paisley wallpaper, and followed it until he came to a second door. It creaked as he opened it and his torch beam slid over dozens of bookshelves. They had reached the main part of the library.

The large, high-ceilinged room with its hidden corners and curtains of shadow was strangely unnerving. Joe had never imagined that an empty library could be so spooky. He longed to flick the light switch and banish the darkness but he knew it would give away their illegal presence in the building, so he held out his torch and stepped cautiously over the wooden floor, in the direction of the children's section. Twiggy followed close behind him. She spoke soothing words to Tadpole in a nervous voice. After every few steps, Joe swung his torch in a circle like a beam from a lighthouse. He could not shake off the feeling that someone was watching them.

'Here we are,' whispered Joe, shining his torch on a couple of bookshelves filled with children's fiction. 'We're looking for *Pigeons in Peril*, remember. Esme said that the author's name was Jennifer Johnson.'

They found *The Adventures of Hengist the Stag Beetle* and *The Mystery of the Disappearing Pencil Case*, both by Jennifer Johnson, but there was a worrying gap beside them on the shelf. 'It's been borrowed!' said Joe in disgust. 'Maybe we could find a record of who –'

Somebody sneezed.

It was a delicate muffled sound but in the stillness of

the library it was as noticeable as a thunderclap. Joe directed his torch at the farthest wall and its beam landed, for a moment, on a hooded figure who had a book wedged under their arm. The figure scurried past the front desk and headed for the main entrance.

'Logan Dritch!' said Joe. 'Stop her! She's got the page!'

They were just about to chase after her when two pairs of yellow eyes glided across the floor towards them. 'Dunkel and Fleck,' said Joe as he shone his torch on two large grey rats with long whiskery snouts. Their claws clattered over the parquet floor and their naked tails slithered behind them.

'Run!' shouted Joe as one of the rats launched itself at Twiggy and knocked her wand out of her grasp. 'Hey!' shouted Joe, throwing his torch at the rat. He missed his target by inches and the torch made an ominous crunching noise as it hit the ground. Its light flickered before going out.

'Come on!' yelled Joe, grabbing Twiggy's arm as she groped around for her wand. 'Time to *go*!'

They ran blindly across the room. Joe knocked his shoulder against a bookcase but he did not pause for a moment. He knew, by the scrabbling sounds at his heels, that the rats were right behind him.

Squinting ahead, through the darkness, Joe saw a strip of moonlight fall across the wooden panels of a door. He dashed towards it and his fingers slid feverishly over its surface until he found the doorhandle. The rats seemed to hesitate as Joe opened the door and then one of them sprang at Joe.

'Quick, Twiggy. You go first,' said Joe as the rat's teeth sank into his leg. He felt razor-sharp needles piercing his skin and shook his leg wildly. The rat was swept off its feet and lost its grip. There was a ripping sound as the rat fell to the ground with a piece of Joe's tracksuit bottoms lodged between its jaws. Joe slipped through the door and slammed it shut. He heard the frenzied scratching of claws on the other side of the door and a distant shout. The rats stopped and the night became silent once more.

Joe limped down the corridor after Twiggy. They stumbled through the room filled with cardboard boxes and burst into the courtyard. Twiggy snatched up her broomstick and they rode it along the dark alleyway until they reached the brightly-lit street, where a few over-burdened shoppers were struggling homeward. Joe looked up and down the street but there was no sign of the hooded figure or the rats. He felt a curious mixture of disappointment and relief.

'Joe, you're bleeding.'

Joe glanced at his leg. Shredded material fluttered in the breeze and he glimpsed a ribbon of red blood sliding down his calf. Twiggy produced a black handkerchief and knotted it tightly over the wound. 'Thanks,' said Joe.

'I can't believe it,' said Twiggy, her voice wavering. 'We were so close to getting the page. How did Logan Dritch find out where it was?'

'I think I know,' said Joe. 'Just before we left my garden, I saw a couple of rats on the woodpile –'

'Dunkel and Fleck,' said Twiggy bitterly.

'Yes,' agreed Joe. 'They must have been eavesdropping. I suppose Logan recognised me last night, when we were in her garden. It wouldn't have been too difficult for her to work out that the Vipers gave the page to me.'

'But how did she find you?'

Joe shrugged. 'The Pipistrelles tracked me down, didn't they? Well,' he said, patting Twiggy's shoulder, 'we gave it our best shot ... but it's over.'

'What do you mean?' she said, stepping away from him, a look of horror on her face. 'It's not over! We know where she lives.' Twiggy drew her wand from her bag. It had a long scratch down one side and rat's teeth marks around the tip. 'We've still got time to stop her!'

'No,' said Joe stolidly. 'I'm going to Scotland, remember.' He gripped the handle of Twiggy's broomstick and stared at her with a blank expression on his face.

'But you can't!' said Twiggy, trying to tug the broomstick out of his grasp. 'What about the spell on page five hundred and thirteen? If Logan Dritch has a chance to use it, she could cause terrible suffering!'

'You don't know that for certain.'

'Oh, really,' said Twiggy, glaring at Joe. 'Fleur Fortescue ripped out that page for a reason. Are you suggesting that we stand back and do nothing until we're absolutely sure? Joe, if Logan Dritch uses that spell, it might be too *late* to do anything about it.'

Joe yanked the broomstick out of Twiggy's hands. 'Where's the Thawing Potion,' he growled.

'But you said that you'd give me Mabel's page –'

'No,' said Joe. 'I said I'd *show* you where it was. I've kept my side of the bargain. It's not my fault if someone else swiped it first. Now, give me the potion and the Flying Ointment. I've got to set off for Scotland. I can't afford to waste another second. My dad could be *freezing to death* right now.'

Twiggy bit her lip and her eyes glistened as she held out a tiny bottle. Joe snatched it from her and examined it closely. 'It's empty!' he roared.

'No,' said Twiggy, tearfully. 'There's one drop in there. That's all I had time to make. It will be enough for one person.'

'Fine,' said Joe, opening a tube of Flying Ointment. He began to smear it over the broomstick.

'You won't need much,' said Twiggy in a timid voice.

'Bye, then,' said Joe as he trod into the dark alleyway

and sat astride the broom.

'Treat it kindly,' said Twiggy, cradling Tadpole in her arms, 'and hold on tight. Good ... good luck.'

'Yeah,' muttered Joe and he told the broomstick to hover. It began to rise off the ground and his feet dangled in midair. 'Fly due north,' commanded Joe, and the broomstick gained height until it had cleared the roof of the library. He glanced below and saw Twiggy's tiny upturned face looking at him. Then Joe patted the broom handle and shot into the night sky.

Chapter Nineteen

North to Tillygrundle

Joe could not keep his eyes open. The snowflakes surged into his face like a swarm of wasps, stinging his cheeks and the tips of his ears. He had lost his hat with the furry ear-flaps. It had been whipped from his head when the broomstick looped-the-loop to avoid some power cables about fifty miles back.

Joe had been clutching the broom handle so tightly that his arm muscles throbbed with pain. He did not dare to relax a single finger in case he lost control of the broomstick. There was a compass in his coat pocket but he had not referred to it once. The broom dropped lower and Joe pulled weakly on the handle, powerless to stop its descent.

'Keep north,' urged Joe, through cracked lips.

The broom spiralled downwards and the snowflakes began to swirl lightly around Joe. He opened his eyes just in time to see a dark shape looming beneath him. It was a tree. Swerving skilfully to avoid the branches, the broomstick sank lower and touched down beside a white post which seemed to glow in the dark.

'No,' breathed Joe, wiping his eyes with a sodden glove. 'I didn't tell you to land, you stupid thing.' The broomstick wriggled its birch twigs feebly and lay on the ground as if it were worn out.

Joe undid the straps on his rucksack and searched for the tube of Flying Ointment. As he began to apply it to the handle of the broom, a light shone in his eyes and moved steadily towards him. Joe picked up the broomstick and clung to the white post. With a roar, a car sped past him, shining its headlights on the white signpost. Joe read the words which were painted in black above his head.

'Blakeney Point. Two miles,' he murmured.

Joe waited for another car to pass by. The pages which he had torn from the atlas were in his hand. As he stood by the signpost, his ears caught the far-off rasping noise of waves lapping a shore and he smelt salt in the air. He guessed that he must be somewhere near the coast.

Another pair of car headlights appeared and threw a beam of light over the map of Central England in Joe's hand. His eyes scanned the page. 'Blakeney Point,' he said, finding the spit of land at the tip of Norfolk. It poked into the North Sea like a hooked finger. Joe's heart sank; he realised that he had completed a tiny fraction of his journey. The car braked and whined in reverse gear until it came to a stop beside him. The driver's window slid open and a woman stuck her head out.

'You lost or something?'

'N … no,' replied Joe.

The woman did not seem convinced.

'You look half frozen. Live locally, do you? Can I give you a lift anywhere?'

'No, thanks,' said Joe, looking longingly at the comfortable passenger seat next to her. 'I can walk from here.'

'OK,' said the woman, raising her eyebrows at Joe. 'Well, good luck to you.'

The car's rear lights grew dimmer and dimmer. Even after the car had vanished into the darkness, Joe continued to stare after it. The woman had wished him good luck. About an hour ago, another person had expressed the same sentiment.

'Twiggy,' said Joe and he felt the broomstick quiver under his palm.

He had tried so hard to keep her out of his thoughts. He had told himself that his father mattered far more than a bunch of silly witches and he believed it still. Joe's fingers tightened round the broom handle as he struggled with his conscience. The truth was – they both needed him.

Joe thought about his father buried in a snowdrift,

clinging to life. He had been missing for over forty-eight hours and a rescue party had failed to find him. Doubts began to creep into Joe's mind. If he had found the journey difficult already, would he be able to make it to Scotland? And how would he succeed in locating his father when trained experts had not managed it? Joe had left his broken torch lying on the floor of the library. Even if he reached the area around Tillygrundle, it would be impossible to begin searching before daybreak.

Joe pressed a button on his watch and its face lit up. It was nearly half past seven. He remembered how rudely he had spoken to Twiggy. She had wished him good luck and he had neglected, selfishly, to give her any words of encouragement in return. Joe had stranded her in the middle of Canterbury without her broomstick. Would she have returned to Dead-nettle Coven and tried to persuade Winifred that one of the Monsters of Much Marcle had not abandoned her evil ways – or would she have walked to Two Hoots and faced Logan Dritch on her own?

Twiggy was a novice witch. She lugged *Mabel's Book* with her wherever she went and only knew one spell off by heart. What chance would she have against a witch who had captured two experienced members of Viper Coven?

It had taken Joe less than an hour to reach the north coast of Norfolk. If he added a couple of hundred miles to his journey, he could still make it to Scotland before dawn. Joe climbed on to the broomstick and asked it to rise.

'South,' he said in a firm voice, 'to Swingletree Lane.'

Joe leaned the broomstick against the crumbling brick wall, its birch twigs drooping like the leaves of a thirsty plant. Seeming to understand that its mistress could be in danger, it had flown low and fast all the way back to Canterbury. The return journey had taken them no longer than thirty-five minutes.

His limbs stiff with cold, Joe climbed clumsily over the wall. More snow had fallen since Joe's last visit to Two Hoots and, as he dropped into the garden, the snow reached past his knees. He saw two lighted windows. One was in the roof, which, Joe supposed, was an attic room, and the other belonged to the kitchen on the ground floor. He waded through the snow and pressed his back against the wall of the cottage. Then he strained his neck to peer through the kitchen window.

The room was dimly lit. Joe saw a shattered lantern on the kitchen tiles. Inside it, a flame fluttered weakly, the candle a stub of misshapen wax. The flame threw a wavering pool of light around the room but it was unable to penetrate the darkest corners.

Joe moved closer to the window and saw Twiggy with her face turned away from him. She was standing with her legs slightly bent as if she was poised to pounce. In one outstretched hand, she held her wand. Joe noticed that the tip of the wand was trembling, like a pencil scribbling in the air.

A movement in a shadowy corner caught Joe's eye. He squinted through the misted glass and managed to see the vague outline of a person. Someone was standing there. Joe realised that Twiggy was pointing her wand at the concealed figure. The flame inside the lantern flared briefly and Joe saw a black hooded cloak hanging from a hook on the back of the kitchen door.

'Logan Dritch,' muttered Joe.

Twiggy leaned to her left and Joe saw her fingers struggling to pick up a paperback copy of *Mabel's Book* which she must have dropped on to the floor. His eyes slid back to the dark corner. Joe breathed in sharply.

There was not one person skulking in the shadows: there were two.

As they shuffled forward, Joe saw that the larger figure was holding someone around the neck; someone small and ashen-faced whose eyes were fixed on a knife hovering inches from her own throat.

It was Esme.

Joe began to shake with anger. His fists clenched and, before he knew what he was doing, he had lifted a heavy

227

clay plant pot and thrust it at the windowpane. The glass smashed and, reaching carefully through the jagged hole, he unlatched the window. In a couple of seconds, he had scrambled over the window ledge and landed with a loud crunch on the broken glass below it.

'Let go of my sister!' Joe said fiercely.

Esme's captor laughed, her face still veiled by shadow. 'Quite the little hero,' she said in a sneering voice.

'Joe!' Twiggy gave him an exasperated smile. 'What are you doing here?'

'Have you come to take me home?' said Esme hopefully.

Joe was dumbstruck. It was starting to occur to him that his dramatic entrance through the window had not been a very intelligent move. 'Please don't hurt her,' he said. It sounded rather lame. 'I ... I'm not afraid of you, Logan Dritch,' he added bravely.

Harsh laughter echoed around the kitchen.

'That isn't Logan –' hissed Twiggy.

'Shut up!' The mysterious woman clasped Esme tightly to her chest. 'If you don't put that wand down this instant, I'll spill this little girl's *blood*.'

Twiggy released her wand and it fell to the floor.

'Now, kick it over here,' said the woman and Joe tried to catch a glimpse of her face as she stooped to pick up the wand. He recognised the line of her jaw, and her voice sounded very familiar.

Joe remembered that Logan Dritch had been talking to someone in the teashop. A horrible thought struck him. What if the Monsters of Much Marcle had been reunited? What if Rose Threep had only pretended to change her ways? What if she had remained as wicked as she had always been?

An icy blast of wind blew through the broken window. The candle went out and the kitchen was plunged into darkness.

A moment later a dazzling light caused Joe to cover his eyes. He parted his fingers cautiously and saw the woman standing by the door with her finger pressed against a light switch. She had fine, lustreless hair crammed into a tight bun, and a disapproving look on her face. Joe recognised her instantly.

It was Lydia the librarian.

Chapter Twenty

Logan's Accomplice

Joe watched Esme as she stood beside the old-fashioned stove, stirring a large saucepan with Twiggy's wand. The hotplate hissed as a few drops of beige liquid spattered upon it.

'Useless child,' snapped Lydia from her seat at the kitchen table. She tapped the knife idly against the table leg, while she turned the pages of a book. 'Don't stir so fast. You're slopping it over the sides.'

'How dare she!' muttered Twiggy, straining against the ropes which bound her wrists and ankles. 'Using *my* wand to stir her stupid supper!' Twiggy spat out the words in disgust.

Joe smiled sympathetically at Twiggy. He had been shoved on to a chair in front of the kitchen sink while Twiggy had been ordered to sit on a stool against the opposite wall. A noticeboard covered with postcards hung above her head. Joe wriggled his hands, trying to loosen the rope which had been tied around his wrists, but Lydia had knotted it too tightly. His ankles had been bound with equal expertise.

'Where's the page?' said Twiggy crossly.

'Ask nicely and I might tell you,' said Lydia, looking up from her book. 'A little politeness goes a long way.'

Twiggy snorted and pursed her lips together.

'Please would you be so kind as to tell us where it is,' said Joe, as courteously as he could manage.

'Very well,' said Lydia, nodding appreciatively at Joe. She left her chair and walked briskly over to the noticeboard, neatly stepping over Twiggy's ankles. By dwindling candlelight, Lydia had been a sinister, frightening figure. However, in the brightly-lit kitchen, she looked perfectly ordinary. She was dressed in a tweed skirt and powder-blue cashmere sweater, with a modest string of pearls looped around her neck. The large knife seemed strangely out of place, clutched in her dainty hand.

'Here it is,' said Lydia, patting a scrap of yellow paper. It was pinned between two faded postcards.

Joe squinted. 'But I can see writing on it,' he said. 'That can't be the page from *Mabel's Book*. She used witchy ink. The words should be invisible.'

Lydia made a tutting noise. 'I assure you that this is the genuine article. The original words have been merely over-written in ordinary ink. After all, how can you expect me to translate Mabel's words if I cannot even see them?'

'You're not a witch, then?' said Joe.

'Alas, no,' replied Lydia. 'I do not possess the gift of magic.'

'And *have* you?' asked Twiggy fearfully.

'Have I what?' snapped the librarian.

'Have you translated the page?'

'Oh, yes,' said Lydia with an air of self-satisfaction. 'It was a simple task for someone as *educated* as myself.'

Twiggy groaned and the librarian hushed her. Joe heard creaking sounds coming from the ceiling, as if someone was walking about above their heads.

'She's coming,' said Lydia, opening a door and popping her head out of the kitchen for a second.

'How could Lydia decipher it so fast?' hissed Joe. 'I thought Mabel's handwriting was unreadable.'

'It is,' said Twiggy in a low voice. 'Before now, only one person has been able to understand a word.'

'Then how –'

'Didn't you see the book she was reading?' said Twiggy, nodding towards the kitchen table.

Joe peered at the book. He read the words along the spine. '*Grappling with Graphology* by Fleur Fortescue.'

'It's the book from Julius's trunk,' said Twiggy. 'I thought it was a boring old maths book about studying graphs … but it's not. I managed to read a few lines when Lydia was turning the pages. Graphology is the

232

study of *handwriting*.'

'That explains a lot,' said Joe.

Twiggy nodded. 'Fleur Fortescue was the translator of *Mabel's Book*. Lydia's been getting advice from an expert.'

'So, now we know who burgled Dead-nettle Coven,' said Joe. 'Squib told us that the culprit didn't have a wand and Lydia admitted that she's not a witch. It's all starting to make sense.'

'Aah, it's a kitten,' said Esme. She abandoned the steaming saucepan and knelt under the table where Twiggy's bag lay. Tadpole had squirmed her way out of the red cardigan and was sitting on the tiled floor, gently patting a woodlouse with her paw. Before Esme could reach out and stroke the kitten, the door was thrust open and Logan Dritch marched into the kitchen.

'Ah,' she said, her scarlet lips stretching into a smile, 'I see the guests have arrived. Good evening, Prunella. Good evening, Joe.'

'You were expecting us?' said Twiggy.

Standing next to a frumpy, sensibly-dressed librarian, Logan Dritch looked even more stunning than usual. While Lydia had squeezed her hair into a bun, Logan had allowed her chestnut curls to flow freely, and they tumbled past the shoulders of her blood-red silk dress. Lydia's pearls looked bland and inexpensive next to the sparkling rubies nestling at Logan's throat. The small, plain librarian seemed to shrink in stature beside the tall, sleek figure of Logan Dritch.

'Do you approve of my ensemble?' said Logan, smiling at Joe and Twiggy. 'I only wear this outfit on very *special* occasions. I do apologise if I kept you waiting. I hope my sister has been entertaining you.'

'Your *sister*!' said Joe, his mouth falling open.

'My twin sister, in fact,' said Logan, seeming to revel in the look of sheer astonishment on Joe's face. His eyes flicked from one twin to the other. He found it hard to believe that twin sisters could be so unalike.

'Unbind them, Lydia,' said Logan curtly, sliding a wand from the sleeve of her silk dress. 'I am here now. There is no need to restrain them.'

Lydia began to unpick the knots that tied Joe's wrists together. 'Keep stirring,' she muttered to Esme, and Joe watched as his sister grasped the wand and revolved it in the saucepan.

'What is that vile-smelling muck?' said Logan, wrinkling up her nose in disgust.

'Soup,' said Lydia nervously. 'Halibut soup. It's a new recipe that I –'

'Eugh,' said her sister. 'Well, don't expect it to pass *my* lips. It smells positively putrid.' Logan's attention shifted to the broken lantern on the floor, and she frowned. 'Fetch some more lanterns,' she said to Lydia. 'I detest electric light, as you well know. A naked flame is so much more *atmospheric*. Oh, and after you've done that, you can remove these two children.' She gestured towards Joe and Esme. 'I want to have a few words with Prunella, *witch to witch*.'

'Joe's a witch, too,' said Twiggy obstinately. 'He's in Dead-nettle Coven –'

'Don't insult my intelligence,' snapped Logan. 'He's not in *Which Witch* – unlike you, my sweet – and he doesn't own a wand. He has no more magical talent than my poor incompetent sister.'

Lydia produced two more lanterns from a cupboard and lit their candles before untying Twiggy and sliding the saucepan off the hotplate. Then she grabbed Esme's hand and prodded Joe in the back with the tip of her knife.

'Take them to your study,' ordered Logan. 'I left Dunkel and Fleck in there. If these two give you any trouble, set the rats on them.'

Joe recognised the study. He and Twiggy had peered through its window on their first visit to Two Hoots. Esme climbed into a rocking chair and gazed sleepily at him, her eyelids beginning to droop. Joe leaned against a mantelpiece. The gentle heat of a dying fire warmed his legs. There were two objects on the mantelpiece. One was a framed photograph of two babies lying at opposite ends of a pram. The smaller baby was asleep while the other had a delighted smile on its face, partially obscured by a smudge. Joe rubbed the glass with his finger but the fuzzy mark remained.

'Is this you and your sister?' Joe asked Lydia.

'Yes,' said Lydia in a subdued voice. She bent down to unlatch the wicker cat basket. Joe tried not to appear afraid when the two rats slid out of the basket and slunk underneath a chest of drawers. He turned to the second object on the mantelpiece. It was a small, square tin with pictures of dense forest on three of its sides and the word 'Schwarzwald' printed on its fourth.

'Don't touch that!' said Lydia sharply as Joe's fingers brushed over the lid of the tin. She smiled at Joe and gave a trembly laugh. 'It's just a silly souvenir my sister brought me from the Black Forest. Used to contain chocolates but its empty now. *Quite* empty.' She sat down in a worn leather armchair, still clutching the knife in her hand.

Joe moved over to a crowded bookcase. He could not help feeling a little bit sorry for Lydia. She had behaved cruelly, but it seemed as if she was merely carrying out her sister's commands.

'It was very clever of you to translate that page so quickly,' he said.

Lydia blushed. 'Yes, well ... I've been studying witch-craft for a long time. It's a hobby of mine. Even though I don't have any magical skills, myself, I'm very interested in the subject. My sister isn't a scholar. I have an agreement with her, you see. She provides me with all the literature and when I've found out something useful for her, she pays me.'

'How much?' said Joe, glancing at the shabby furniture in the room. There was no filing cabinet, no anglepoised lamp and not the slightest whiff of a computer. Lydia's study was very poorly equipped. Joe suspected that Logan had not been overly generous.

Lydia gave an amused titter. 'Oh, not with *money*. She catches windsprites for me. I keep them as pets. They're fascinating creatures, don't you think?' She waved her hand towards a glass tank which spanned an entire shelf on the wall. Before, Joe had presumed that it was empty but, as he stared at it, he saw the flicker of tiny faces pressed against the glass. It sickened him to see the windsprites imprisoned in such a small space, but he did not think that it would be prudent to show his feelings. Antagonising Lydia could only serve to worsen the situation.

'How lovely,' said Joe, forcing himself to smile.

'I started collecting them years ago,' said Lydia. 'My sister bought me a book about them when she was on holiday in Ilfracombe. I kept my first windsprite in an empty milk bottle but, naturally, as my collection expanded ...'

'Ilfracombe ...' murmured Joe, trying to recall why that place sounded familiar.

'Witches flock to Ilfracombe every year,' said Lydia. 'On the last day of August, there's a big witches' auction in the cellar of the local fish and chip shop. The year that my sister attended it, there was quite a crush, I believe. Every single lot in the auction had belonged, at one time, to Fleur Fortescue. She's rather a famous witch, you know.'

'Fleur Fortescue?' said Joe, rubbing his chin. 'That book on windsprites must be quite valuable, then.'

'Oh, no, dear,' said Lydia. 'Logan wouldn't buy me anything expensive. She got it for a pittance. There were no other bidders, you see.'

'Why not?' asked Joe.

'The subject matter didn't grab them. To a witch, a windsprite has its uses, but no witch in her right mind would want to read about the little creatures. On top of that, the book was written by Algernon Fry.'

'Who's he?'

'One of Fleur Fortescue's relatives, as it happens ... and, more importantly – *a man*. Male witches have been treated as an underclass for centuries. Attitudes are beginning to change but – even five years ago – no self-respecting female witch would have touched Algernon's book with a ten-foot broom handle.'

Joe's eyes rested on the glass tank. The windsprites were crammed together with barely enough room to move.

'I've got over three hundred,' said Lydia proudly. 'My sister thinks I'm quite potty.' She gave a sigh. 'We couldn't be more different. Logan has always been the adventurous one. When the missing page of *Mabel's Book* was found in the Black Forest, she flew to Germany immediately. Ever since then, she's travelled all over the world to find that page. It's been her obsession, you see. She's jetted off to far-flung places and I've never strayed from this corner of England. I'm quite content in my little cottage with the windsprites to keep me company.'

'So Two Hoots belongs to *you*?' said Joe.

'Oh, yes,' said Lydia. 'Logan lives in a plush apartment in Kensington. Dear, oh dear, my tongue is running away with me.' Lydia frowned. 'Sit down, boy, and stop quizzing me.'

Joe perched on one arm of the rocking chair. He was careful not to disturb Esme, who had fallen asleep.

'Why is Esme here?' said Joe softly. 'How did she get mixed up in all this?'

'No more questions,' said Lydia, waving the knife threateningly.

'Please,' said Joe. 'I'd like to understand ...'

'Oh ...' Lydia shook her head from side to side. 'Very well! I like to see a child with an enquiring mind. I was always pestering my mother with questions when I was your age. Let's see ...' She took a deep breath.

As the orange glow in the fireplace faded to a dingy grey, Joe learned how Harriet and Aubrey had been overpowered by a complicated curse on the train at Stubble End station. He heard about the vicious fight between Harriet's snake and the two rats. (Facing defeat, the injured snake had turned itself back into a fountain pen and rolled underneath a seat.)

Joe listened without interrupting as Lydia described how she had hunted all over Dead-nettle Coven without finding the missing page. The rats had been equally unsuccessful at Pipistrelle Coven. It had been Lydia's idea to use the Re-growing Potion on *Mabel's Book*, but when the potion failed to reproduce Mabel's words, the Dritch sisters had been close to despair.

'Then we had a stroke of luck,' said Lydia, smiling at Joe. 'When she met you on the train, Logan thought you were an insignificant schoolboy; but then you showed up at my little cottage with your friend, Prunella, and Logan put two and two together. She realised that the Vipers must have given you the page. When you escaped, she sent Dunkel and Fleck after you –'.

'I *wondered* if someone was following us,' said Joe. 'So, that's how you found out where I lived.'

'From then on, the rats watched your every move,' said Lydia.

Dunkel and Fleck poked out their hairy noses from

underneath the chest of drawers and made an excited snittering noise.

'I saw a couple of rats on the woodpile in my garden,' said Joe, eyeing Dunkel and Fleck warily. 'They overheard me telling Twiggy that the page was in the library, didn't they?'

'Of course,' said Lydia. 'Logan sent me to the library to retrieve the page. Dunkel and Fleck came with me in case there were any ... *problems.*'

Joe winced, remembering the moment when one of the rats had attacked him. 'You still haven't explained why Esme is here,' he said.

'She was the bait, dear,' said Lydia patiently. 'We couldn't be sure that you'd have the nerve to come after the page, so Logan kidnapped your sister and left a little message for you at your house. We needed to lure you here.'

'But why?' said Joe. He did not receive an answer. Then Joe asked the question he had been burning to ask since they had entered the study. 'What does it do – the spell on page five hundred and thirteen?'

Lydia tapped the side of her nose with her forefinger. 'You'll see,' she said mysteriously.

The door of the study creaked open and Logan Dritch stood in the doorway with Twiggy standing awkwardly by her side. 'We've finished our little chat,' said Logan. 'It's time –'

'No!' shouted Twiggy and she rushed towards the glass tank. 'Cuthbert! Oh, Cuthbert ... it's me,' she cried, pressing her nose against the glass. She turned to face the twin sisters, her eyes blazing. 'That's a *wicked* thing to do! Let them out of there, you horrible beasts!' The rats scuttled across the floor and snapped at Twiggy's ankles.

'Stop that tantrum immediately!' roared Logan. 'Lydia, bring the children to the attic. It is time to play the Spillikins of Doom.'

Chapter Twenty-one

The Spillikins of Doom

Joe stood beside Esme in a dark attic room that smelt strongly of wood shavings and fresh paint. A rafter jutted above him and he had to stoop slightly to avoid bumping his head on it. Through an open skylight he caught fleeting glimpses of the moon and, every now and then, a flurry of snowflakes wafted into the attic on an icy breeze. Candles flickered, and a lantern hanging from a nail creaked back and forth, its beam of light lurching into every cobwebbed corner. Joe reached for his sister's hand and clasped her damp palm tightly.

Underneath the lantern was a small circular table, at which Logan Dritch was seated. She rested her elbows on a battered shoebox and made a steeple with her hands, her long scarlet nails making the tiniest clicking noise as they touched together. Opposite her was an empty chair.

'Sit down, Prunella,' she said in a crisp voice.

Lydia prodded Twiggy between her shoulder blades,

and stepped back against the closed door. As Twiggy sank on to the chair, the rats began to scamper around the attic. 'Be still,' commanded Logan and the two rats crouched next to the pointed toes of her black boots, squeaking softly and twitching their whiskery noses. The smaller rat sat up on her haunches and dared to press a paw against Logan's leg. 'Not *yet*, Dunkel,' snarled the witch, grabbing the rat by the scruff of her neck and tossing her across the room. 'If you keep pestering me, I will *change my mind*.' The rat landed by Joe's feet and squatted there, her whole body quivering.

Joe tried to catch Twiggy's eye, but she did not seem willing to look in his direction. He had not had a chance to speak to her as they had climbed the two flights of stairs to the attic, and the subject of her chat with Logan was still a mystery to him. However, Joe could tell that Twiggy was frightened, even if she was trying not to show it. She was biting her bottom lip and her hands were trembling in her lap.

'The Spillikins of Doom,' Joe muttered. He had heard their name mentioned several times. Finally, it seemed he was going to discover what they were.

Logan lifted her elbows from the shoebox and carefully removed its lid. Slipping one hand inside the box, she withdrew a bundle of thin sticks which had been sharpened to a fine point at each end. A length of silver thread had been wound around them. Logan knocked the shoebox on to the floor and, with one hand, she held the bundle of sticks upright in the centre of the table. With the other hand, she slowly unravelled the thread. Then, with a sudden motion, she released the bundle, letting the sticks fall on to the table in a jumbled pile. Joe noticed that the two pointed ends of each stick had been painted a particular colour.

'What's going on?' said Joe.

'These are the Spillikins of Doom,' said Logan proudly.

'She's been making them all evening,' explained Lydia. 'As soon as I'd translated page five hundred and thirteen, my sister began to collect up everything she'd need: a spear of wood from thirty-three different types of tree, the same number of paint pots – all of them containing a different colour – and nine inches of spider silk. Mabel was very specific in her instructions.'

'So it's not a spell at all,' said Joe in amazement. 'It's a *game*.' He smiled with relief. 'Is this what everyone's been so afraid of? It doesn't look very dangerous to me!'

'That is where you are wrong, boy.' Logan flicked a lock of chestnut hair over her shoulder and glared at him. 'You are about to witness an historic moment.'

'What do you mean?' said Joe.

'The winner of the Spillikins of Doom receives the Ring of Tor Dree. It gives the wearer tyrannical powers

'– what were they again, Lydia?'

'The ability to bring about mass destruction, eternal suffering … basically it enables you to enslave an entire planet,' droned her sister.

'And … and … the loser?' stuttered Joe.

Logan smiled slyly. 'The loser … *is doomed*.'

'Plunged into a fiery furnace, to be precise,' said Lydia, fiddling with her pearl necklace.

Joe gulped and stared at Twiggy. 'Refuse to play!' he shouted. 'If she doesn't have an opponent, she can't win! Don't take part in her stupid game.'

Twiggy shook her head and smiled sadly at Joe.

'She has no other choice,' said Logan nastily. 'If she does not compete against me in the Spillikins of Doom, I have told her that I will kill you and your precious little sister.' The witch shook her sleeve and a wand slid into her palm. She waved it menacingly at Joe.

Joe put his arm around Esme, who had begun to sniffle. 'Is that what you've done with Aubrey and Harriet?' he said coldly. 'Have you *murdered* them?'

'No,' said Logan. 'They were far too useful to me. All I did was turn them into fat black slugs.'

Tears streamed down Esme's face.

'Stop snivelling,' said the witch sharply, 'or I'll turn *you* into a slug, right now. A little plump juicy one.'

Esme started to wail.

'Shh,' said Joe, putting his hand over her mouth, but

he was unable to stop Esme from filling the attic with high-pitched shrieks. 'Please be quiet, Esme. It'll be all right,' he said, but she wriggled out of his arms and ran towards the door.

'Stop that infernal racket … IMMEDIATELY!' shouted Logan, her pale blue eyes filled with loathing. She stood up and pointed her wand at Esme's head. 'You wretched child – you're ruining everything. I've waited *years* for this moment … AND NOW YOU'RE SPOIL-ING IT!'

Esme's eyes widened and she screamed at the top of her lungs, overcome with terror.

'Right,' said Logan, seething with rage. 'That's it. Prepare to die!'

As a flare of green sparks erupted from Logan's wand, Joe yelled and lunged at Esme. At the same time, Twiggy sprang out of her chair and tried to pull Esme out of the way.

But neither of them would have been quick enough.

Like a small hairy grenade, the rat who had been sitting at Joe's feet hurled herself into the air and sank her teeth into Logan's hand. The witch dropped her wand and roared with fury as the green sparks spluttered on to the floor, burning a neat hole in it. In one swift movement, Logan wrenched Dunkel from her wrist and lobbed the rat through the skylight. Fleck circled Logan, baring his teeth. Then he ran to the door, nudged it open with his nose, and disappeared.

The witch glowered at Esme, who had fallen silent, her face frozen in shock. Joe grabbed his sister's hand and tried to soothe her.

'Now, perhaps we can proceed uninterrupted,' said Logan, taking her seat at the table. 'You know the rules,' she said to Twiggy.

'Let me play instead,' said Joe fiercely.

'Shut up,' said Logan. 'This is a game for witches … not for untalented beings like *you*.' Joe shrank against the wall and gazed worriedly at Twiggy. 'Let us begin,' growled Logan.

Beads of blood were visible on the witch's hand as she pressed her finger on to the pointed purple tip of a spillikin. She lifted it out of the pile without disturbing the other sticks and attempted to ease out another.

'Hey, isn't it Twiggy's turn?' said Joe.

'Shh,' said Lydia, moving closer to him. 'In one turn, a player can remove as many spillikins as she likes. It becomes the turn of her opponent when she dislodges another spillikin and causes the pile to move.'

'Oh,' whispered Joe. 'How do you win the game?'

'The tips of the spillikins have been painted with different colours,' explained Lydia. 'Certain colours are worth more points than others. At the end of the game, each player is left with a small heap of spillikins which they have extracted from the original pile. The one who has scored the most points is the winner.'

'Does Twiggy know how many points each spillikin is worth?' asked Joe.

'I'm inclined to think,' said Lydia, as Twiggy slid an orange-tipped spillikin from the pile, 'that my sister has omitted to tell her.'

It was a helpless feeling, watching Twiggy leaning over the table, her tangled hair falling in her eyes as she tried to pick up a single spillikin without moving the others. Joe could not help noticing that Logan's pile of spillikins was far larger than Twiggy's. As every minute passed, Twiggy's movements became clumsier and Logan's smile grew wider.

'This is like torture,' said Joe. He tugged Lydia's sleeve. '*Please* tell Twiggy how much each spillikin is worth. It isn't *fair* otherwise.'

'Shh,' said Lydia, putting a finger to her lips. 'It's too late. They've nearly finished.'

'Oh, *Twiggy*,' said Joe as she lifted the final spillikin and laid it neatly on her modest pile. Despite a valiant effort, Joe was convinced that Twiggy had lost. He placed his hands over his sister's eyes. 'Don't look, Esme,' he said as the spillikins began to jiggle frenetically on the table.

While Logan crowed about the glory of victory and world domination, Joe gazed at Twiggy. It will happen any moment now, thought Joe miserably. She'll be plunged into the fiery furnace.

There was an ache in his throat and his eyes felt hot and prickly. The spillikins stopped moving and Joe squeezed his eyes shut.

There was no enormous crash or deafening boom; just two soft fizzes as if someone had snuffed out a couple of candles. When Joe opened his eyes, Twiggy was still sitting at the table, but she had a rather gaudy ring on her finger. On the seat of Logan's chair, there was nothing but a lump of coal.

'That's that,' said Lydia briskly. She snatched up the piece of coal and spoke to it. 'What use are your magic powers, now, my darling sister? Useless and incompetent, am I? Ha! I think *not*.' She picked up Logan's wand which was lying on the table.

'What ... how ...' stammered Joe as Lydia swept past him and opened the door.

'That'll teach her to leave all the hard work to me,' she said. Then she looked directly into Joe's eyes. 'It can be all too easy to concentrate on *one* and overlook the *other*,' she said cryptically. Before Joe could ask her what she meant, Lydia left, shutting the attic door behind her. Joe heard a key turning in the lock.

'Oi! Don't point that thing at me!' said Joe, cringing against the wall as Twiggy studied the ring which had materialised on her left forefinger. 'You heard what Logan said. That's the Ring of Tor Dree. It gives the wearer tyrannical powers. Don't *touch* it, for heaven's sake! Twiggy, are you mad? You could cause an earthquake or something.'

His sister ambled over to the table and peered at the ring. 'Ooh,' she said. 'It looks like the ring I got out of a cracker last Christmas.'

'*Esme!*' shouted Joe. 'Get back over here, right now. That's not some worthless piece of plastic. It's an extremely dangerous weapon.'

'There's no need to panic,' said Twiggy. 'I don't think I'll be enslaving the planet any time soon.'

'What do you mean?' said Joe suspiciously.

'Take a look for yourself.' Twiggy removed the ring and held it out on her palm. Joe edged towards it and prodded it gingerly with his finger. It was a lightweight ring made up of a translucent turquoise band and set with a small unspectacular gem. 'It could be an opal,' she said, 'or it might just be milky glass. At any rate, it's completely harmless.'

'But ... but *Logan* thought –'

'She believed what Lydia told her,' said Twiggy, shrugging her shoulders.

'Then Lydia tricked us all,' said Joe. 'That's absolutely shameful! I thought you were going to *die*! I still don't understand how you managed to win the game.'

'Lydia told her sister how much each spillikin was worth,' said Esme. She fixed her large grey eyes on Joe.

'I think she might have lied.'

'It was a ploy,' said Joe in a bewildered voice. 'Lydia *wanted* her sister to fail ...'

'And she was turned into a lump of coal,' said Twiggy gravely. 'Maybe the loser *will* end up in a fiery furnace after all.'

'But why?' said Joe. 'How could she do that to her own twin?'

'You saw how badly Logan treated her,' said Twiggy. 'Some witches are like that. They despise anyone who isn't magical. Lydia wanted revenge, I suppose. What do you think she meant by "concentrating on one and over-looking the other"? Was she taunting us because we underestimated her?'

Joe shrugged. 'I don't know ...'

'It's so pretty,' said Esme, picking up the ring and slip-ping it on to her stubby finger. The gem winked as she held it up to the lantern.

'You can keep it if you like,' said Twiggy kindly. 'I think you've earned it. You've been very brave.'

'Oh, thank you,' said Esme. 'Twiggy, are you a *real* witch?'

'Yes ... not a very good one, I'm afraid.'

'Why haven't you got any warts?'

Twiggy laughed. 'Maybe I'll get one when I'm older ... a big hairy one on the end of my nose! I've got a black cat, though. Joe gave her to me. And a broomstick, too. Oh, Joe!' Twiggy put a hand to her mouth. 'You're meant to be on your way to Scotland. What happened? You didn't crash, did you?'

'No,' said Joe defensively. 'Even though I'm just one of those useless non-magic types, I did manage to hang on, thank you very much.'

'Then you changed your mind?'

'Not exactly,' said Joe, folding his arms and frowning. 'I was making such excellent progress, that I decided I'd have enough time to double back and make sure you were OK.'

'How gallant of you,' said Twiggy, narrowing her eyes. 'Did you think I was too feeble to cope on my own?'

'Well, you didn't appear to be doing very well when I arrived.'

'Oh really?' She put her hands on her hips. 'I had everything under control before you crashed through that window like a pint-sized yeti.'

'A yeti!' Joe was appalled. 'I didn't *have* to come back, you know. My dad could be freezing to death right now and I'm stuck in this stupid attic with you. I'm sick of Mabel Crump and her rubbishy old book. Who cares about page five hundred and thirteen, anyway? Don't just stand there with your mouth hanging open! Get us out of this locked room! Go on,' roared Joe, 'or can't you remember the spell?'

'I haven't got my wand,' said Twiggy, trembling with anger.

'Oh,' said Joe, feeling a little sheepish.

'Excuse me,' said Esme, her ear pressed against the door. 'I think I heard a noise outside.'

Chapter Twenty-two

flabbergasted

Joe held his breath and listened. A sudden gust of wind rattled some roof tiles and the lantern squeaked as it swung like a pendulum from its nail. Joe's heart quickened as he heard a third sound. It was a faint high-pitched mew.

'Tadpole!' said Twiggy. She lay on her stomach and poked her fingers through the gap underneath the door. 'Did you find us, then? Aren't you clever?' The kitten gave an anguished mew and Joe saw a brief flash of black fur as her paw brushed Twiggy's fingers. 'I'm sorry, Tad. I wish I could give you a cuddle, but we're trapped in here.'

Joe leaned over and squinted through the keyhole. He could not see anything. The keyhole was blocked. 'I've got an idea,' he said, snatching a spillikin from the table. 'Lydia's left the key in the lock. If I can manage to dislodge it, do you think Tadpole could slide it underneath the door?'

'Oh ... er ... I don't know,' said Twiggy. 'She likes patting things with her paws and she's a very intelligent kitten. We could give it a try.'

Twiggy wriggled her fingers to distract the kitten so that she did not wander underneath the keyhole, while Joe slid the spillikin into the hole and jabbed at the key until it fell to the floor with a loud clunk. 'She's sniffing it,' said Twiggy, her head jammed against the crack under the door. 'Nudge the key towards me, Tadpole. I know you can do it!' She drummed her fingers on the floor. 'Look ... over here, Tadpole. Good girl!'

Joe heard the sound of metal grazing the wooden floorboards. 'I can see it!' said Twiggy, thrusting her fingers into the gap. 'Nearly there ... got it!' She scrambled to her feet and dropped the small rusty key into Joe's hand. 'Good thinking,' she said.

Joe smiled at her. 'Even an Amber-eyed Silver-tip couldn't have done better,' he said, turning the key in the lock.

Holding the lantern in front of him, Joe led the others down a steep staircase and on to a narrow landing. 'Can't you keep that kitten quiet?' hissed Joe.

'Sorry,' said Twiggy, hugging Tadpole tightly. The kitten purred even louder.

Joe shone the lantern down the next flight of stairs. 'OK, there's no sign of Lydia. Keep close to me and try not to make any noise.'

'I don't know why you're being so cautious,' said Twiggy. 'She can't do any magic.'

'I know,' he said. 'But she's still got that knife, hasn't she?' Joe glanced over his shoulder. 'Where's Esme got to?'

'I'm here,' said his sister's voice, and Joe lifted the lantern, illuminating the landing. Esme was kneeling on a window-seat, staring out into the darkness. 'I wonder what happened to that poor little rat,' she said. 'It saved my life, didn't it, Joe?'

Joe grunted, reluctant to admit the truth. He remembered his tussle with one of the rats in the library. His leg throbbed painfully underneath Twiggy's makeshift bandage. Joe could not look Esme in the eye. He knew that she was right. For some reason, Dunkel had turned on her own mistress. If the rat had not attacked Logan at that precise moment, his sister would have been killed. Dunkel had been prepared to sacrifice her own life to save Esme's, and Joe had no idea why.

'Come on,' he said grumpily. 'Stop hanging about.'

They did not meet any knife-wielding librarians on the stairs. Joe left Twiggy and Esme huddling in the hallway with the lantern while he nudged open the kitchen door and peered round it. The saucepan had been removed from the stove and the room appeared to be empty.

'OK,' said Joe, beckoning to the others. 'She must be

having her supper. We'll nip through here and climb out of the window. I left the broomstick outside. By the time Lydia realises we're missing, we'll be halfway home.'

Joe slung his rucksack over his shoulder and unlatched the window. 'What about my wand?' said Twiggy as she crouched under the table to retrieve her bag. 'Can I have a quick look for it?'

'No. Forget it,' said Joe impatiently. 'You can get another wand. We need to leave *now*.' He brushed the broken glass from the windowsill and prepared to lift up Esme.

'Hang on. What's this?' said Twiggy as a piece of paper wafted off the table. She snatched it out of the air.

'Hurry *up*, Twiggy.'

'Yes, in a minute,' she said, her eyes darting over the page. 'This must be Lydia's translation of page five hundred and thirteen. "The Spillikins of Doom requires two or more players",' read Twiggy. '"You will need –" … gosh, her handwriting is so neat. Here we are. "The winner receives the Ring of Tor Dree, which, when rubbed … looks very shiny." Oh.' Twiggy shrugged and grinned. '"And the loser is transformed into carbonised plant matter. It is recommended that the defeated player is turned back to her original form using the Disenchantment Spell on page one hundred and two, rather than being burnt to a cinder."'

'Why on earth did Fleur tear out that page?' said Joe,

shaking his head. 'Now, put it down and let's get out of here.'

'Turn over,' said Esme eagerly. 'There's some more writing on the back.'

'She's right!' said Twiggy, and she slapped herself on the forehead. 'Oh, Joe ... we're such idiots! Every page has writing on *both sides*. When Fleur ripped out page five hundred and thirteen, she removed the five hundred and fourteenth page as well!'

'It's easy to concentrate on one and overlook the other,' repeated Joe slowly. *'That's what Lydia meant!* Read it out, Twiggy. Quick.'

'Oh,' said Twiggy in a disappointed voice. She handed the page to Joe. 'It's a Flabbergast Potion, which renders someone speechless. Doesn't sound very dangerous to me. Come on. Where'd you say you left my broomstick?'

Joe grabbed her arm. 'The saucepan! It wasn't halibut soup. I'll bet you anything that it was Flabbergast Potion. The instructions here say that the ingredients should be mixed together with a wand. She made Esme stir it with *your* wand. Don't you remember? Lydia's going to use the potion on someone and *it can't be reversed*. Look ... it says so at the bottom of the page.'

'I'll admit that it would be awful to lose your voice,' said Twiggy, 'but it's hardly the global catastrophe that I was expecting.'

'We've got to stop her,' said Joe.

'Hang on … a minute ago you said –'

'I've changed my mind,' said Joe stubbornly.

'You seem to be making a habit of that,' said Twiggy, and Joe glared at her. 'All *right*, then,' she said. 'We'll go and investigate.'

As they crept into the hallway, they heard muffled bumping noises coming from Lydia's study. Joe put his eye to the keyhole and saw Lydia wobbling precariously on a small stepladder with the glass tank clasped in her arms. 'She's got the windsprites,' hissed Joe.

'Oh!' Twiggy gasped and squeezed Joe's shoulder. 'I forgot about Cuthbert! How could I be so *thoughtless*? We have to set them free! What's she doing, now, Joe?'

'I can see the saucepan!' said Joe. 'She's putting the tank on her desk. Now, she's wiping her forehead with a handkerchief … and opening a drawer. Oh! She's taking out a giant pair of tweezers, I think. They look like something a surgeon would use.'

Twiggy made a retching noise as if she was going to be sick. Joe turned to her. 'Are you OK?'

'Yes,' she said, handing Tadpole to Esme. 'Look after her for me,' said Twiggy as she rolled up her sleeves and took a deep breath. 'I'm going in.'

'Wait,' said Joe, squinting through the keyhole. 'I think she's holding a windsprite in those tweezer things. Yes! I can see it struggling. Now, she's dipping a ladle into the saucepan … I don't get it. I thought you said that windsprites couldn't speak.'

Joe fell forwards, banging his knees against the floor as Twiggy kicked the door open and barged past him into Lydia's study.

'Let go of that windsprite, *right now!*' she shouted, striding towards the startled librarian. Lydia's right hand released its grip on the ladle and drops of syrupy liquid splattered on to a faded Persian rug. Twiggy grabbed hold of the large tweezers at the same time as Lydia seized the knife. The librarian jabbed it in the air, missing Twiggy's face by a few inches.

'Keep away from me, little girl!' screeched Lydia insanely. 'Don't try and stop me.'

Twiggy let go of the tweezers and took a step backwards, her eyes twinkling with unshed tears. 'What are you doing to them?' she said in a trembling voice. Twiggy faced the glass tank. The cowering windsprites had pressed themselves into the corner furthest from Lydia. 'You must have *hundreds* in there.'

'Three hundred and two,' said Lydia proudly. 'No … I'm forgetting the latest addition to my collection. My sister caught it only a few days ago. Make that three hundred and three.'

'Cuthbert,' breathed Twiggy. She leaned closer to the tank. Joe knew that she was trying to spot her favourite windsprite amongst the mass of cringing little creatures.

261

'Get back!' said Lydia warningly, waving the long pair of tweezers at Twiggy. The windsprite squirmed, its neck pinched between the tweezers' silver tips.

'You're wasting your potion,' said Joe from the doorway. 'Windsprites can't talk.'

'That's right,' said Twiggy. 'What you're doing is pointless.'

'Pointless?' Lydia threw back her head and laughed hysterically. 'Pointless, is it? You foolish witch!' The librarian glared at Twiggy. 'You think I'm an idiot, don't you: a poor, untalented, useless wretch who isn't fit to lick your hobnailed boots. Well, my sister thought the same … and now look at her!' Lydia gazed triumphantly at the mantelpiece where the lump of coal sat between the small tin and the framed photograph.

'You witches are all alike,' said the librarian bitterly. 'You think you're better than the rest of us. Do you know how many years of humiliation I had to suffer at the hands of my loathsome sister? I knew that if I was patient, if I studied every book on witchcraft, I would find a way to exact my revenge.

'Logan has been searching for the missing page of *Mabel's Book* for twenty years, and I've been assisting her,' said Lydia, perching on the desk. She balanced the pair of tweezers on a pile of notepads. 'I trawled through every book I could find, trying to provide her with clues to its whereabouts. My stupid, lazy sister! She couldn't be bothered to do any research herself ... and that proved to be her downfall! I spent years poring over books on handwriting and I visited the National Museum of Witchcraft a dozen times to look at Mabel's original book. It was an added bonus when I came across *Grappling with Graphology* at your coven. Fleur Fortescue was an exceptional talent in the field of linguistics. When I finally had that page in my hand ...' Lydia clicked her fingers, '... it took me a quarter of an hour to decipher it.'

'But ... but that's impossible,' blustered Twiggy. 'You're talking rubbish. You couldn't have translated the instructions for the Spillikins of Doom and the Flabbergast Potion in fifteen minutes flat!'

'Shut up, Twiggy,' hissed Joe as Lydia turned to Twiggy with an evil glint in her eye. Joe took a few steps into the study and Esme followed him with Tadpole struggling in her arms.

Lydia raised her hand and nodded calmly. 'You're perfectly right, Prunella,' she said. 'But I didn't need to translate both of them. I already knew how to play the Spillikins of Doom.'

'How?' said Twiggy. 'I don't believe you!'

'A few days ago something rather peculiar happened to me,' said Lydia. 'At first I thought I'd had a strange vision. One moment, I was shelving books in the library, and the next ... I found myself in an old-fashioned study, staring at a page of neatly-written instructions which explained how to play the Spillikins of Doom. Then a young woman in a feather-trimmed bonnet snatched the piece of paper out of my hands, screwed it into a ball and pointed a wand at me. The next thing I knew I was standing in the library corridor.

'It took me a few hours to put a name to the woman's face. I'd seen photographs of Fleur Fortescue before, but only as an old woman. Imagine my excitement when I realised that I'd glimpsed her translation of the missing page of *Mabel's Book*!'

Joe caught Twiggy's eye. Her face had flushed rhubarb pink and she was looking extremely guilty. Joe knew that she shared his suspicions. Unwittingly, they had been responsible for the librarian's 'strange vision'.

'Bizarre as it may seem,' continued the librarian, 'I think someone must have tampered with my mind and inserted a memory that Fleur Fortescue extracted all those years ago. It's the only explanation I can think of. I suppose someone must have been snooping around in Fleur's study and she burst in on them and changed their memory ... quite unnecessarily, as it turned out, because they hadn't read a word of the Flabbergast Potion. When I find out who meddled with my memory,' said Lydia, eyeing Twiggy's burning cheeks suspiciously, 'I intend to thank them very much indeed.'

Twiggy backed nervously into a bookcase.

'It was you, Prunella, wasn't it?' said Lydia. 'You three children were in the library when I had my funny turn. I distinctly remember you passing me in the corridor while I was on the phone to my sister.'

'Hmm ... don't think so ... dunno,' mumbled Twiggy, staring at her boots.

'Well, it was most helpful,' said Lydia. 'I realised, of course, that the Spillikins of Doom was just a silly game and that the dangerous spell must have been on the other side of the page.'

Joe rubbed his chin thoughtfully. He felt as if someone was waving a flag in his brain, trying to get his attention. 'F.F. ...' he murmured. 'F.F. ...' Joe stared ahead of him, his eyes unfocused. 'Ilfracombe!' he said suddenly, remembering a few words written in indigo ink in Julius's journal. He looked excitedly at Twiggy. 'When I was putting Julius's belongings back into his trunk, I saw a diary entry. Something about F.F. ... that must mean Fleur Fortescue ... and an auction in Ilfracombe. That's where he must have bought the jar with the purple mist inside!'

'Shh!' said Twiggy, her pink face darkening by several shades until it resembled a ripe plum.

'No wonder Julius was heartbroken when he noticed the jam-jar was nearly empty,' said Joe, ignoring Twiggy's frantic pleas for him to be quiet. 'It must have cost him a packet.'

'Thanks to you,' said Lydia, glancing pointedly at Twiggy, 'I was able to formulate a rather ingenious plan. I built up my sister's hopes, making her think that she would become incredibly powerful if she won the Spillikins of Doom, and then I made sure that she would suffer a humiliating defeat!'

'You gave her false information about the values of the spillikins,' said Joe. He clapped his hands slowly. 'Very clever.'

Lydia straightened her shoulders and beamed at him. 'I'm glad you think so, but that is nothing compared to what I am about to achieve! Fleur was wise to tear out page five hundred and fourteen.'

'Why?' demanded Twiggy. 'How can a potion that strikes you dumb be so terrible?'

'Because, you unsuspecting little fool, it will wipe out witchcraft. You are the last of your kind, Prunella Brushwood. By the time I am finished, witches will be an endangered species … and before this century is out, *there will not be a single witch left in the world.*'

Chapter Twenty-three

Within a Whisper

'Lost for words?' said Lydia smugly as Twiggy collapsed into the rocking chair with a horrified look on her face. 'In a few moments, that is precisely what will happen to these windsprites.'

'I don't understand,' wailed Twiggy.

'That's because you don't read enough,' snapped the librarian. 'The answer lies in a definitive work by Algernon Fry. Third shelf down,' barked Lydia, pointing with her tweezers at the bookcase.

'Who on earth is Algernon Fry?' said Twiggy in a puzzled voice.

As Joe went to fetch the book, he passed within inches of the windsprite. It had exhausted itself and dangled limply from the tweezers, but Joe felt a faint breath on his arm as if the little creature had tried to reach out to him.

A Hundred and One Things You Never Knew About Windsprites was a heavy book with mouldy splotches on the flyleaf. Written elaborately in sepia ink were the words:

To dearest Auntie Fleur. Happy Birthday. Love from Algy.

Joe remembered what Lydia had told him about the book. It had been purchased by Logan at the witches' auction in Ilfracombe. Owing to the book's unpopular topic and the fact that its author was a man, *A Hundred and One Things You Never Knew About Windsprites* had been a universal flop, shunned by witches everywhere. It seemed that Fleur Fortescue had owned a copy, but only because the author was her nephew, Algernon, and he had given it to her as a birthday gift.

I expect she would rather have had a pair of socks, thought Joe as he began to leaf through the book.

Joe stopped at a paragraph which had been highlighted in luminous pen. '"Fact twenty-six",' read Joe out loud. '"The windsprite is not completely mute but its vocabulary is restricted to a single word. This word is unknown and is whispered exclusively into the ears of infants."' He replaced the book on the shelf and turned round slowly.

'I don't know if you've noticed,' said Lydia in a gloating voice, 'but the witch population has been diminishing steadily in recent years. Ever since I started my collection of these charming windsprites, in fact.' She tilted her head in an exaggerated fashion and placed one finger on her cheek. 'It's a funny coincidence, don't you think?'

Twiggy gripped the arms of the rocking chair. 'What

are you trying to suggest?'

'Take a look at the photograph,' said Lydia tartly. She made stabbing motions at the glass tank and there was a ripple of movement as the windsprites recoiled. 'Go on, then!' she screamed at Joe, her face pinched with hatred.

Joe gulped and dashed over to the mantelpiece. He seized the picture of the Dritch sisters lying in their pram. In his haste, he nudged the small tin with his elbow and it fell on to the floor.

'Oops,' said Esme, squeezing next to Twiggy on the rocking chair. She watched her brother with large, frightened eyes.

'You'll find a magnifying glass in the top drawer of my desk,' said Lydia, shifting from one foot to the other beside the glass tank.

Joe wondered why Lydia had become so agitated. He stepped towards her nervously, his eyes fixed on the knife which she held in her clenched fist. The windsprites squashed their faces against the see-through wall of their prison as he opened the drawer of the desk and selected a large magnifying glass. As Joe closed the drawer, he glimpsed Twiggy's wand wedged between a slide rule and a pencil tin. For half a second he was tempted to grab it, but Lydia seemed to notice his hesitation. She walked round the desk and slammed the drawer shut.

Retreating to the rocking chair, Joe handed the photograph to Twiggy and held the magnifying glass over it. Joe, Twiggy and Esme peered through the glass, their heads knocking together.

The smaller baby was sleeping contentedly, two tiny fists resting either side of her hairless head. At the opposite end of the pram lay the other twin, who was wide awake. She was smiling gleefully at the camera and it would have been a perfect photograph if a smudge had not blurred one side of her face. Joe tilted the magnifying glass. He gasped, and Esme gave a surprised hiccup.

'Wow!' said Twiggy.

The smudge which rested against the baby's head was a windsprite. Its pointed face and shimmering hair were clearly visible. Nestling against the baby's cheek, the windsprite cupped one gleaming hand around its mouth. There was no doubt that the windsprite was whispering something in the baby's ear.

'Why did it have to choose *her*!' said Lydia viciously, slashing through the air with her knife. 'What was wrong with *me*? That windsprite made my life a misery! I have always been in the shadow of my gifted sister.'

'You mean that windsprites give us our magical powers?' said Twiggy, a smile brightening her face. 'Oh, that's lovely!'

'Lovely?' spat Lydia. 'It's *cruel*, that's what it is. They flit about, whispering their stupid word to the chosen few ... and then reject the rest of us.'

'I wonder if Cuthbert was the windsprite who made me a witch,' said Twiggy wistfully. 'Oh, I hope he was.'

'SHUT UP, SHUT UP, SHUT UP!' screamed Lydia. She rested the knife on the desk and raised the ladle of Flabbergast Potion to the windsprite's translucent lips. 'This is it!' she said with relish. 'This is the moment that Fleur Fortescue dreaded would happen. No one had ever found out how witches acquired their magic gifts until Fleur read her nephew's book and guessed the secret. *I* am only the second person to discover the importance of a windsprite's whispered word. It takes *brains* to solve a mystery like that,' said the librarian, swelling with pride. 'No amount of wand waving can match the power of a keen intellect!'

A wicked smile spread across Lydia's face and, just for a moment, she looked exactly like her twin sister. 'Now, watch as I silence these windsprites for ever, and rid the world of magic!'

'Eugh!' shrieked Esme, causing Lydia to spill Flabbergast Potion down the front of her powder-blue cashmere sweater. 'Something's trying to climb up my welly!'

Joe glanced down at his sister's boots and saw a large black slug creeping up the side of her wellington, leaving a glistening trail on the yellow rubber. He flicked it off with his finger and caught sight of a slimmer slug emerging from the small, square tin which must have burst open when it hit the floor.

'I think you've just knocked out Aubrey White,' said Twiggy, peering at the motionless slug. 'Don't step on him, whatever you do.'

Lydia refilled the ladle and was just about to tip its contents down the throat of the windsprite when she was thwarted again. This time, however, the interruption was considerably louder than a child's scream – and it came from outside the room. The walls of the study trembled in the wake of a sizzling noise and a thunderous crash. Unlike Lydia, Joe did not pause to wonder what had caused the deafening sound. Instead, he took less than two seconds to run to the desk and yank open the top drawer. He snatched up Twiggy's wand while Lydia was still fumbling for the knife, an astonished look on her face.

'Catch it!' he called, flinging the wand at Twiggy.

Lydia gave a strangled scream as Joe dodged out of her reach and shoved the glass tank across the desk with all the strength he could muster. It smashed into the wall and cracks streaked across the glass.

'NO!' roared Lydia, as the windsprites began to squeeze through the cracks in the glass tank.

The curtains billowed and flapped as the stuffy room filled with swirling breezes. Joe felt his hair being ruffled by hundreds of grateful hands and, out of the corner of his eye, he saw a windsprite with its arms fastened around Twiggy's neck.

The windsprites swarmed towards Lydia, loosening her bun and lifting her hair so that it rippled above her head like a waterfall. Her necklace snapped and pearls bounced into every corner of the room. She dropped the knife and the tweezers, thrashing her hands frantically in front of her face. Joe bent down and forced the tweezers apart, freeing the last windsprite. It pecked Joe's fingers affectionately before wriggling into the air to join its friends. Joe put his hands over his ears, trying to drown out Lydia's screams. Then the door of the study flew open.

'What on earth is going on?' said Winifred, brandishing her wand. She ducked through the doorway and a little heap of snow slid from the brim of her black witch's hat and dropped on to the fat slug. The snow seemed to revive him and he twitched his antennae feebly.

'Watch it, Winifred,' said Twiggy. 'You're about to squish Aubrey White.' She scooped the two slugs into the tin and Winifred gave her a questioning look. 'Logan Dritch turned him into a slug along with Harriet Perkins,' Twiggy said.

'Did you say *Logan Dritch*?' Rose strutted into the room and squinted at Lydia through her butterfly-shaped spectacles. 'Well,' she said haughtily. 'It's been a long time, hasn't it Logan?'

'Oh, that's not her,' said Joe, lifting the lump of coal

from the mantelpiece. 'This is Logan. I expect she's changed quite a bit since you last saw her.'

'Don't be cheeky,' said Rose, snatching the piece of coal out of his hand and examining it closely. 'You'd better not be fibbing to me, boy.'

'Charlie!' said Esme, as Squib dashed into the room, followed closely by Patsy, who was breathing rather heavily. As Esme crouched down, Tadpole sprang out of her arms and Squib jumped into them. He rubbed his head against her chin, a loud purr rumbling in his throat.

'Hey ... are you Esme?' said Patsy grumpily. 'What have you done to my cat, huh? He won't come near me. Wouldn't even ride on my broom –'

'Good evening,' said Julius politely, popping his head round Patsy's broad frame. His hair looked even whiter than usual, owing to the snowflakes that had settled in it. 'My, my. I've never seen so many windsprites. Are you all right, Twiggy, dear? And what about Esme? We heard that she was in terrible danger.'

'I'm fine,' said Twiggy, 'but I'm very glad to see you. Patsy, your hat is squashed flat!'

'Bit of ceiling fell on it,' said the witch. 'I blasted the front door clean off its hinges, but I think I might have overdone it. The hallway is ankle-deep in rubble.'

'I told you to use the Unlatching Spell,' said Rose huffily, 'but oh, no ... you had to show off and make a spectacular entrance.'

'The little girl was in trouble, wasn't she?' Patsy clenched her fist and glared at Rose.

'That's enough from you two,' said Winifred. She clicked her fingers twice and the windsprites stopped circling Lydia. The librarian flopped into the leather armchair and stared blankly at the new arrivals, her bottom lip trembling as if she was about to cry. Lydia's hair was a tangled mess and there was a brown splodge on her cashmere sweater where she had spilled the Flabbergast Potion.

'Who is that scruffy-looking individual?' said Patsy rudely. 'Is she the one who kidnapped Esme?'

'How did you know about that?' said Twiggy in a bewildered voice. 'And how did you know where to find us?'

'It was Squib,' said Winifred, and Joe noticed that her tongue was stained black. 'He turned up on our doorstep in a terrible state. Naturally, I swallowed some Lingo Liquorice to find out what was the matter. Squib told me that a witch had snatched a little girl. He'd managed to leap on to the back of the witch's broomstick as she was taking off. Said he'd clung on upside-down until they reached a cottage in the middle of a wood. Then he ran all the way back to fetch help.'

'Good old Squib,' said Joe, stroking the cat's head.

'His name's Charlie,' said Esme, burying her face in the cat's fur, 'and he's the bravest cat in the whole world.'

Winifred sighed heavily. 'Joe, you seem to be the most sensible person in this room. Could you please tell me what this is all about?'

Chapter Twenty-four

Transformations

Joe explained about the Dritch twins, the missing page of *Mabel's Book* and the Flabbergast Potion, while Rose and Patsy argued about who was going to cast the Disenchantment Spell on Aubrey and Harriet.

'I know how to do it,' said Twiggy hopefully, clutching the tin to her chest. She was preparing to point her wand at the biggest slug when Tadpole made a hissing noise and arched her back. The kitten's black fur stood up like the bristles on a shoe brush as she spat at something which had appeared in the doorway.

It was a rat.

Scuttling out of sight for a moment, Fleck reappeared with his jaws fastened around the scruff of Dunkel's neck.

'Eugh,' said Rose. 'Nasty, fleabitten rodents. I'll soon dispose of them.' She raised her wand and began to mutter a spell when Joe stepped in front of her.

'There's no need to kill them,' said Joe firmly.

'Besides, I think one of them is already dead.'

'No!' cried Esme, tears welling in her eyes.

Fleck struggled to the fireplace with Dunkel hanging lifelessly between his jaws. He laid his motionless friend on the hearth and looked pleadingly at Joe. Despite having been bitten by one of them, Joe felt genuinely sorry for the rats. He knew that Esme would have been killed had it not been for the selfless bravery of Dunkel.

'Poor thing,' he said, crouching beside Dunkel's inert body. He touched her gently and Fleck made no move to stop him.

'This rat saved my sister's life,' said Joe, looking up at the members of Dead-nettle Coven. 'Then Logan Dritch grabbed her by the tail and threw her out of the attic window. Fleck must have searched for her in the snow.' Joe hung his head sadly.

Winifred knelt down beside him and ran her fingers over Dunkel's stiff fur. 'She's still breathing,' said the witch, 'but her heartbeat is very faint.' Winifred squeezed Joe's shoulder tenderly. 'There are no bones broken. The snow must have cushioned her fall. Her body has been frozen, though. I doubt that she will live.'

Esme began to cry and Joe continued to crouch on the hearth. He stared at the fireplace, his eyes resting on the heap of pale ashes lying in the cold grate. The room fell silent around him.

Without a word, Joe slid the rucksack off his back and unzipped one of the pockets. He plunged his hand inside and withdrew a little bottle.

'No, Joe ... don't,' breathed Twiggy as Joe unscrewed the lid. 'What about ... what about your *dad?*'

Ignoring her, Joe opened Dunkel's mouth with his finger and tipped up the bottle. A single drop of Thawing Potion fell on to the rat's tongue.

The snow, which had clung to every hair on Dunkel's body, began to melt with a soft hiss. Joe felt a gentle heat brush his face as a warm glow radiated from the rat. Her waxen tongue became flushed with colour, turning from pallid rose to rich, healthy pink. Dunkel flexed her toes, opened her yellow eyes and lifted her head.

Fleck could not keep still. He licked his friend's face until Dunkel pushed him away with her nose. Then Fleck turned round in circles, chasing his tail, before sinking down beside Dunkel, his whiskers quivering.

Joe sat back on his heels, holding the empty bottle in his hand. He was pleased that the rat's life had been saved but, at the same time, he felt inconsolably wretched. His shoulders drooped and the bottle slid from his grasp, making the softest of thuds as it hit the hearthrug. Joe avoided Twiggy's eyes. He knew what she was thinking. He had just thrown away the only chance of saving his father.

Fleck lifted his chin and squeaked at Joe.

'He says "thank you",' said Winifred, traces of Lingo Liquorice still visible on her tongue.

Joe nearly overbalanced as Esme flung her arms around his neck and hugged him tightly. 'You did magic, Joe!' she said. 'That was *wonderful*.' He felt his sister's heartbeat thudding against his shoulder and remembered the terrible moment when Logan had pointed her wand at Esme. Twiggy caught Joe's eye and she nodded at him.

'I won't ask how you got hold of that potion,' said Winifred, raising her eyebrows at Joe.

Twiggy coughed and her face turned pink. She studied the slugs inside the tin with exaggerated concern. 'I think Aubrey and Harriet are getting pretty restless,' she said. 'Shall I turn them back into witches now?'

'You?' scoffed Rose. 'Don't be ridiculous. Are you even familiar with the spell?'

'Oh, yes,' said Joe and he saw a heap of paperclips in his mind's eye. 'She knows it, all right.'

'Very well,' said Winifred, 'you may try – but I think it's probably best if you remove them from the tin, first.'

Twiggy wrinkled her nose as she pinched each slug between her fingers and set them down in the doorway. Then she cast the Disenchantment Spell twice, without mumbling or forgetting any of the words. Joe felt extremely proud of her, and even Rose looked impressed when the slugs metamorphosed into Aubrey White and

Harriet Perkins.

'I'm much obliged, young lady,' said Aubrey, brushing the dust and grime from his pinstriped suit. 'I'd got rather fed up of crawling along on me belly. Phew!' He straightened his tie and winked at Joe. 'All right, lad?' he said, patting Joe on the shoulder. 'You came up trumps, didn'tcha?'

'I should say he did,' said Harriet, probing in the pocket of her salmon-pink jacket. She produced a lacy handkerchief and dabbed her eyes with it. 'I took such a risk when I gave you the page from *Mabel's Book*,' she said in a high, tremulous voice. 'I never dreamed that you would turn out to be … well … such a *hero*.'

'Oh … er … thanks,' said Joe, his face burning with embarrassment.

'On be'alf of the witches of the world, I reckon I oughta thank you,' said the leader of Viper Coven, beginning to sniff.

'Yes,' said Harriet, passing her handkerchief to Aubrey. 'You saved us from extinction, by the sound of it.'

'Madam!' Aubrey seized Winifred's hand and shook it enthusiastically. 'I don't believe we've met. What coven do you belong to?'

'Dead-nettle,' said Winifred quietly.

'Dead-nettle, eh?' Aubrey beamed. 'I guarantee that you'll be receivin' the Coven of the Year award. Well done, me dear!'

'What is it?' hissed Twiggy as the rats frisked around her ankles, tweaking her bootlaces and clawing holes in her woolly tights. 'Joe, I think they've gone loopy. They won't leave me alone.'

'They want you to do something for them,' said Winifred. She crouched down and listened to the excited twittering noise that the rats were making. 'I think they're asking you to do the spell again.'

'The Disenchantment Spell?' said Twiggy. 'Why?'

'I don't know,' said Winifred, shaking her head with frustration. 'The Lingo Liquorice is wearing off. Sorry – that's all I can understand.'

'Might I suggest that we ask this lady?' said an elderly voice. The study had become crowded and Joe had to squeeze between several people before he caught sight of Julius, standing guard over Lydia at the back of the room.

'Well?' said Julius, prodding the librarian with his wand. 'Can you shed any light on the proceedings?'

'They want to be changed back,' said Lydia sulkily.

'Back into what?' asked Joe.

'How should I know? You'd have to ask my sister. She captured them in Germany, years ago, just after the missing page turned up in the Black Forest –'

'Schwarzwald,' said Julius, nodding. 'That's what the Germans call it.'

Lydia scowled at him before continuing. 'Logan told

me that she'd had to change Dunkel and Fleck into rats so that they'd fit inside her suitcase. She promised that she'd return them to normal once she'd found the missing page.'

'Only she didn't keep her promise,' said Joe thoughtfully. 'That's what the rats were pestering her about in the attic.'

'Breaking promises never bothered my sister,' said Lydia moodily. 'She'd probably have kept those rats as her slaves until the end of their lives.'

'They realised that they'd been double-crossed,' said Joe. '*That's* why Dunkel attacked Logan.' He turned and looked at Twiggy. 'Let's do the spell right now.'

'Give the girl some room,' said Patsy, self-importantly, pressing everybody back into the doorway. Joe moved several pieces of furniture until he had cleared a sizeable area in the middle of the study. The rats ran into the space and sat up eagerly on their hind legs while the windsprites swooped and somersaulted above them.

'Oh,' said Twiggy, her eyes swivelling from Dunkel to Fleck. 'Which rat shall I do first?' She glanced over her shoulder. 'Winifred ...'

'We'll do them together, shall we?' said the leader of the Dead-nettles. Twiggy nodded and looked a little relieved. They held out their wands and repeated the Disenchantment Spell together:

'By the Stones of Fate
and the Spillikins of Doom,
your former self
you must resume.'

Green sparks showered over the rats and they began to scratch themselves feverishly as their hair thickened and became a softer, glossier grey. They grew fatter and taller, reaching the size of Joe's terrier, Hamish, and cinnamon fur sprouted on their slender legs. Their muzzles broadened and each pointed snout became a wet, black nose. The colour of their eyes deepened from yellow to amber and their ears swelled, filling with snowy hairs.

Dunkel and Fleck continued to grow until they were the size of young deer. The fur around their necks became thick and shaggy and charcoal hairs spread down their backs, covering their powerful hind quarters. Dunkel wagged her bushy tail and Fleck let his mouth sag open, revealing a set of gleaming white teeth.

'Wolves,' said Joe. He stepped backwards and seized Esme's hand.

'Aren't they beautiful?' she said, trying to hold on to Squib's tail as he scrambled over her shoulder.

'They certainly are.' Joe nodded.

Dunkel and Fleck padded around the room, their nails clicking on the floorboards. They whined and yelped but no one seemed able to understand what they were saying. The larger wolf placed his front paws on the windowsill and gave a mournful howl.

'I ... I *think* they might want to go *home*,' said Joe, 'but how are they going to get back to Germany?'

'Have you got any Flying Ointment left?' said Twiggy, grabbing Joe's arm.

'Yeah, loads ... I only used a tiny bit. Why?'

'We could rub it on their paws and the windsprites could show them the way.' Twiggy's hair flickered around her face as Cuthbert danced excitedly on her shoulder.

'Would the ointment last all the way to Germany?'

'Oh, yes –'

'I should say so,' said Patsy. 'Flippin' waste of jolly good stuff if you ask me. You could make a return trip to the North Pole with a whole tube of Flying Ointment. Never seen it used on anything other than broomsticks before, though.'

Displaying the obedience of trained dogs, the wolves stood patiently while Joe and Twiggy applied the contents of the entire tube of Flying Ointment to their paws. It sank into their pads, leaving the merest hint of silver glitter on their skin. Joe, Twiggy and Esme dared to rub their hands over the wolves' soft fur. Joe heard Twiggy muttering something to each of the wolves.

'Thank you, and good luck,' said Joe as he stared into the golden eyes of Dunkel and Fleck. Then he walked over to the window and unlatched it.

'Have a safe journey,' called Twiggy as Cuthbert left her shoulder and darted into the shimmering clump of windsprites which had surrounded the wolves. Dunkel and Fleck leaped through the window and floated over the garden, stabbing at the air with their paws and whimpering nervously. Joe leaned out of the window and glimpsed the wolves rising past the topmost branches of the trees, their airy escorts streaming silently beside them. Then they dissolved into the darkness.

'Quite a spectacle,' said Patsy. 'Brings a lump to your throat, doesn't it?' The wart wobbled on her chin and she gave a contented sigh.

Aubrey blew his nose on Harriet's lacy handkerchief. Then he turned to Rose and made a reproachful clicking sound with his tongue. 'I'll 'ave to break up your little reunion, I'm afraid.'

'What?' said Rose, adjusting her spectacles. She glared at his outstretched hand.

'The Monsters of Much Marcle,' said Aubrey. 'I 'aven't got it wrong, 'ave I? You *are* Rosemary Threep?'

Rose nodded, the colour draining from her face. She began to tremble all over, and her fingers tightened round the piece of coal.

'Hey!' Winifred elbowed Joe in the ribs as she pushed through the little crowd of people. She stood in front of Aubrey and folded her arms. 'I don't think there's any need to dredge up the past,' she said fiercely, narrowing her eyes.

'I didn't mean to cause offence,' said Aubrey, looking rather hurt. 'Fact is, I'm really chuffed to meet such a top-notch celebrity. To meet one Monster of Much Marcle was thrillin' enough ... if a little scary ... but to bump into both of 'em ... well, I wish I 'ad my autograph book.' He smiled encouragingly at Rose, who was peering round Winifred's waist.

'I'll be poppin' into Head Office, tomorrow,' said Aubrey, 'to drop off *Mabel's Book* and that blinkin' page. I'm sure they'll want to 'ave a word with Logan Dritch. I reckon she'll be wingin' her way to Papua New Guinea in a very short time.'

'The Penitentiary for Wayward Witches,' muttered Rose in a horrified voice. Winifred stepped to one side and Rose dropped the lump of coal into Aubrey's palm, before shrinking away from him.

'I don't think I'll change 'er back to 'er radiant self just yet,' said Aubrey, wrapping the coal in Harriet's handkerchief and slipping it in his pocket. 'She'll be nice 'n' easy to transport like this – and there won't be any chance of 'er escapin'!'

'What are we going to do with the other Dritch sister?' asked Harriet.

'It will be a complicated job,' said Julius, lifting a carpet bag on to the desk and delving inside it. He held up a

Fundibule and an empty jam-jar. Lydia clamped her hands over her ears and shook her head violently.

'Now, now … don't worry,' said Julius. 'I'm very experienced at this type of thing. I don't think it will be necessary to do a *complete* mind-wipe.'

Chapter Twenty-five

Cuthbert Returns

A small fleet of broomsticks sped along Swingletree Lane towards Canterbury. Overburdened by extra passengers, the broomsticks flew low. Every so often, Joe's trainers brushed the top of a hedge or scraped against a fence post, coating his soles with snow. Esme was flying alongside him, her arms wrapped around Winifred's waist. Squib crouched behind her, digging his claws into the birch twigs, his tail snaking from side to side. Joe reached out and shook Esme's arm, afraid that she would fall asleep and slip off the broom.

'Car!' yelled Twiggy as a pair of lights flashed in the distance. She steered her broom over the hedge, and dropped so low that Joe's trainers dragged along the snowy field, leaving parallel tracks behind him. The rest of the witches made the same manoeuvre. 'All clear!' shouted Twiggy a couple of minutes later, and she pulled on the handle of her broomstick, rising above the hedge once more. Luckily, they did not have to perform this feat very often, because it was almost eleven o'clock and there was not much traffic about.

When they entered the outskirts of Canterbury, they were forced to dismount because streetlamps lined every road and vehicles passed by far more frequently. The witches removed their hats and they all walked together, in a rather strange procession. They received a few odd looks and someone mistook them for carol singers, demanding a few verses of 'Ding-Dong Merrily on High' but they marched wearily onwards, not pausing until they reached the headquarters of Dead-nettle Coven.

Twiggy yawned and blinked her eyes slowly. 'Right,' said Winifred, taking her firmly by the shoulder and guiding her through the crooked front door. 'Time for bed … No arguing,' she said, as Twiggy opened her mouth to protest. '*I* can see Joe and Esme safely home.' Winifred turned to Patsy. 'Could you magic up a couple of beds for Aubrey and Harriet?'

'Sure thing,' said Patsy, 'but I'd like to have a little word with Esme first.' The witch bent over and stretched out a hand to stroke Squib, who was lying in Esme's arms. 'Well, I reckon I'll have to admit defeat,' said Patsy as the cat pressed his claws into her hand. 'Ow! You little so-and-so! It's obvious that he prefers you, Esme. Why don't you keep him?'

'Yes, please,' said Esme, planting a kiss on the witch's

check. 'I think my dad might change his mind about cats when he sees how *adorable* Charlie is.'

'Let's hope so,' said Joe without much confidence.

As Joe walked through the snowy streets, one hand on his sister's shoulder, he was reminded of the night that Winifred had altered his memory. He kept glancing at her anxiously but he could not hear any clinking noises or see any jam-jar-shaped bulges in her cloak. When they turned into Cloister Walk, a police car was sitting outside his house, just as it had been three nights ago.

'This is where I leave you,' said Winifred. 'Goodnight, you two.'

His mum must have been watching through the cur tains because she had run halfway down the front path before Joe managed to unlatch the gate. She threw her arms around Joe and Esme and held them very tightly. Squib wriggled out of Esme's arms and dashed through the open front door.

'Oh, thank goodness!' said Merle when she finally stopped crying. 'Gordon's been searching the streets for *hours*.'

Joe recognised the policeman who stood on the front doorstep, holding a walkie-talkie to his ear and speaking to someone called 'Sarge'.

'Hello, Constable Atkins,' said Joe, cringing slightly.

'Hello, Joe Binks,' said the policeman. 'Been out in your rowing boat again, have you?'

Before Joe could reply, the cathedral clock struck midnight. 'It's Christmas Eve,' said Joe. He turned to his mother. 'I don't suppose ...' Joe took a deep breath. 'Has there been any news about Dad?'

Joe had not needed to think up a story on the spot. When the policeman had asked them where they had been, Esme had seemed to understand that no one would believe the truth.

'I was sleepwalking,' she said with conviction. 'My brother followed me and brought me back.'

'Sleepwalking?' said the policeman doubtfully. He tapped a pencil against his notebook and raised one eyebrow. 'In your coat and wellington boots?'

'No,' said Esme, twisting a toggle on her dove-grey duffel coat. 'You've got it wrong, Constable Atkins. My brother gave me these clothes to put on. He thought I might catch cold.' Joe saw Esme crossing her fingers behind her back. 'I'm wearing my pyjamas underneath.'

'Hmm ...' said the policeman. 'Got an answer for everything, haven't you, miss?' He pointed his pencil towards the sky. 'Suppose you tell me how *that* got up there, then. Sleepwalking on stilts, were you?'

Joe and Esme glanced upwards at the roof of number two, Cloister Walk. They saw Esme's yellow scarf knotted around the television aerial, flapping in the wind.

Esme shrugged and smiled innocently at the policeman. For a moment, Joe was as bemused as Constable Atkins. He could not imagine why somebody would choose such a bizarre place to display Esme's scarf – and how had they done it? Surely they would have needed an extremely long ladder …

Or a broomstick, thought Joe, suddenly.

A few seconds later he had worked out the scarf's significance. It was the message left for him by Logan Dritch earlier in the evening. To anyone else, a scarf tied to an aerial would have communicated nothing – but it would have told Joe, straightaway, that his sister had been kidnapped by a witch.

The policeman scribbled something in his notebook before tucking it in the breast pocket of his uniform. 'Well,' he said to Joe, his face softening, 'I know you're having a rough time of it, what with your father and all, so I won't give you a lecture about wasting police time as long as you promise me that you, and little miss smartypants, won't wander off again.'

It was half past four in the afternoon on Christmas Eve and the lamps were already lit in Becket Gardens. Joe linked arms with Esme as they trudged along a path beside the river. 'That was pretty impressive,' he said.

'What was?'

'The enormous great fib you told the policeman last night. Sleepwalking, indeed!'

'Oh, that,' said Esme. 'Well, I couldn't tell Constable Atkins what *really* happened. Grown-ups don't understand about that kind of thing.'

'True,' said Joe, grinning at his sister. He heard a clomping noise and, glancing over his shoulder, he saw Twiggy running towards him. She was dragging her broomstick through the snow.

'Hey!' she called breathlessly. 'Wait a minute!'

Joe stopped and looked ahead. His mum and Gordon were sauntering up to a park bench and brushing the snow off the seat. 'What is it?' he said.

'It's taken me ages to find you!'

'Yeah.' Joe sighed. 'Mum and Gordon took us shopping this morning and we've been at the cinema all afternoon. I think they wanted to keep my mind off … you know … my *dad*.'

'He hasn't been found, then?'

Joe shook his head miserably and gave a heavy sigh. 'He's been missing for almost three whole days now. Nobody seems to think that he could have survived for so long in such cold weather. I suppose I should accept that he … he won't be found alive.' Joe blinked rapidly, his eyes misting with tears. 'It was stupid of me to think I could have found him. Anyway, the Thawing Potion's gone and, well ...' His voice dropped to a whisper. 'It's too late, now.'

Twiggy patted his arm. 'Don't give up hope,' she said.

Joe nodded and wiped his eyes. 'Did you want to tell me something?'

'Yes.' Twiggy unbuttoned her overcoat and Tadpole peeked out from her cardigan. The kitten was nibbling the end of a rolled-up piece of parchment. 'How's Squib – I mean Charlie?' said Twiggy, sliding the parchment past the kitten's nose.

'He likes knocking over Christmas cards and sleeping on them,' said Esme, 'and Dad hasn't sneezed once.'

'Good,' said Twiggy. She unrolled the parchment and thrust it at Joe, a smile spreading across her face. 'What do you think of *that*?'

'Not very much,' said Joe. 'It's blank.'

'Oh no!' said Twiggy. 'I forgot the magic specs. Never mind ... I'll read it to you. The Governor of Covens delivered it, *personally*. It's a certificate for you, Joe.' Twiggy cleared her throat and read the invisible words. '"In recognition of his Services to Witchcraft, Joe Binks is hereby permitted to be an honorary member of Dead-nettle Coven" – and it's signed by Freda Snaggletooth.'

'An honorary member?' said Joe.

'Oh, yes ... Head Office knows you're not a witch but

they said it doesn't matter! It's such an honour, Joe. A non-witch has *never* been allowed to join a coven before.'

'That's great,' said Joe, trying to sound enthusiastic.

'Ooh, look,' said Esme. 'It's Lydia.'

The librarian passed them, with tinsel tied around her hair and baubles hanging from her ears. She was carrying a small inflatable Santa Claus, and did not give any of them a second glance as she hurried over a bridge and headed for a bus stop outside the railings of Becket Gardens.

'I wouldn't have recognised her,' said Twiggy. 'She looked so different ... and she didn't know us at all. I think she'll be much happier, now. Oh, Joe ... look out!'

At the last minute, Joe saw a large sheet of paper swoop towards him. It slapped against his face and wrapped itself around his head. He pulled it off and felt a little breeze whizz past his ear.

'It's Cuthbert!' said Twiggy. 'He's brought you something.'

'It's the front page of a newspaper,' said Joe in a puzzled voice. '*The Aberdeen Evening Express.*'

Twiggy leaned over his shoulder and whistled. She prodded the page with her finger. 'Wow ... read this, Joe!'

'What – "Loch Ness Monster Sighted in Swimming Pool"?'

'No!' said Twiggy in an exasperated voice. 'The col-
umn next to it. The one that's headed "Englishman
Found in the Nick of Time".'

Joe read the article aloud. '"Rescuers were astounded,
this afternoon, to find the missing Englishman, Nicholas
Binks, *alive*. Mr Binks, who had been feared dead after
straying from a broken-down taxicab in the middle of a
blizzard, was found in a rocky outcrop, five miles from
Tillygrundle, after surviving for over sixty hours in the
open."' Joe beamed at Twiggy. '"Rescuers were alerted
to the whereabouts of Mr Binks when they heard the
sound of dogs howling. They discovered the Englishman
huddled in a hole with two husky dogs pressed against
him. Rab MacFee, who led the rescue, said 'Mr Binks is
a lucky man. He owes his life to those dogs'."'

'That's fantastic!' said Esme, jumping up and down.

'Yeah,' said Joe, smiling broadly. He stared at Twiggy's
blushing cheeks. 'Huskies?' said Joe suspiciously. He
remembered how Twiggy had whispered in the wolves'
ears before they left for Germany.

'You *didn't* ask Dunkel and Fleck –'

'Why not?' said Twiggy. 'It was only a *few* miles out of
their way.' She squeezed his arm. 'Merry Christmas,
Joe.'

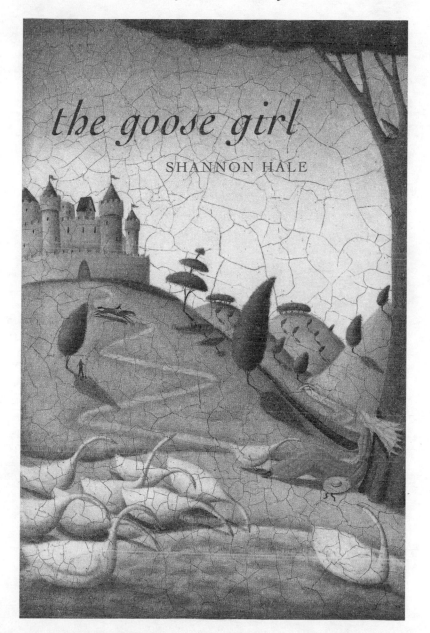

the goose girl

SHANNON HALE

Also from Bloomsbury

DRAGON'S Breath

E.D. BAKER

The sequel to THE FROG PRINCESS

Also from Bloomsbury

'An astounding blend of fantasy, mythology and science.
Brennan is a master of all three' *Eoin Colfer*

Faerie WARS

Herbie
Brennan